Dear Reader:

Timothy Michael Carson has penned a novel, *When the Truth Lies*, which tackles the topic of whether one lives a life of truth or of lies.

We follow the characters Marcus, Tyrone, Brandon and Uniyah—four individuals who intermingle as they explore the streets of Atlanta on a mission for true love and success.

What they find will be an amazing discovery that will either set them free to experience passion at its fullest, or keep them trapped in the search for love.

The backdrop is the music industry in an urban setting. Timothy keeps us craving to find out what follows on the next page in this fast-paced debut novel.

Love, lust and friendship blend as these characters forever search for their real identities. But one answer appears to be elusive: Can true happiness ever be achieved?

Thanks for supporting all of the Strebor Books authors. You can contact me directly at zane@eroticanoir.com and find me on Twitter @planetzane, and on Facebook at www.facebook.com/AuthorZane.

Blessings,

Zane

Zane
Publisher
Strebor Books International
www.simonandschuster.com

ZANE PRESENTS

When The
TRUTH
Lies

A NOVEL

Timothy Michael Carson

SBI

STREBOR BOOKS
NEW YORK LONDON TORONTO SYDNEY

SBI
Strebor Books
P.O. Box 6505
Largo, MD 20792
http://www.streborbooks.com

ISBN 978-1-59309-308-2
ISBN 978-1-4391-8740-1 (e-book)
LCCN 2010925106

First Strebor Books trade paperback edition August 2010

Cover design: www.mariondesigns.com
Cover photograph: © Keith Saunders/Marion Designs

10 9 8 7 6 5 4 3 2 1

Manufactured in the United States of America

For information regarding special discounts for bulk purchases, please contact Simon & Schuster Special Sales at 1-866-506-1949 or business@simonandschuster.com

The Simon & Schuster Speakers Bureau can bring authors to your live event. For more information or to book an event, contact the Simon & Schuster Speakers Bureau at 1-866-248-3049 or visit our website at www.simonspeakers.com.

THIS NOVEL IS DEDICATED TO THE FOLLOWING:
Linda A. Volley,
my siblings,
&
Anthony T. Brown, Sr.,
may you rest in peace.

ACKNOWLEDGMENTS

Writing *When the Truth Lies* has indeed been a journey for me— a journey that was definitely worth traveling. This novel allowed me to express parts of myself that I thought I'd never share with anyone as each character, regardless of their gender or sexual orientation, has a part of me living inside of them.

Being able to open myself to bring forth this story was at times just as scary as it was liberating and, for that, I have no regrets. Therefore, I would like to acknowledge those who persistently encouraged me to give my all to this story and, thus the world:

Thurman Lily, thank you for being such a great friend and great emotional support.

Erica Kennedy, fellow writer and editor, thank you for everything. Your editing has made this project come alive! More importantly, you allowed me to tell my story in my own words. Thank you also for your advice and support. I wish you the best in your future writing endeavors.

Lee Hayes, author of *Passion Marks*, I don't have many

in this industry that I call a friend. Even though you didn't have to, you took the time to facilitate my writing journey with your guidance, support, and advice when times got rough.

Tyran Weldon, of Ty Xavier Weldon Photography, you are a really gifted individual. Your eye for detail is indescribable. Thank you for all of the visual contributions you've provided. You took my ideas and materialized them into an attention-grabbing head-turner. Thank you for being a part of the original *When the Truth Lies* 2009 project.

Lorenzo Turner, of NZO Designs, thank you for designing the 2009 *When the Truth Lies* website. Because of you, I've been able to reach the masses all over the world. I appreciate your time, dedication, and creativity.

To the FosCO Media Group, thank you for revamping and maintaining my website.

To all of my family, thank you for your undying support as I procrastinated with completing this project. I couldn't have done it without you all.

To my "children" Nylah and Davinci—my two Boxers, thank you for understanding when I couldn't give you the attention you needed. You two are always there when things are good and when they are bad.

Thank you, Charmaine Parker and Zane for believing in this project and giving it new life and the opportunity to reach a broader audience.

Lastly, to those individuals in my past who crossed

my path and "encouraged" this story, I thank you, for as a great person once said, "Pain nourishes courage. And you can't be brave if you've only had wonderful things happen to you." Without these individuals, I wouldn't be able to deliver a story rooted in so much truth.

Finally, I'd like to thank all the readers who purchased my novel to help make my dream a reality! You are truly appreciated.

Much love!

Timothy Michael Carson

One
MARKUS

"Come on, Markus. It's time to come and play with your favorite cousin."

Still groggy from being awakened in the middle of the night and slightly disillusioned, I began to gain focus of my surroundings. Slowly my mind processed my older cousin's whispered words. There was no need to fight or argue. There wasn't any other way around what I had to do to protect my little brother from this pain. Fighting would be futile, yet my seven-year-old mind still hoped; even though I had already learned that hope meant nothing.

"Markus, don't play with me tonight! I'm not in the mood for these damn games!" My cousin chastised me in a stern voice. Seeing the fear in my eyes, he softened his tone as he continued to coax me out of bed.

"Don't you want to come and play with me? I thought I was your favorite cousin?" he asked, pulling me from under the sheets and out of the comfort of my bed. Holding my hand, he forced me down the hall toward the guest bedroom where he slept. He instructed me to lie on the queen-size bed as he turned to close and lock the door. As frightened as I was, I *didn't bother to run and, instead, I followed his every command.*

Slowly, the tears began to fall from my eyes. Then, as the realization of the pain I was about to endure entered my mind, the water gushed from my ducts like a broken dam.

"Markus, stop crying. I thought you liked playing with me. What's wrong, cuz? Please, don't cry."

The sound of my cousin's false sincerity now caused me to sob uncontrollably. Part of me still hoped that he would eventually grow weary of trying to calm me down and allow me to go back to bed untouched. Unfortunately, something told me that tonight wouldn't be one of those nights where sympathy would save me.

"Markus! Are you a fucking punk now? I told your ass to stop all that damn crying!" he screamed.

It was evident my cousin wasn't going to relent until I gave him what he wanted, so I forced myself to stop crying and allowed my mind to zone out as my cousin's hands tugged at my pajama bottoms. I figured the sooner we started, the sooner the ordeal would be over.

Lying on my back, I tried to think of something that would take my mind far away from where I was; away from the reality that my cousin was toying with my juvenile body. I could no longer process the words he spoke about my manhood: "Damn, Markus, you're a big boy. You still got some growing to do, but the girls and little boys are going to love you when you get older. When you grow up, are you going to still remember me and what we do?" he questioned.

I nodded my head "yes." After all, it was the same routine and the same questions he would ask every time he forced me to do this. My cousin continued to utter more "compliments;" an attempt to put me at ease as he forced me to turn onto my stomach. As his lips made contact with my body, a cold shiver ran down the small of my back and my mind went blank.

I had made my thoughts void so that I wouldn't have to feel the pain that my body was about to endure as my cousin penetrated me with his fingers. I tried to remember what my mother had always taught me. She would always tell me that whenever I found myself in trouble, I should pray. I did. But God never showed up.

Now my eyes were dry from crying, and my body was numb to the pain and weight of my cousin's massive frame. Physically, I was in bed with my cousin; mentally I was elsewhere. Tonight my wandering thoughts put me alongside my mother as she worked her second job at the nursing home. While she was passing her meds to her patients, I was sitting at the nurse's station reading a book, waiting for her to finish so that we could talk. I loved when she used to take me to the nursing home because it was always so quiet, and I was safe from my cousin. Those days were long before the birth of my younger brother; those were days long gone.

I tried to ignore the pain that my cousin was causing, but there were moments when it became unbearable. Letting out a pain-filled cry as I squirmed, I continued my attempt to escape from reality. I wanted to fly to a place where I never had to feel pain or hurt. I wanted to run into the comfort of my mother's arms. There I would always find comfort and love. But tonight my mother was unavailable. She had been working double shifts for the last few months to make ends meet so my brother and I could have a decent Christmas. This is why she allowed my fifteen-year-old delinquent cousin to move in, so that someone could "protect" my little brother and me at night. Little did she know.

I was jerked from my thoughts as I was tossed onto my back, and a hand gripped my throat, restricting my airflow. Finally I concluded that it was over, as I felt the wetness from my cousin's ejaculation run down the side of my body. His grip on my throat became tighter, and I could feel his face coming closer. Smelling the morning breath and the mild funk of an active adolescent that had not showered, he lowered his mouth to my ear and spoke in a whisper.

"Markus, you know if you tell anyone about how we play at night, they'll try to hurt me, right?" I did my best to nod my head while he continued. "But before they hurt me, you know I'll kill you first…"

❖❖❖

I lurched up from beneath the covers, my body soaking with sweat and my clothes clinging to me. Glancing at the alarm clock, I noted it was only a quarter to four in the morning. Wiping the sweat from my forehead, I took a deep breath to calm my nerves. I was really getting tired of these damn nightmares that forced me to relive my traumatic childhood over and over again. It seemed that their occurrences were more frequent than ever before. I was getting to a point where I didn't want to close my eyes to go to sleep. I'd even contemplated going to a shrink to obtain a prescription that would knock me out so that my body could finally get some rest. Yet something was telling me that no matter what the doctor prescribed, the nightmares would continue to visit me night after night.

Climbing from beneath the sheets, I pulled off my drenched undershirt and boxers and headed toward the bathroom. Feeling for the toilet in the dark, I took hold of my penis, aimed, and prayed that I would hit my unseen target as I fired and released the built-up tension in my bladder attributed to my late-night drinking. Hearing the breaking of water, it was obvious that I had hit my mark. Shaking my penis to make sure I got rid of the excess urine that lingered on its tip, I headed toward the sink.

I rinsed my hands in the cold water, cupped them, and brought them to my face, letting its refreshing coolness relax my jumping nerves. Reaching under the sink for some mouthwash to rinse out the bile taste of my morning breath, I could swear that I heard noises coming from my bedroom. I waited a second to see if it was my imagination and, not hearing any more noise, I proceeded to gargle. Then I heard the noise again; this time louder. Now there was no denying someone was in my crib. Slightly panicked, I tried to remember if I had locked the door when I had stumbled through it that evening after returning from the club. Not like it mattered now. Someone was in the apartment and I was going to have to go out there and deal with him or worst—them.

Butt-booty-naked, I crept out of the bathroom, not sure if the intruder was armed or not. Part of me wanted to go back into the bathroom and hide in the shower; to wait until the intruder left. But then I heard my cousin's voice in my head shouting at me: *"Markus! What? Are you a fucking punk now?"* That was all the motivation I needed. There was no way in hell I was going to allow someone to come into my crib and strip me of my manhood without putting up a damn good fight.

Shit! I should've put some damn clothes on! I thought aloud as my limp penis swung from side to side.

As I tiptoed toward my bedroom, I turned on the light and stood in the doorway, flabbergasted at what lay before me: a female changing her sleeping position. I had to be drunk and hallucinating. I had no idea who this woman was. All I knew for sure was that she was gorgeous. I quickly turned off the light, after grabbing a fresh pair of shorts, and headed toward the living room to sleep on the couch until the sun came up. Thoughts flooded my mind as I plopped down on my sofa. *Did I have sex with her? Did I use a condom? Was it good?* Unfortunately, the answers eluded me.

It was evident the woman was nothing more than a

club hopper that I had randomly brought home. She probably was another one of those overtly anxious women that gave up their goods to any man that showed interest. Shaking my head, I couldn't understand why any woman would give herself so freely to a mere stranger. Then I wondered what this said about me, being that I often zealously took their offerings with no hesitation. I closed my eyes and decided an answer to that question would have to wait until after the sun rose. I felt my eyes grow heavy and my senses numb as I succumbed to sleep. It was going to be a rough day, and I'd need all the energy I could muster to get through it.

Brandon pulled the earphones from his ears and took a deep breath. He had just replayed his supporting background vocals. Earlier in the week, he had written this song for me to record; and from the expression on his face, he seemed quite satisfied with his production. I had to admit the song was tight, and I kind of wished I had written it myself. At the rate that he and I were writing and producing, we'd have the demo finished within a couple of months and could begin shopping it around to record companies, radio stations, and anyone else willing to give it a listen. With chemistry like Mariah Carey and Jermaine Dupri, Brandon and I were on our way to big things.

Looking at Brandon through the studio window, I couldn't help but smile as I thought of our first meeting through a guy my girl, Janelle, tried to hook me up with: to my surprise, Brandon was dating the guy's cousin. I had never personally known anyone that was gay or, as Brandon called himself, a "same gender-loving brother." I initially thought talking and being around Brandon would be awkward; but to my dismay, things easily flowed between the two of us. We had so much in common. He reminded me a lot of myself when I was his age, trying to find love.

It seemed like Brandon was journeying down some of the same roads that I had already traveled along, so I felt it was my responsibility to step in and assist him on his quest for happiness. I sort of adopted Brandon as the younger brother that I never had. The more time we spent together talking, laughing, and cutting up, the closer our friendship grew. And having shared interests like poetry and a passion for music didn't hurt either.

One day, while chilling at Brandon's crib, I shared my goal with him of trying to complete a demo and acquiring a record deal, and he asked me if I'd let him write a song for me. I was flattered but a bit skeptical until he got up, went to his keyboard, and began playing a beautiful melody that made my heart skip a beat. It was then that I realized not only was he was serious about his offer, but he was talented as well.

Brandon didn't have a hard, sexy voice. His tone was more soft and sensual, yet masculine. Either way, his intonation was perfect for the song he was singing to me. I was completely mesmerized with the song's lyrics; and the vibe Brandon would bring to the table would help me establish the sound I was looking for—the sound that would individualize me and make me more than a girl with a pretty face. From that day forward, we had been kickin' it and writing beautiful music together.

"Niyah, can you play that track back for me so I can hear how it sounds?" Brandon asked, interrupting my thoughts and bringing me back to reality.

"All right, give me a second. Now I hope tonight isn't going to be one of those nights where you want to keep re-recording the same tracks over and over?" I jokingly whined.

Brandon shot me a nasty look to let me know he wasn't in the mood to hear my nagging, but I could not have cared less. The studio time was costing us a grip. And after all the money we'd dished out, we only had three songs completed. But that wasn't bad, seeing that we'd only started recording merely a month ago. We probably could've had more, if Brandon wasn't such a perfectionist. With him, everything had to flow perfectly and every note had to be right; not a little too sharp and not even a little bit flat. If that was not bad enough, Brandon also played all of the instruments on his tracks so those, too, had to be perfect. And when it came to critiquing, forget about it: Brandon was his own worst critic.

I had heard of producers being obsessed with their work, but Brandon took things to another level. One time he had me record a song seven times for reasons that are still unbeknownst to me. He would always say that if his name was going to be on something, it needed to be tight. But I couldn't blame him. I felt the same way when it came to singing.

As the track played through the speakers, Brandon

swayed back and forth along with the music and directed an invisible band that only he could see. I watched him in amusement until my cell phone began to pulsate against my hip and pulled my attention away from Brandon's impromptu "concert." I reached down and unclipped the phone from my belt buckle to check its caller ID. When I saw it was my Boo, I quickly flipped the phone open and pressed it close to my ear so I could hear over the song's crescendo.

"Wassup, baby?"

"Nothing much. Thinking about you and wondering when a brother can come through to kick it?"

"Hmm, is that right? Well, I'm about to lay down some vocals on this track and should be done in about an hour."

"Damn, Uniyah, I gotta wait a whole hour? Why can't you handle that tomorrow or afterwards? You know a brother is on borrowed time," David griped.

I rolled my eyes in my head. "Borrowed time" was the wrong term; "married" was the right one. And his call only meant one thing: "wifey" had let him out for a few hours and he had to hurry up and do what we needed to do before curfew. Our fling was starting to get old, and I really didn't want David as my full-time lover. When I got an "itch," he was there to scratch it, and I didn't have to worry about him being in my bed when the sun rose. However, his whining as of late had been incessant. I don't know why I believed him when he told me that he was legally separated from his wife; and the two of them were waiting for the right time to tell their kids. I didn't have to be a genius to know that this wasn't happening anytime soon.

Ironically, if he actually did finalize their divorce, I didn't want him *because* he was kicking it with me. I was a true believer in Karma, and with him married with three kids, I could easily be in his wife's shoes, if I chose to love him beyond "a few hours." Besides, at twenty-five, I was still interested in seeing what else was out there.

"Look, David, if an hour is too long for you to wait, then we can always get together some other time. This studio time isn't cheap and I've already paid for it, so I'm not going to waste it because you want to come through and *chill.*"

"So, it's like that, Uniyah?"

"David, it's always been like that so don't act surprised." *Yeah, I'm definitely going to have to ditch this brother*, I thought to myself. He was nothing but dead weight. Plus, I hated a whiny brother like I hated a whiny infant—regardless of how fine he is.

"I'll just have to wait then. Can I at least come through and get the keys to your crib?"

He had to be tripping. I didn't know him like that, to have him all up in my house unsupervised. Knowing him, he'd probably go though my stuff to find something he could give his wife since his jobless ass couldn't afford to buy her anything decent. Women like her always amazed me. I'd never understand why she chose to toler-ate him and his antics just for the sake of saving face amongst her family and peers.

I mean there were evident signs that their marriage was over, but like most women, she chose to overlook them. Call me callous, but if I were her, his ass would have to go—kids or no kids. After all, the last time I kicked it with David, I left a hickey on his neck so large, the blind could've seen it. And when he left wearing the brown moniker I'd "tattooed" on his neck, he didn't seem to have a care in the world. Separated or not, it was plain out trifling.

"Look, David, I got to go. I'm being signaled to come in and put down these lyrics. I'll call you when I'm done," I lied. I quickly hung up the phone before David had a chance to protest. When I looked up, I saw Brandon staring at me impatiently with his arms folded across his chest.

"I'm glad to see you're finished. Now do you think that we can get back to work before our time runs out?"

"My bad, Brandon; I had to take care of something. So does the track get your stamp of approval?"

"It'll do for now. There's still something missing from it that will make it stand apart from everyone else's. It's missing something that'll make people know what it is as soon as they hear the first few notes. Are you ready to come in here and do your thang?"

"You know it!" I replied and quickly entered the studio

so I could prepare to lay down the lead vocals to the song. I dimmed the lights and burned some vanilla-scented candles to set the mood, and then read over the lyrics so that I could mentally get myself in the right frame of mind. I closed my eyes and waited for Brandon to play the track.

As I sang the lyrics, my emotions began to pour out of my heart. I wanted to give the song everything I had, yet I didn't want to oversing it so that it lost its effect. As I neared the end of the first verse, Brandon stopped me and had me redo it, telling me where to make changes and where to watch my pitch. *Yeah, it's going to be a long night*, I thought as I watched Brandon sit at the console and tinker with the levels. That "itch" I had wasn't going to get scratched after all.

Three
BRANDON

It was almost one a.m. by the time Uniyah and I left the studio. She gave me a lift to the MARTA train station and then zoomed off to do whatever the hell she'd been pressed to do all night or, more accurately, *whomever* the hell she'd been pressed to do all night.

Lately, I didn't know what was going on with her. It seemed that after her volatile engagement, which ended three years ago due to her fiancé sleeping with her maid-of-honor the eve before their wedding, she's been recklessly giving her heart away. Her latest conquest was a man that had duped her into believing that he was separating from his wife and going to leave her when the time was right. Now wasn't this some *Waiting to Exhale* type of shit? I couldn't help to think about how ironic Uniyah's situation was; I mean the mere mention of me being involved with a married man, or dating one already involved with a woman, would frazzle her. Call me naïve, but I didn't see the difference between a man cheating on his lady with another woman, or with another man. To me, cheating was cheating.

As the train approached, I tried to clear my mind. The last thing I wanted to do was think about Uniyah and her rendezvous with a married man. Today had been a good day, and I was still a little high from our studio session.

I stepped onto the train and headed toward the back where no one else was seated. I wanted to clear my thoughts as I allowed the train to take me to my destination. Pulling my notebook and pencil from my book bag, I took a deep breath to calm my nerves and clear my mind. I didn't really have anything to write about and my time could have been better spent on studying for my Principles of Music Theory final exam, but it was a Friday night and I figured my studying could wait until Sunday evening. I was the type of student to wait until the night before an exam to begin studying but, somehow, I always ended up with good grades on them regardless.

I tried to focus, but I couldn't stop my mind from wandering back to my cyber conversation with a guy named Tyrone. We had been talking back and forth via the Internet for almost two weeks, and from the start he had caught my attention. I was anxious to meet him, but he didn't seem too pressed to meet me. I couldn't figure out why I was so attracted to him. I had never seen a picture of him because he was on the DL, the down low, or as he says, "just private." But I still felt some type of connection with him.

We shared a lot of common interests and it only seemed appropriate for us to meet face-to-face to see if we shared the same connection in-person, but he seemed apprehensive about an in-person encounter. I think he was still attempting to feel me out, to see if I was one of those "messy" brothers that ran around telling everyone's business. If that was the cause of his apprehension, then he definitely didn't have anything to worry about. Who I slept with was my business only. Well, I might choose to share some minor details with Uniyah; but she could be trusted.

The train operator's voice announced the train was approaching the Decatur Transit Station, which was my stop. I quickly gathered my things and grabbed my notebook. Before closing it, I noticed that the opened pages were blank. I hadn't written a thing in it during the commute. I climbed off the train and headed toward the buses, where I'd wait another ten minutes, and then make the twenty-minute ride to my apartment.

As I waited for the last bus to arrive, I checked my cell phone for messages. The first three—from my mom, Uniyah, and, an old highschool friend, Trent—were no surprise. However, the fourth was. A smile broadened across my face as the unfamiliar voice announced itself as belonging to Tyrone.

I had given Tyrone my number almost a week prior, but he always had an excuse as to why he couldn't call me. So, I had become content talking via Yahoo! instant messenger. There had been many nights when I had rushed home to my laptop to read an email from Tyrone, or to see if he was active on my Friends List.

I listened to the message and became somewhat entrapped by Tyrone's deep tenor voice, informing me he'd be at a gym located on Metropolitan Parkway the next day around seven a.m. and, if I was game, we could work out together. He informed me that he'd also sent an email, and to email him back to let him know if I'd be able to make it.

Now I grew impatient waiting for the bus to come and take me back to my place so that I could email Tyrone and confirm our face-to-face meet 'n' greet. I checked my wallet to see how much cash I had and, seeing that I had enough to afford the ten-minute cab ride home, I headed over to the waiting taxis.

I climbed into the first vacant cab and told the driver my destination before asking him to put a rush on it. The cab driver sped down the highway like a madman. If I got home without a scratch, it'd truly be by the good grace of God. I released my grip on my seatbelt as the cab driver slowed down in front of my apartment complex and checked the meter: $8.70. I slapped a ten-dollar bill into the driver's extended hand and jumped out of the taxi.

I quickly ran to my apartment building and up the stairs two at a time. Fumbling with my house keys, I finally got the right one into the lock and opened the door. I flipped on the light switch, quickly closed the door, and headed to my bedroom where I kept my laptop. I had it already powered on and my account was still logged onto the Internet. I stripped down to my fitted boxer briefs and climbed into my bed with my laptop sitting in my lap.

I sifted through the spam mail, daily e-mails from friends, and saved Tyrone's for last. As I deleted each e-mail and watched Tyrone's elevate to the top, my excitement elevated as well. Finally, his untitled message sat alone in the mailbox and I exhaled deeply before I clicked on it.

To: Brandon
From: Tyrone
Subject: [none]
Wassup Brandon? I tried to get at u earlier this evening but I got your voicemail. Guess u were a lil busy. Was hoping we could meet somewhere public 2moro morning. I usually work out at the gym on Saturdays and since u said that u wanted to start lifting weights, I thought we could work out together. Hit me back with an email and let me know if that's cool with u. Also hit me with a picture so that I will know that it's u when I see u.

A smile broadened across my face. I was a little disappointed that Tyrone didn't include his number so that I could call him back and converse with him on the phone, but I'd deal with that tomorrow. I wondered why he was so apprehensive about meeting. He was making things more difficult than they had to be. I re-read his email and then clicked on the reply button to respond to the invitation.

To: Tyrone
From: Brandon
Subject: Meet 'n' Greet
No lie, Tyrone, when I heard the message u left on my phone, I couldn't stop smiling. It was totally unexpected and couldn't have come at a better time. I was hoping that we'd meet soon but you seemed to be moving at ur own pace. I'd luv to get up with you 2moro at the gym. I hope that my inexperience with the equipment doesn't interfere with ur workout. I'll be there around 7:00 a.m.

I looked over at my alarm clock and saw it was already 1:48 a.m. If I was going to be at the gym by seven, I needed to turn in for the night. The new song I was working on for Uniyah would have to wait until later. I did a final run through the house to make sure the doors were closed and locked, the fish were fed, and my alarm clock was set for 5:00 a.m. I climbed into my bed and attempted to go to sleep, but it was difficult. The only thing that was on my mind was meeting Tyrone.

"Yo, Markus, this club is banging. So what you got planned tonight, son?"

"I don't know," I replied to Jay halfheartedly while scanning the dance floor. Jay, short for Jason, was my assistant but also doubled as my running buddy when I needed someone to roll with.

As I struggled to make out "pretty faces" underneath the hypno- tizing strobe lights, I grew slightly annoyed with myself for being at the club again searching for another "sleep aid." I hadn't even figured out who the one I'd brought home a few nights before was. Yet, I needed my fix. As Jay rambled on, I peeped a honey across the way and contemplated whether or not to approach her.

"Hey, what do you think of honey over there?" I asked Jay and pointed to the sister I was checking out.

"Honey is fly and all, but look at the way she's moving on the dance floor. Those hips, the way she's wearing that dress, the look she's giving every brother in the club, is all saying one thing: first-class freak! I say you holla at her," Jay joked.

"Yeah, that's exactly what I was thinking." I laughed.

It had been two hours since I arrived at the club, Jay had disappeared, and I was still posted up against the wall, checking the scene and sipping on my drink, a concoction of Red Bull and Grey Goose. I was in the mood to straight-up freak with no strings attached. I'd been feeling that way for the last couple of weeks, and it seemed like every night I had a different girl up in the crib. If I hadn't told each of them upfront that I wasn't interested in anything requiring commitment; that it all was about the physical and they could go home to their boyfriends, husbands, or, for some, their girlfriends afterward worry-free, then maybe I could feel guilty about my actions. However, I was always completely honest and it seemed to make no difference in their decision to "give it up." And if they didn't care, neither did I, as long as they weren't lying next to me in the morning when I awoke. But regardless of how straight-up and direct I always was, there were always a few women thinking they could talk me into being more than the night's freak, and some even had the audacity to state that they would like to be in a relationship with me. But the only thing that happened for sure, in the end, was their feelings getting hurt.

The truth of the matter was because of the night-mares I was having as of late, I hadn't had a decent night's rest in what seemed like weeks. It was getting to the point where I was afraid to even close my eyes for fear that the past would come back to haunt me. To escape the dreams, I went out to the clubs and danced until I was exhausted. By the time I got home, I had only enough energy to bust a quick nut and then fall asleep. This routine was quickly becoming my new "sleep aid." And although it made me forget my nightmares, I knew that I was still having them due to my perspiration-drenched clothes the next morning.

But the long hours I was forcing myself to work at the office, the late-night clubbing, and the constant freaking were all taking a toll on my health and my appearance. I was looking haggard like a homeless drunk, and bags were beginning to show under my eyes. As the thought of the nightmares entered my mind again, I cringed. I couldn't understand how I could still physically feel the pain that I was enduring in my dreams. It reminded me that I definitely didn't want to feel that pain again any time soon, and I decided to push up on the honey that was working the dance floor like she was at her nine-to-five. Tonight, I would need someone to hold.

As Atlanta's signature bass-infused music blared out of the club's speakers and the sound reverberated against the walls, I allowed the alcohol running through my veins to influence my movements and I began to loosen up. Dancing alone, I slowly inched my way over to my choice of the night. As I moved in front of her, I pretended not to notice her watching my gyrating hips.

I decided to tease her by turning my attention to the average-looking female that was dancing beside her. This sister paled in comparison to the honey I really wanted. Besides, a brother could always get extra points for giving some sista a pity dance. It was a tactic I had picked up and employed after watching the movie, *How to be a Playa* with comedian Bill Bellamy.

The song ended and the DJ threw on a slow groovin' reggae cut that had a heavy bass line. This was what I needed to show off my moves. Ms. Average Sista grinned from ear-to-ear as I moved my lean six-foot-three-inch, mocha brown body close to hers and swayed her hips from side to side. Like a magnet, her backside was stuck to my groin. Determined not to let me steal her spotlight, Ms. Honey dug deep into her Caribbean roots and began to wind and grind on the thigh of some undeserving brother, thrusting herself into his hip bone along to the beat of the rhythm. She and I were putting on a show so sensual it seemed to arouse everyone that was watching us. Even though we had different dance partners, we kept our eyes fixated on one another.

I decided to turn up the temptation by allowing a big booty girl that had made her way over to me to rub her butt up against my growing manhood. I hoped that the big booty girl didn't think that she was the cause of my arousal; she was only a pawn in my game to capture the "queen." Growing bored and annoyed that Ms. Big Booty had spent more time stepping on my new

Timberland boots than on the dance floor, I headed toward the exit and left her "backing her thang up" to the air. I didn't bother looking back, but I could feel Ms. Honey's eyes burning a hole in my back. I could tell from the look in her eyes earlier and from the way she moved her body that she wasn't going to allow me to leave the club without me stepping to her.

I slowed my pace when I reached the outside of the club to allow my prey of the night enough time to catch up with me. I casually looked at my watch and waited for her to come outside and approach me. Pretending to search for an imaginary friend so I could survey my surroundings, I locked eyes with Ms. Honey as she headed my way. We both smiled and as she approached me, she made a sudden beeline toward the parking lot. Game recognized game.

I watched as she proceeded to the parking lot and headed toward a white Mercedes CLS550 Coupe. Hearing my footsteps coming up from behind, she nervously dropped her keys on the ground, and then bent over to pick them up. She barely was able to balance herself in the tight dress and six-inch stilettos she was wearing. Looking back and feigning a look of surprise, she observed my eyes watching her every move like a lion stalking its prey. She turned to face me and waited for me to spit my game. Feeling the effects of the alcohol still running its course, I let my pseudo-confidence work its magic.

"So, you were going to bounce without properly introducing yourself to a brother?"

"Seems to me a true gentleman and *real* brother would have had the nerve to step to a woman properly and introduce *himself*," she replied with mock attitude. "Tell me, do you always follow women to their cars in the dark? I could've brought out my tae kwon do or mace." Her Caribbean accent was thick and sensual, even when laced with sarcasm.

"I'm sure you would have a better time kissing this handsome face rather than bruising it."

"A little cocky, aren't we?"

"Not at all, baby girl. You can call it…being confident. If I don't think that I'm attractive, how can I expect anyone else to think so?"

"I guess," she replied and turned up the corner of her lip. "So, are we going to stand out here all night in the dark with the big-ass Georgia mosquitoes attacking us, or are we going to take this conversation indoors somewhere?" she asked.

"My bad, *Ms. Thang*. Would you like to go back to my place and chill, or would you prefer we ride around and find some place that's still open?" From my experience in dealing with women, they always preferred an option.

"Well, Mr. Confident, you and I both know that everything is practically closed, so we can go to your place, as long as you are on your best behavior," she coyly teased.

Damn, I love her accent! "Okay, then my place it is," I replied, smiling coyly myself. "Are we riding together, or separately?"

"We can ride together."

"By the way, my name is Markus," I volunteered while extending my hand to her.

"The pleasure is all yours, I'm sure," she replied, almost causing me to lose my cool. "You can drive, but let me run inside to give my girl my car keys so that she won't be stranded here all night. I'll be right back," she stated, looking back over her shoulder.

I watched her ass sway from side-to-side as she made her way back into the club. I couldn't deny that I was somewhat feeling her confidence and cockiness. The way she flaunted her sex appeal was enamoring. I liked my women feisty, and that she was. As I pondered over her long-term potential, I watched her head out of the club and back in my direction. The street light reflected off of the lip gloss on her pouty lips and made the glitter on her lashes sparkle. They were such unnecessary cosmetics as she was one of those women that didn't need makeup. She had natural beauty. But I knew better than to challenge her style and possibly ruin what I was sure would be guaranteed booty coming my way.

"Shall we?" I gestured as I bowed down at the waist like a humble servant.

"Where is this broken-down hoopty of yours?" she asked.

"Hoopty? My ride can't be that much of a hoopty, if it caught your attention," I interjected.

"What are you talking about? I don't know what you drive."

"Sure you do. You were posted up in front of it when we talked." I smirked and chirped the car's alarm. The lights on my white Mercedes coupe flashed twice, and I couldn't help but snicker.

"Funny," she replied and settled into my butter-soft leather seats after I opened the passenger-side door. "I knew this was your car. That's why I chose to stand in front of it."

"Uh-huh. Sure you did. Buckle up," I replied and tossed her a wink.

She smiled and reclined back in her seat, causing her already too short dress to rise and expose her left thigh even more. I glanced over and unconsciously gripped the steering wheel, feeling myself grow heated in rising anticipation of a night of bona fide freakin'. I had already decided she wouldn't be more than a one-night stand, but I was certainly ready to stand all she was going to give me for one night.

Five
MARKUS

I pulled my luxury sports coupe up to my condo's private gates and stopped short as I hit the remote attached to the sun visor. As the gate slowly retracted, I looked over at the passenger seat to give my little "club piece" the once-over one last time. Debating on whether or not I should call the entire thing off, I decided to go ahead with it. Well, my body decided for me. As I pulled through the gates, I caught a look of puzzlement on her face.

"What's wrong?" I inquired.

"Nothing, but I can see mommy and daddy are still taking care of their little baby boy."

"Is that what you think? Baby girl, believe me when I say, it's not even like that. I work hard for everything I have. Unlike most of the brothers you're probably used to messing with, I'm not afraid of actually working— legally, that is."

"Who do you think you're fooling? You can't be a day over twenty-two, probably just graduated from college, wearing a designer outfit to the club, *and* driving a Benz.

Now either you getting some help on the side, you got some mad skills with a ball, or you slinging some dope on the low."

I opened my mouth to defend myself but knew any attempt to do so would be pointless. She seemed to have her mind already made up. After all, this was only a fling. She didn't need to know that I was a twenty-eight-year-old college graduate who had just finished my Executive MBA at Georgia State University and worked for one of the most prestigious advertising firms in the Southeast, which was paying me more money in a year than she'd probably ever see in a lifetime. Everything I had acquired was from the fruits of my labor, sacrificing, and some plain good ol' investing. I grew up struggling and wanting. That alone was motivation enough.

"Okay, since you know so much about me, why don't you tell me something about yourself?" I asked, attempting to change the subject.

"What would you like to know?" she asked without much enthusiasm.

"How about the basics? You know, your name, your age, where you're from?"

"Now, I know your mother taught you to never ask a woman her age."

"Is that your way of telling me that you aren't going to answer the question?"

She paused, and then smirked. "Twenty-nine," she replied.

I stopped climbing the steps leading to the lobby of my condo building and looked at her with bewilderment. She must've really thought her high school tight dress and all of her clown makeup was hiding the truth. After all, I could see crow's feet beginning to form around the corners of her eyes; she had to be somewhere in her mid-to-late thirties. "Okay, let's try something else. How about you tell me your name?"

"Markus, right?" she asked. "Why don't we stop all this small talk and do what we came here to do?" she flatly stated as the elevator door opened and she stepped in.

"Damn, you're straight to the point, aren't you?" I asked, somewhat intrigued but a bit turned off as well. It was just a fuck, but I was trying to do my best not to make her feel like the hoochie I was starting to discover she was.

"Believe me when I say there's no need for you to pretend with me. When it comes down to all the games, I've been there and done that. So all this getting to know each other isn't necessary. Let's just get down to business."

The elevator doors opened, and we stepped out onto the twelfth floor. She followed me to my door and I allowed her to enter first. Silently, I watched as she made her way through my condo—sizing up my financial worth—until she made her way to the last door down the hallway. She smiled at me coyly, and then pushed the door open.

"Are you coming or should I start without you?" she asked rhetorically.

My footsteps following behind hers was my answer. I entered the bedroom and watched her slowly undress. She enticed me as she pried off each piece of clothing while staring me straight in my eyes. It was like watching a striptease, and I was so captured by her beauty that I couldn't look away. The slight disdain I had felt toward her up to this point started to slowly dissipate.

I walked over to assist her with removing the few remaining garments, which was just her bra and panties. Her body shuddered when my hands connected with her skin. I made sure to take my time. I was never one to rush lovemaking. I wanted her anticipation to build; so I started removing her thong. As it dropped to her feet, I grabbed the small of her back and seductively began to rub my growing manhood against her ass. As she stood with her back to me wearing nothing but a purple pushup bra, I couldn't help but admire her physique. Her legs were muscular, probably from dancing, her stomach was flat with a hint of a six-pack emerging, and her ass was the shape of an apple.

I continued to tease her, moving my hands in circular motions down her spine and she reciprocated by arching her back, showing me her approval. Her breathing grew heavier as my fingers made their way to the front of her bra and unclasped the hook.

"You're stimulating parts of my body that haven't

been touched in forever," she leaned back and softly cooed into my ear. Finally, the lioness was putting away her claws and allowing her softer side to surface. My fingers softly pinched her firm nipples, and she grabbed one of my hands and moved it between her legs. Dry humping my dick through my pants, she made it no secret that she wanted to feel me inside of her; but I didn't want to rush things. I wanted her to relish the moment.

Pulling my hand from between her legs, I placed two of my fingers into my mouth to taste her sweetness. Removing my fingers from my mouth, I once again began to fondle her breasts. I tenderly rubbed both of her nipples, and then nibbled on the small of her neck, all the while grinding against her backside. I was at half-attention and growing harder with every pant of her breath.

Observing the effect I was having on her body, I decided to run my tongue from her neck to her butt cheeks where I lightly nibbled on both. I was anxious to end this foreplay that was torturing me as well. As my tongue flickered across each cheek, I firmly bent her forward to let my tongue explore every crevice of her body. As I reached the warmth between her legs, she flinched in anticipation. I teasingly blew in between her legs and she let out a lust-filled moan. She reached back and guided my head and tongue back to her spot, and I gave in to her unvoiced request. She arched her butt up and stood on the tip of her toes trying to maintain her balance by leaning forward on the dresser. I wanted her to beg me to stop. I wanted her to see that even my "young ass" had enough experience to work her body like a pro. As I continued to lick her kitty, she continued to moan and suffocate me with the depths of her love.

"Oooh…stop…oh yeah…please…oh my God," she moaned. "Stop before you make me cum."

I honored her request and pulled away, not wanting to get myself into a Kobe situation. I understood what "stop" and "no" meant. Grabbing my head once again, she forcefully pushed it back between her legs. There was no question what she really meant after that. Embedding my tongue deep within her womanhood, I began to spell out my name with it. As I formed the "s" in Markus, she almost lost her balance from grinding her pelvis so forcefully in my face. I could tell that my tongue had sparked a flame and now her entire body was on the brink of being set ablaze.

Quickly, she turned around and pushed me onto the carpeted floor. Straddling my midsection, she gently lifted me so that she could remove my shirt. She then slowly and seductively rubbed her manicured finger-nails down my hard stomach, and I could tell she was impressed with how smooth my skin felt. Now she was back in control as she began her journey down south.

Loosening my jeans with her hands, and then unzipping my pants with her teeth, she teased me with her tongue through my boxers before hungrily pulling my penis out from inside of them. The mere contact of her hand made me stand at full attention as she ran the top of her tongue down my shaft. When she reached the base, I felt her hesitate and draw back.

"What's wrong?" I asked, confused.

"I was wondering if you were one of those brothers that could give a sister lockjaw," she replied with widened eyes.

"Is that right?" I asked with laughter, as she continued to stare at my throbbing manhood. Ignoring my laughter, she took a deep breath and engulfed my manhood before drawing back to twirl her tongue in the head's slit. She moved her mouth down my shaft, stopping halfway so she could swallow to release the tension in her jaws before continuing down the length of my penis. With her face buried in my trimmed pubic hair and her ass suspended over my face, I tickled the back of her throat with the head of my penis. Slowly she worked her mouth up and down as she teased my sensitive head.

"Damn, girl," I gasped. Not wanting me to climax yet, she removed her mouth from my penis and moved down to my scrotum. She gently ran her tongue over my sac and I began pulling away from her. It was now my turn to squirm. Wrapping her legs firmly around my torso, she continued to work her magic. As she pushed her goods in my face, I was beginning to see colorful circles. The attention she was giving my scrotum and the finger she used to massage my perineum was making me dizzy.

"You're going to make me cum," I managed to utter.

When she heard my comment, she eased up. The last thing she wanted was for me to "finish" before I penetrated her walls. She raised herself up from my groin and walked over to her purse to grab a condom. She tore the tiny gold and black wrapper open and placed the lubricated sheath on the head of my penis with her mouth. Aligning her hips with mine, she pulled herself up on her knees, hovered over my body, and slowly lowered herself on top of me until my penis made contact with her juicy gates.

My eyes rolled back in my head, and my toes curled. I couldn't believe I was having sex on the floor and was still practically fully dressed. If this was how she liked it, we didn't even need to leave the club. We could've hit a sidestreet and handled our business there.

Finding her rhythm and matching her thrusts stroke for stroke, I reached up and grabbed her bare breasts, attempting to suck them. She pushed me back and continued to ride me like a madwoman. Her muscles clenched and released and I thrust up and down, in and out. She was telling me how good she felt while her moaning became unintelligible as her body tensed and shuddered, and her legs clenched tightly around my body. I felt like I was in a death grip. Her breathing became intense and erratic as her body moved back and forth like a snake. She looked like she didn't have a spine. Intrigued, I pulled her close to me as she began to go through her post-orgasmic twitches.

After her twitching ceased, she raised herself from my penis, gathered her clothes, and ran into the bathroom, slamming the door behind her. Minutes later, she exited fully dressed. I was wondering what the hell was going on. If I had known she was the type to rush and get hers before the other person could get theirs, I would have busted a nut twenty minutes earlier.

"Are you okay?" I asked her, the concern evident in my tone and etched onto my face.

"I'm fine, but are you going to drive me home with your dick hanging out like that?" she asked crudely.

"You know, you don't have to go home; you can spend the night if you want." I was breaking my number one rule by extending an invitation for her to stay over, but I was still hoping to get mine.

"I'd rather sleep in my own bed," she replied flatly.

I couldn't believe how cold she had become in the blink of an eye and noticed how she refused to look at me. I pulled myself up and went into the bathroom to discard the used condom before shoving my now limp penis back into my pants. I followed her out of the bedroom toward the front door, grabbing my keys along the way.

The ride to her apartment was filled with a silence you could have cut with a knife. Pulling up to her apartment building, she uttered an inaudible "thank you" and hastily made her way to her building without so much as a glance back in my direction. I was confused and feeling like nothing more than a simple fuck; although those were my intentions for her back at the club. I backed my car up, turned it around, and made my way home back across town. The shoe was definitely on the other foot this time, but I didn't quite like its fit. Tonight I was going to have to release the growing tension in my loins myself by administering a little "self love."

couldn't believe I was heading to the gym to meet this brother. I'd never kicked it with a guy before, so you could say that I was curious *and* nervous. I wasn't gay and I was extremely into women sexually. After all, I never had a problem getting women to kick it with me. All I had to do was hit the club, throw a little game their way, flash a little ice, and they were hooked. Lately though, I had a desire to follow my curiosity and see why I was becoming more attracted to dudes. In the past, I used to ignore these feelings, thinking there was nothing wrong with me and that every guy had them. I figured every guy checked out the next to size up his competition.

I was constantly staring brothers up and down, checking to see who was tighter, cuter, and, if I was in the locker room, who was packing more. And although a brother would never admit it to anyone, he always needed to know if someone else had something that could make his girl want to stray. Not that I had to worry about the latter. I had more than enough to satisfy the ladies.

Call it what you want, but I'd been thinking about being with a dude non-stop for a while. Sometimes when

I was with a girl and we were freaking, I'd start imagining that I was with a dude instead. I always heard lesbians say that only another woman could know how to truly love a woman, and I'd spent many hours wondering if it was the same with guys. That is, if it took another man to satisfy a man for him to obtain complete sexual gratification.

I'd started doing a little research on brothers who crept on the low. That is, guys kicking it with women *and* men. I wasn't even sure I wanted to be with a guy like that. I could see myself allowing one to give me a little head, but that's about it.

Even when I wanted to ignore my growing feelings and concentrate on being with a woman, it got hard. It seemed like everywhere I went someone was always talking about brothers on the DL, the down low. If I turned on the television, there was Oprah and Tyra talking about it; if I turned on the radio, the V-103 deejays were dishing out their views about it; and if I went to the grocery store, *Essence* and *Jet* had the "phenomenon" flashed in bright letters across their covers. Regardless, I decided to stop ignoring my feelings and go with the flow, wherever it led me.

To assist me in finding out what the deal was with this lifestyle, I'd utilized the best tool for this kind of research—the Internet. The net helped me tremendously with finding out what this alternative lifestyle was truly all about. I'd met all kinds of brothers in the chat rooms with Atlanta being one of the biggest, black, gay meccas in the country. I wouldn't lie and say that I didn't once stereotype all gay brothers as the girl acting-switch walking-soft talking-limp wrist-makeup wearing faggots that society defined them as. Not that those types didn't exist, but there were equally, if not more, gay guys that played sports, worked out, and dressed like any other brother around. I was more attracted to those types.

Climbing into my ride, I tossed my gym bag in the backseat and made my way to the gym. I was supposed to meet this Brandon guy that I'd been vibing with the past few weeks over the Internet. He'd been educating me on what to expect from this lifestyle and offered to help make my transition as smooth as possible. On the real, judging from the picture Brandon sent me, it was going to be hard to not want to kick it with him sexually. He was definitely the type of brother I was physically attracted to: tall, slim, but not too skinny, with a chocolate complexion, pretty eyes, and a sexy smile. Basically, he was cute as hell.

After two weeks, Brandon finally convinced me to meet up with him for a face-to-face encounter. He suggested we meet somewhere public so that I would feel comfortable. I suggested we meet at the gym since he mentioned wanting to add a little mass to his size and tone up a little. He had no idea what I looked like but from the picture he sent, I knew exactly what he looked like.

At twenty-one, Brandon was a little younger than what I was looking for. Broaching thirty myself, I would have never considered talking to someone that young—man or woman. But something about Brandon made me overlook his age. Maybe it was his level of maturity. When I read his emails, I always got the impression I was talking to someone my own age, if not older. Now I was ready to see if that held up in person as well.

I pulled up to the gym, put the car in park, grabbed my bag, and then hesitated. I wasn't sure if I was ready to make this move. Once I went in and met Brandon, there'd be no turning back. My curiosity would intensify and soon it would lead me into acting on my desires, thoughts, and feelings. I was scared to death.

I couldn't imagine my mother finding out that I kicked it with guys. God only knows how my little brother or the rest of my family would react. I never gave up my dreams of having a wife and kids. I'd always wanted three boys and two girls and maybe a dog. I still wanted the house in the suburbs, the white picket fence, and all the bullshit that we've been taught was the American Dream. I wasn't sure if I was ready to throw all of that away. And there'd be no way I could have a wife and a male lover on the side; although there were many men that did.

I looked at my watch and saw I was already fifteen minutes late for my scheduled meeting time with Brandon. I definitely didn't want to stand him up. After all, there was definitely a vibe there, but I wish that I didn't allow him to rush me into meeting him. What if he was clockable? That is, easy to track? I worked out at this gym on the regular, my homeboy worked out here also, and I'd even slept with some of the women here. I couldn't even imagine what would happen if the ones I'd slept with found out I kicked it with men, too. They'd never forgive me for that—or let me forget it.

Finally, I took a deep breath, wiped the sweat from my palms on my pants, and calmed my nerves. I convinced myself that there was nothing wrong with working out with another brother and people would not care less if we were workout partners or lovers. Climbing out of my car, I headed toward the gym's entrance and braced myself. People say curiosity kills the cat; I was willing to see if the cat would survive.

I couldn't shake the previous night's events from my thoughts. I continued to ask myself what it was that I had done wrong or said that caused the sexcapade to go so awry. I pulled my gym shorts up and sat down to lace up my Nike cross trainers. Trying my best not to allow the encounter to disrupt my daily morning workout, I cleared my mind and prepared for the rigorous workout I was about to undergo.

Tightening my MP3 player around my bicep and strapping my Timex sports watch on my left wrist, I grabbed my towel and water bottle and headed upstairs to the stretching room. I let the jazz playlist and neo-soul mix blare in my ears as I began to relax for the first time since the night before. Music always seemed to calm the beast within me.

As I stretched my hamstrings, my mind began to wander back to my dreaded nightmares. I couldn't rationalize their repeated occurrences or why they had become so frequent all of a sudden. I told myself as I stretched my back muscles, that the nightmares were the work of the devil trying to enter my spirit. Things had finally begun to look up for me, and this was the devil's way of trying to break me down.

I was never the church-going type of brother, yet I was very spiritual. I believed in God and I believed in the basic foundation of Christianity, but didn't allow religion itself or the Bible to interfere with my personal relationship with God. I used the Bible as a guide, sort of like a teaching manual. Most often I found that people spent so much time trying to live by the Bible or by the church's standards that, in the end, they forgot to devote their direct attention to the Lord. Not wanting to get myself engrossed with my own religious views, I refocused on finishing up my stretching session.

After completing my last set of stretches, I climbed onto the treadmill and prepared my body for what it was going to endure physically.

I started the treadmill at a mid-tempo pace and began my workout. My spirit was heavy and I was getting a bad vibe internally. I had hoped that the day would be one where I could reach a zone where any and everything became null and void. As I watched the treadmill's display slowly make its way to the one-minute mark, I anticipated the two-minute mark so I could adjust the machine's incline and speed until I was sprinting at a steady pace.

Thinking back to the night before, I told myself that maybe after my workout, I'd go by the little honey's place. She was only a club piece, but I still felt the need to apologize for whatever I had done wrong. Who knows, maybe my act of chivalry would possibly allow me to get "mine" since I hadn't the night before.

Then I realized not only did I not know her name, but I also didn't know what apartment she stayed in. I only knew her building and I definitely wasn't going door-to-door asking everyone where a middle-aged Caribbean woman lived. For all I knew, she could have been happily married with kids.

I continued to run but I couldn't escape the fact that not knowing the sister's name wasn't what was really bothering me. I was bothered by how reckless I had been in my attempts to escape my nightmares by sleeping with so many women I didn't know. Besides wondering if she was married, I now wondered if she had any sexually transmitted diseases, or even worse, if she had HIV.

The questions kept plaguing me, regardless of how fast I ran or how hard I tried to push the thoughts aside. I began thinking of all the other girls I had slept with and how I couldn't even recall many of their names. They had served their purpose and that was to assist me with achieving my sexual gratification. The little honey from the club was no different. She would be another nameless girl that had come and gone. I decided I wouldn't try to find her, I wouldn't attempt to apologize, and chances were good I'd probably never see her again.

I closed my eyes in an attempt to block everything out

of my head. I regretted my decision as soon as I did so. The image of my nude, seven-year-old body came into view. With my mind's eye, I could see myself lying on the bed scared; the look in my eyes calling out for help from someone, anyone. Yet, no one bothered to come to my rescue; not even God.

Memories of me lying helpless and defenseless angered me to the point of nearly breaking down and crying right there on the treadmill. Without opening my eyes, I reached down to increase the treadmill's speed. I didn't want to lose focus of my thoughts. I always ran from my nightmares and this time I wasn't going to run. I was going to face them head on.

I could feel the eyes of the other gym members watching me as my size thirteen Nikes slapped down on the treadmill's belt. I was probably creating a spectacle, but I didn't allow this to deter me. I continued to run. I felt my heart rate increase and my breathing become unmanageable. Thoughts came at me from every corner of my mind, overlapping and not enabling any one particular thought to take root.

Running…breathing…thought…running faster…new thought. I tried to elude the memories. The pain I felt as a child; the emotional distress that my past caused; the hatred I contained for my cousin fueled me on and brought me to my desired destination: the zone. When I got into this zone, nothing mattered. Time had no control and pain didn't exist. When I entered into this frame of mind, I was safe from everything. And to assure I stayed there, I continued to run, ignoring my body's signal to slow down. The music blasting in my ears became mute, and I was finally at peace. I was in a mental state that I hoped to remain in. Harder and faster I ran.

Suddenly, without warning, my legs began slowing down as the treadmill automatically decreased its speed. *No!* I screamed to myself. I didn't want to stop, and I didn't care how tired I was. I continued running at a vigorous pace, even though the treadmill had slowed to a walking speed.

Slowly, I opened my eyes and began to regain focus of my surroundings. Reality had resurfaced and all was real again. The high had ended and disappointment had set in. The machine came to a halt, and I continued to stand there, trying to control and manage my breathing.

Waiting for my breathing and heart rate to return to a manageable pace, I climbed off the machine and proceeded to wipe it free of my body's perspiration. I tossed the towel around my neck and headed over to the free weights. Still reeling in the aftermath of having reached my zone, I felt victorious in beating my mind at its own game. It gave me a second boost of energy, and I decided that pumping some iron would be the best way to end my day's routine. And if I was lucky enough, maybe, just maybe, I could find that zone one more time and hold the nightmares off a little while longer— at least, until they found another way to return.

I groggily reached for the phone as its shrill ring woke me out of my sleep. Before answering it, I glanced at the alarm clock that sat on my dresser and wondered who in their right mind could be calling before noon on a Saturday. The caller ID answered my suspicions: It was Janelle. I should've known. Janelle was the type to wake up early, go to work, go out and party after work until the wee hours, and then be up before sunrise.

I answered the phone on its fifth ring. "Hello?"

"Girl, I know you are not still in the bed and it's a quarter to nine?"

As much as I adored Janelle, I was regretting not pulling the covers over my head and allowing the call to go into my voicemail. Her loud, ghetto talk was not what I wanted to wake up to. "Yeah, Janelle, I was in the studio until midnight with Brandon and, afterwards, I had to handle something."

"Umm-hmm. Something or someone?"

Janelle was one of my closest friends and no matter how hard I tried to avoid the topic, she wouldn't give up until she was completely in my Kool-Aid and could tell you what flavor it was. I tried to keep things on the low and not put my business out there, but lately I'd been itching to talk to someone about my so-called relationship with David. In any other circumstance I would've only talked to Brandon, but he made it clear to me that he had no interest in hearing me talk about any married men.

"Janelle, let me bring you up to date on my escapades."

"I'm sure by the time you're done, it's going to be more like sexcapades," Janelle teased.

I was now fully awake and the lack of energy in my body was rejuvenated by the previous night's events I was about to share. I pulled myself up and cradled the phone between my ear and neck as I stretched my arms over my head. I could tell Janelle anything, and she would keep it confidential. I was sure this would be no exception, so I began. "Well, for the last couple of months, I've been kicking it with this brother named David."

"Months? All right, Ms. Thang, thanks for keeping this on the hush for so long," Janelle shot back with feigned sarcasm. "Seriously, I'm glad you've found someone that makes you happy; especially after you and Broderick broke up. I didn't think you would ever bounce back."

"Well, I've bounced back; sort of. There's one small problem."

"Which is?" Janelle asked quizzically.

"He's married. Well, legally separated so he claims."

"Oh hell no, Uniyah! Now why would you want to be kicking it with a married man? Please tell me that homeboy ain't got kids!"

"Just three," I quickly revealed, and then braced myself for the verbal attack I was certain was going to be released upon me. I was shocked when all she did was let out a big sigh.

"Uniyah, you're a grown woman and you're free to make whatever decisions you want, but you already know some of my experiences with married men. All I got to say is don't fall in love."

"Fall in love with David? You trippin', right?" That was almost too funny. All David was to me was something to do for fun. I wasn't going to be one of those naïve women that became involved with a married man with the hopes of him falling hopelessly in love and leaving his wife for me. I'd seen enough in my lifetime to know all I was to David was a moment's relief and that was all he was to me—if that.

"Then why are you messing with him, if you aren't looking for anything long-term?"

"Janelle, to keep it real with you, at first, I tried to convince myself that he was just something to do. When I needed someone to hold me or when I needed someone to scratch my itch, I'd have someone. And when I don't want to be bothered with anyone, I don't have to be. But I think it goes a little bit deeper than that. I don't mean deep like I'm *feeling* him, but deep as in finding myself looking for a way to keep my heart protected."

"Uniyah, it sounds like you're playing with fire and asking to get burned."

"Janelle, I hear you, girl. But after Broderick did what he did to me, I can't see myself getting involved with another so wholeheartedly. Don't forget, he didn't just cheat on me with some skank from the club. He did it with my childhood friend, Regina. I trusted her with my life. Imagine my dismay when I went into the bathroom where my bachelorette party was being held, and caught her, my maid-of-honor, in a stall with her mouth glued to my future husband's dick.

"I had to undergo the embarrassment of telling my family and friends that the wedding was off, and in the end, I was the only one who suffered. I lost my future husband and I lost a friend. I was so ashamed that I dropped out of college my senior year and relocated here to Atlanta to pursue my singing career."

"So forgive me if I hold little regard for love, let alone marriage. Broderick knew I wanted to save myself for marriage, yet he talked me into giving my virginity to him with the promise of loving me until death did us part. So if you ask me, fuck love, fuck marriage, and simply fuck men! They are only good for one thing— and that is helping me to get mines."

"I know you don't really mean that. After all this time, I can see that you are still feeling the hurt."

"If you say so, these last three years have allowed me to grow in so many ways." Deep down I knew that Janelle was right. I wanted to feel what it was like to be loved again. I wanted to know how it felt to have someone love you for better and for worse. I wanted my soul mate.

"Niyah, I have a question for you?"

"Go ahead."

"Does he know how to treat the kitty?"

"Does he?" I laughed. "Girl, please believe me when I tell you that I've never had a brother that could eat it like he does. He has me climbing the walls when he's down there, and I find myself begging him to stop because it feels so good."

"Begging? You? Now I know he got skills, to have Ms. Saditty climbing the walls and begging."

"There ain't no shame in my game. Brother got skills but I'm definitely not falling in love with someone based on that. I need the whole deal and if he's married, then there's not much he can offer me."

"I hear you, and you make sure you remember that. By the way, how is Brandon doing, with his cute self?"

"Brandon is okay and still being a pain in my ass. But I think he's talking to someone; he's been going to the gym and talking about putting on some weight. Not to mention the smile he's been wearing on his face for the last few days. I think something is up, but he won't tell me yet."

"It's a shame that all three of us like the same thing. A guy like Brandon would definitely make some woman out there happy. It's rare that you find a brother nowadays with his conviction for commitment. Not to mention he's cute as hell!"

"Yeah, I have to admit when I first met Brandon, I wished that he had been a little bit older—and straighter!"

"You ain't lying," Janelle cosigned. "So what you got planned for this evening, girl?"

I went over my social calendar in my head to see if I had made any prior commitments. I hadn't and, since I hadn't hung out with her in a while, I let her know I was free after I performed at the new nightclub in midtown called Club Chillax.

"Okay, I can get with that, but afterwards let's hit the clubs," Janelle replied. "I'm on the V.I.P. list over at Club Xtasy, and you're more than welcome to roll through with a sister."

"Sounds like a plan. I'm needing a girl's night out anyway."

"Oh, you aren't bringing Brandon?"

"Are you kidding? Brandon is our competition! Plus, I believe he already has plans." My nosey self wanted to know what his plans were but, knowing Brandon, he'd only tell me when he was ready.

"So what time are we talking, Ms. Saditty?"

I hated when Janelle called me that. I definitely didn't act like I was better than anyone else, or walk around with my nose tooted up in the air. Now, I wouldn't lie and say that I didn't enjoy the finer things in life, or that my standards in men weren't high, but that was just me. I've had my share of brothers that I've used strictly to assist me with my, well, let's call them "maintenance issues," and then there were the guys that I saw as being much more. The latter usually were bankers or executives. But, hey, if my higher standards made me saditty, then I guess that's what I was.

"How about we get up around eight tonight and you can come with me to my performance? Then we can go hit the club."

"No doubt; I'll see you later then."

Before Janelle hung up, we chatted a bit about my performance. That was one thing I truly loved about her. She always was supportive of my dreams, of becoming either a well-known singer or a renowned writer. I informed her that the new club I was performing at was offering studio time and a chance to work with an established producer. And after everyone performed that evening, all the contestants would be brought out and the audience would select the winner for the night. To get the studio time, a performer had to win three performances and place first in the finals. I had already won twice.

I hung up the phone and, with my back rested against my headboard, I debated whether or not to go back to sleep or get up and do something productive. Glancing at the clock and seeing it was already a quarter to eleven, I decided to drag myself out of the bed and begin handling some of the issues that I'd put off all week.

The day was going to be a pressing one, with vocal lessons and dance lessons scheduled. After all, a singer like me had to keep up with the latest moves if I was going to sell myself as the total package. In the past, record labels would have an artist development department that would prep an artist. They'd handle the vocal training, the dancing, interviewing skills, and anything else that would make you a success. Now, it seemed like the record companies already wanted you pre-packaged and ready to hit the stage without having to put in any extra effort.

Seeing that dancing was not my area of expertise, I needed all the help I could get so that I didn't appear stiff on stage. Pulling the head wrap from around my matted head, I stretched once more, climbed from beneath the sheets, and headed toward the bathroom. Yep, it was going to be a good day.

Nine
BRANDON

should've known better than to think I could count on meeting someone from the Internet. I'd be lying if I said I wasn't disappointed about being stood up. I stayed at the gym for close to three hours, waiting on Tyrone to show, only to leave sweaty, sore, and alone. The only highlight was being assisted with the free weights by some fine brother. I probably would've forgotten about Tyrone had my spotter made a move but my "gaydar" was telling me the brother wasn't on my team. I even tried to test him by making and holding eye contact, but he didn't notice or wasn't paying me any mind.

This was to be expected. Disappointment seemed to be the one certainty in the gay lifestyle. I didn't understand the games brothers played, even though I was a brother myself. If Tyrone didn't want to meet me, he could've said so and I could've been on my way to meeting someone else. It was hard enough trying to find that special love, so wasted time was something I couldn't tolerate. I'd been in Atlanta for nearly two years and the only things I had managed to find without problems were heartache and pain. Truth be told, I could have given Toni B. and Mary J. a run for their money with all the drama and bullshit I had been through.

As I was leaving the gym, my thoughts brought me back to the brother that offered me some assistance on the floor. I didn't even get a chance to ask his name. Sometimes I wished that I could be straight so I wouldn't have to deal with all the shit that was intertwined with this lifestyle. From my past dealings with women, I knew things didn't have to be this complicated, yet my heart and adoration led me to the same sex rather than the opposite.

I wished all gay men or, as I liked to call myself, "same gender-loving" men, could be like that brother. His attractiveness alone had me caught up, but I liked his masculinity above everything else. It was rare to meet an ATL brother in this lifestyle interested in doing anything that required them to sweat or work, unless they were sweating it out in the club on the dance floor three or four nights a week. And the only working that was being done was them working the room to flaunt the flyest outfit they had put together.

I had to laugh because I was also guilty of doing those same things. But, hell, I was pissed at being stood up and was definitely in a funky-ass mood. I had been looking forward to this meet 'n' greet for quite some time and after all the time I'd invested in getting to know the brother, he'd stood me up.

I started to make my way to the train station so I could take my funky behind home, shower, climb into bed, and sleep this mood away. I was so upset at not meeting Tyrone that I didn't even take the time out to shower at the gym. I wanted to get the hell up out of there.

"Hey, yo', you need a ride or something?" a voice asked, pulling me from my thoughts. I turned around and saw it was the brother from the gym. Hell, I wasn't about to turn down a free ride when the alternative was to take the train.

"I'm catching the train!" I yelled back.

"Where you going?"

"Home."

"What part of town is your crib in?" he inquired with a million-dollar grin posted on his face.

"The Dec."

"Decatur where it's greater," he joked. "Come on, playa; I'm headed to Stone Mountain. I can drop you off if you want."

"That's w'sup. I'll take you up on that," I replied, heading toward his ride. When I reached the passenger side, I opened my bag and pulled out my towel to wrap around my shoulders so I wouldn't perspire on his seats. I was glad that I had wiped down, and put on deodorant and body spray before leaving the gym. I would have hated for his first impression of me to be his last.

"You can throw your bag in the backseat, if you want," he offered.

His voice sent shivers down my spine and made me

secretly wish I was one of those gay men that liked to try and tempt straight men into coming to the other side. I used to call men like that pathetic. Now I wasn't feeling as judgmental. I calmed myself, my hormones, and the stirring in my pants as I climbed into the passenger's seat and buckled myself in.

Homey seemed cool as he sped down the interstate. He made some jokes about me being a novice at the gym and how I reminded him of himself when he first began working out. He said he was so lost, he had to go out and buy the *Weightlifting for Dummies* book to help him learn how to do weight training correctly. I admired that about him. He saw me struggling and instead of doing his own thing, he stopped to help a brother out and show me the ropes.

I told him about my plan on gaining more body mass and bulking up, and he gave me some tips on what exercises, supplements, and vitamins I should try. I was really feeling the conversation and decided, at that moment, that the entire day wasn't a complete bust. Something good was coming out of my gym trip after all.

The conversation turned from working out to music, and we eventually got on the subject of my music. I told him that I was currently in school and when I wasn't there, I was in the studio helping a friend put together her first demo. He was intrigued but seemed to take more of an interest in my writing and playing than my producing.

He told me he did some writing himself but more

along the lines of poetry, and that he wanted to put together a spoken word album with music as its backdrop. I found the passion he exuberated when speaking of his poetry intriguing. There was a fire in his eyes that made me wonder if he had any "lyrical skills." I had him pegged as a jock rather than the artistic type. But I also knew better than to judge a book by its cover.

He told me he'd been writing poetry since his freshman year of college but never had the guts to share it publicly. I told him that if he was serious, I'd take him to some of the spoken word spots in Atlanta like the Apache Café or the new spoken word joint, Club Speak! He appeared to be receptive of my invitation and told me he'd like to see what it was like to watch others perform first so he could muster up the energy to do the same.

I couldn't help but laugh to myself, thinking of the conversation I would have later with Uniyah about my day and how I went to the gym to meet a guy in the life and ended up snagging a straight one instead. The thought took me back to my high school days when all I did was hang out with the jocks trying to be one of the boys. However, since moving to Atlanta, I somehow only hung around other gay people and gay-friendly women. I truly couldn't say that I had one straight male friend. I wondered what he would say if I told him I got down with brothers and not women. I can't say that he'd straight out trip with it being Atlanta, but I wasn't sure. Only time would tell.

Our conversation came to a halt when he pulled up to

my apartment. We gave each other some dap, and I reached into the backseat to grab my gym bag. I thanked him again for the ride since he had saved me almost an hour of travel time on the train and bus, and then closed his car door and turned to head to my crib when he called me back.

"Hey, playa, when you want to go to them poetry spots you were telling me about?"

"Well, what does your schedule look like?"

"Just tell me when and where, and I'll clear my schedule. I mean, you seem like the busy one, with school and your music. Tell you what though, take my cell number and give me a call when your schedule looks free."

"Cool, I'll do that. I'll give you a holler later on this evening," I replied as I took the scrap piece of paper he handed me. I reached into my pocket for my keys, unlocked my door, tossed my gym bag to the side, and headed in the direction of my bedroom. As I kicked off my shoes, it occurred to me that I never asked the brother his name. I opened the piece of paper I was still holding in my hand and chuckled when I read the note:

"Nice to meet you. 555-6487. Tyrone"

I can't believe that I hadn't recognized his voice from his voicemail from the night before. I was so pissed at being stood up, and then so infatuated with his in-person persona that I never thought to put two-and-two together.

Ten
MARKUS

pulled my sore body up from the garden bathtub as I heard my phone ringing in the other room. I was in no rush to answer it; it was only Jay calling to tell me to hurry up and scoop him so we could hit the clubs. I lazily reached for a towel as the water dripped from my body and onto the tiled floor.

I glanced into the steamed mirror and caught a hazy glimpse of my physique. I couldn't help but notice how defined my stomach and chest were. I was never one to be conceited, but I was looking pretty damn tight compared to my high school days. I clearly remembered the girls teasing me about being nothing more than skin and bones with no butt to boot. I turned to the side and noticed the definition of my well-defined ass. I wanted to hear what the ladies would say about me filling up a pair of jeans now.

I heard the melodic tone of my BlackBerry emanating from the bedroom; its unique melody let me know it was Jay again. Still soaking wet, I walked into my bedroom and fumbled around in the candlelight looking for my phone. When I finally located it and hit the TALK button, Jay had already hung up. I didn't bother to call him back because I didn't want to hear his mouth when he found out that I wasn't even close to being ready and that it'd probably be another thirty minutes before I even left the crib.

I headed into my bedroom to get ready for the night and searched my closet for something fly to wear. It was one of the few nights where I wasn't actually in the mood to bring home some club freak. My roundabout with the last sister still lingered in my head and I wasn't trying to go there again anytime soon. I made a promise to myself to go to the club, drink a little, dance a little, and leave—alone.

Forty-five minutes after my bath, I was climbing into the driver's seat of my ride. I reached for my cell phone and hit the voicemail button to see what Jay had to say about my running on colored people's time as usual. I was a little disappointed when I heard him say he was going to have to bail on me so he could get up with some honey he'd been chasing for months. All I knew was if his ass was bailing on me at the last minute, he'd better be getting the panties.

Before starting the car, I debated on whether I should spend the night at the crib by myself. As good as pulling out a DVD and popping some popcorn sounded, I found myself turning the key in the ignition anyhow and heading to the new spot over in midtown—called Club Chillax—a coworker had told me about.

Cruising down the highway with Sade's latest album blaring through my speakers, I bobbed my head along to the beat as I weaved in and out of late-night traffic. I hoped the spot would be on point, because I was definitely in the mood to chill out and relax. I pulled up in front of the nightclub and was surprised to see how packed it was.

I drove through the small parking lot trying to find a parking space but to no avail, so I pulled up to the valet parking attendant instead. Looking at the attire of those entering the club, I was glad I had decided to step up *my* attire. I stepped out of my ride, handed the valet attendant my keys, and began to casually stride toward the club's entrance.

Although I was catching looks from many of the ladies lined up outside, I continued my confident stride to the club's door. I looked good, fully dressed in my black flat-front slacks, a midnight blue silk button-down shirt—halfway buttoned to show off my chiseled chest, black square-toed boots from Aldo, and a black platinum Kenneth Cole *Reaction* watch. To top off my attire, I sprayed on a little of Versace's *Man* cologne. It, along with Armani's *Code*, were my new scents of the season.

After entering the club, I was slightly taken aback by its atmosphere. Contemporary R&B music blared from the speakers and, for the first time since I'd been going to clubs, it seemed like almost everyone was dancing. I was accustomed to seeing brothers posted up against the wall, trying to look cool while four or five women sat at tables looking unavailable and unapproachable. What really caught my attention, however, was the band that was setting up in the back of the club.

Some laid-back, live R&B music was definitely what I needed, and I wondered who would be performing. I made my way over to the bar and ordered a Hennessy and Coke before heading toward the side of the stage where some tables had been set up.

With only a few seats available, I sat down at a table occupied by a young couple and got the four-one-one from them on what was going on. Turns out the club was hosting Amateur Night, which in the past had brought out record label execs looking for the next big star. Even Diddy had come through a time or two. I figured if Diddy enjoyed the show, I would, too.

I sat back and enjoyed the band's rendition of Boyz II Men's "I'll Make Love to You," Toni Braxton's "Let it Flow," and Chrisette Michele's "If I Had My Way." As the band finished warming up, the show's MC stepped to the stage to get the show started. No heckling or booing would be allowed and eight acts would showcase their talents, he stated. The winner would be chosen by the audience's reaction and would go on to the next round to compete for some studio time with a well-known producer. Overall, a person had to win three of the competitions to make it to the final. The competitions were held for a period of nine months. I overheard the guy sitting at the table whisper to his girl that the producer was rumored to be Jermaine Dupri. I figured if that was true, then whomever won was definitely in for some quality work; especially after what he'd done for Mariah Carey, Monica, and Jagged Edge, to name a few.

I got up and headed toward the bar to get another drink as the first performer did his rendition of Maxwell's "Pretty Wings." By the seventh performer, I had no idea who'd win. All were good, but none had anything that would make a producer rush to sign them. I mean they all were doing their best to copy the original works, but none had owned their selections and put their own spin on it. When the last performer was called to the stage, I was stunned by her beauty.

Wearing a red evening gown, stilettos—my favorite—and a full lace front wig that would make Beyoncé envious, she had the look and posture of a diva. I had to get to know her, but first I wanted to hear if she could sing as good as she looked. As the band began to play Whitney Houston's "All the Man That I Need," I crossed my fingers for this sister, whom the MC introduced as Uniyah. Usually anyone who tried to sing anything by Whitney fell drastically short. Hell, after all the drugs, smoking, and alcohol, she herself often was a hit and miss with performing her own songs.

I didn't realize that I was holding my breath until Uniyah let out the first note of the song and I exhaled. Her voice wasn't Whitney's, but it had its own style, and as she began to do the ad-libs and runs, it was evident that it was just as strong. As the saxophonist played the bridge, Uniyah swayed along. She was definitely feeling the music as she grabbed the microphone and belted out the song's lyrics. Her voice was filled with more passion than I thought possible. She was definitely singing her heart out.

As the song ended, she took Whitney's signature note an octave higher, spun around on her heels, and two-stepped to the instrumental. This sister was definitely born to perform. She had a natural stage presence that commanded the attention of the audience. As she danced with her back to the crowd, everyone in the club was on their feet, applauding and whistling. There was really no need for a vote because it was evident that she was advancing to the competition's next level. Following protocol, the MC called for all performers to return to the stage anyway. The light applauses for the other contestants didn't compare to the thunderous ovation Uniyah received. It was well deserved. After she was crowned, nothing else that night would top her performance so I decided to call it a night.

As I headed toward my car, I couldn't get Uniyah's beauty off my mind and her voice out of my head. I would have loved to have met her, maybe have her sing a poem I wrote or, better yet, take her out and see what she was really all about. If I played my cards right, I could get my chance. After all, the brother seated at the table let me know she was a regular at the club and basically known by all the usual patrons. If that were true, I'd definitely be back. She was definitely someone I wanted to know.

"Damn, girl, you tore that song up?" Janelle screamed as we made our way out of the club.

"You think so?" I questioned. I was feeling a little apprehensive about my overall performance and thought it could've been a little stronger.

"Girl, you need to stop tripping. I didn't know your voice was so strong. I'm so used to hearing you sing them songs that don't really show off your vocal range."

"That's right; it has been a minute since you've been to the studio. Brandon has been hooking me up with these ballads that would make Mariah jealous. Brother seriously got some writing skills."

"*Word*? I'm going to definitely have to come through to see what you two have been doing. But did you see the club's reaction when you hit that note and then two-stepped with the band?"

"Nah, I didn't. My back was turned." I laughed.

"Now you got to break it down for me and tell me what the deal really is between you and that married brother. If he was the man that you were singing about, then damn, he's definitely doing something good."

"Honestly, I wasn't singing about anyone in particular. I was singing about a fictitious man. You know that man we all dream about when we're lying in bed alone."

"I feel you, girl. So are you ready to head back to my crib and change so we can go get our party on?"

"You know it." As I climbed into Janelle's ride, my thoughts took me back to a brother in the club I had noticed sitting back in the cut. As I belted out each note, I couldn't help but keep my eyes fixated on him. He had that ruggedly handsome thing going on, which was what I liked. As I sung the lyrics about a man I'd never known, I imagined it was that stranger's arms holding me close and giving me all the love *I* needed.

"Yo', this is my jam!" Janelle yelled, turning Jazmine Sullivan up on the radio and interrupting my fantasy. "I love this song."

"Yeah, it's all right," I replied. *Leave it to Janelle to be a fan of a song about a woman busting the windows out of a cheating lover's car*, I thought to myself before slipping back into my daydreaming state.

We pulled up to Janelle's condo and I climbed out. I didn't really feel like clubbing. I really wanted to go to Club Speak! I had been working on one particular piece of poetry that I felt like sharing, and I wished that I hadn't talked Janelle into going with me tonight with the promise of clubbing afterward. There was no way she was going to let me back out of it now.

As we entered her apartment, I noticed it had been a minute since my girl had decided to do a little house cleaning. "Umm, Janelle, you sure you don't want to stay in and clean this joint instead?"

"Oh, you got jokes, huh? My crib isn't that messy; it's mainly my clothes. Plus, I've hired a cleaning service that'll start on Monday to do the basic housecleaning."

"Look at us, moving on up like the Jeffersons."

"I wish that I was moving up but the truth is I don't have time to dust, mop, and clean while working all these long hours. So, a little assistance will definitely take a sister a long way. I know your place must be spotless; your ass is barely there. When you're not at the studio, you're at dance classes, vocal lessons, or running the streets with your newfound beau," she teased.

"Hey, don't hate me for being able to multi-task," I joked.

We headed toward Janelle's bedroom, where she pulled a new outfit that she had designed for me from her closet. This was one of the benefits of having a friend that was an aspiring fashion designer, and I always rocked an outfit by Janelle whenever I had a performance. I held the outfit out to inspect it before I put it on. Girlfriend had skills; this outfit was definitely on point. I went into the bathroom, to ease out of the evening gown and the heels. As I turned from hanging the pants ensemble on the back of the door, for some reason I couldn't pry my eyes away from the mirror. My jogging and light weightlifting were beginning to show. I hoped to have a body like Janet Jackson's one day and from what my personal trainer told me, if I kept up my dance lessons, jogging, and gym routine, then I'd accomplish that within a couple of months, if not sooner. It's a shame that, even in her forties, she was giving us young bucks a run for our own money in the body department.

Standing in front of the mirror in a matching bra and thong set, I proceeded to remove the lace front wig freeing my own natural hair from underneath. Combing and styling it, I allowed it to fall to the middle of my back. Forty minutes later, I heard a knock on the door, followed by Janelle telling me to hurry my ass up so she could get her groove on.

I quickly pulled the pants ensemble from the hanger and put it on, and then went out so Janelle could critique her own work. Handing me a pair of black high-heeled T-strap sandals to top off the outfit, I let her spin me around so she could see how the garment moved.

"Damn, Uniyah, all that working out is starting to show. You're looking good, girl."

"Really? I feel like Halle Berry in *Catwoman*, child. I'm glad you didn't decide to make this outfit out of leather."

"So, you saying you don't like it?"

"When have I been known not to like something that you made? I'm constantly praising you about your skills. Leather would have been too damn hot," I teased.

"True. True," Janelle replied.

"Well, let's go hit these clubs and see what we can find," I said as I grabbed my purse and headed toward the door. I was stopped as Janelle instructed me to hold on so she could change her shoes. I observed that she had on an outfit like the one I wore, but the one she was sporting showed off a little bit more of her assets than mine. "I see someone is trying not to come home alone tonight," I joked.

"Girl, please, these puppies are going to get us some free drinks," Janelle replied as she adjusted her breasts. "Now let's roll."

Climbing into separate cars, I followed Janelle to her choice club of the night. She'd intended on closing down the joint, and I wasn't in the mood to be up in the club until the wee hours of the morning. I planned to stay long enough for Janelle to find her first "prey," and then I'd make my exit. I was sure she wouldn't have a problem snagging someone. Everyone thought Janelle was gorgeous.

She was slightly shorter than me, about five-eight and, at 130 pounds, still considered petite. She had a chocolate smooth complexion, toned body, and a slim waist with a strong back that held up her oversized breasts. Her features were like that of a China doll encapsulated by her African heritage. She carried herself with class and confidence, mixed with sensuality that only a woman sure of herself could possess. Nope, she'd have no problem snagging a few brothers at the club—or anywhere else.

Pulling up to the club, I mentally prepared myself for all the lame-ass lines that would be thrown my way, the weak-ass game that most of the brothers would shoot, and the cheap feels I'd receive from the bold ones. I could already feel a headache coming on as I walked alongside Janelle toward the club's entrance. "Lord, please let this night end soon," I muttered to myself, as a brother in a tweed sport jacket grabbed me by the arm and delivered the first corny "line" of the night. I knew right then that the night was going to be even longer than I expected.

Twelve
TYRONE

I reached into my pocket to grab my phone as it pulsated against my body. Looking at the caller ID on the display, I quickly recognized the number. I hit the TALK button as a grin spread across my face.

"Hello," I bellowed into the phone, shouting over the wind that was coming through my open sunroof.

"Hello, may I speak with Tyrone?" a young, but masculine voice asked on the other end.

"Speaking. Who is this?" I feigned like I didn't know who he was. I didn't need him knowing that I had taken the initiative to store his number into my phone.

"Brandon."

I'd been waiting for almost two days for him to call me. I hadn't heard back from him since I had given him a ride home after the gym, and I had checked my email and voicemail daily, hoping he'd get in touch with me. Part of me wanted to be mad with him but another part was simply elated that he hadn't written me off. What I had done at the gym was a little messed up.

"Wassup, B? What took you so long to give me a holla?"

I questioned, trying to hide the annoyance in my voice.

"My bad. Between school, trying to work out, and writing some lyrics for my girl, it's been a little hectic for me."

"Cool. I feel you. I thought you were mad at a brother for the day at the gym."

"Nah, I was actually okay with the way it all went down. Why were you scared to let me know who you were?"

"I wasn't scared. I wanted the chance to feel you out without either one of us feeling awkward. So tell me what's good?"

"Well, you told me to give you a call when there was a spoken word show at Club Speak! I was calling to see if you had anything planned. If not, then I was hoping we could get up and check it out."

"Why you wait until the last minute to give me a call?"

"Honestly?"

"Mos' def."

"I was nervous."

I couldn't help but laugh at Brandon's last comment. I was grateful that he was keeping it real and not trying to hide what he was feeling.

"No lie, I had plans to chill with my boy, but I think I can get out of that and hang out with you. You want me to come through and scoop you up?"

"It's on you. I don't mind catching the bus and the train."

Now that was definitely rare in the ATL. It really

caught my attention when someone was willing to meet me halfway and not expect me to cater to them. Brother definitely was earning some points. I was beginning to think that kicking it with a guy wasn't all that bad.

"Nah, yo', I don't want you to go through all that. I don't mind coming through and scooping you up. I'm dressed casual though. Is that cool?"

"That's fine. There's no dress code."

After telling him that I'd be there in fifteen minutes, I disconnected the call. A huge smile was plastered across my face. I couldn't believe that this brother had me tripping the way that I was. Anxiously, I headed in the direction of his crib. I couldn't wait to be in his presence once again. The way I was feeling wasn't natural, yet it felt as if it were. I pushed my feelings aside. I didn't want to be in a debate with myself over something that I'd never have the answer to. Some people would say what I was feeling was wrong; others would say it was right. Tonight I was going to agree with the latter.

As I pulled up to Brandon's apartment, I took a deep breath as I turned off the ignition. Stepping out of the car, I told myself to relax and calm down. We were simply two homeys getting together and chilling. As I raised my hand to knock on the door, it flew open instead. Brandon was obviously as anxious as I was for us to see each other again. Wearing khaki slacks, a maroon cotton shirt, and brown Steve Madden shoes, Brandon was a vision to behold. He almost made me feel as if I were somewhat underdressed as I stood before him in my Sean John blue jeans, button-down shirt, and Timberland boots.

Regardless of my attire, I was determined to have a good time with him. "Wassup, B?"

"I'm good. You got here sooner than I thought. Were you in the area?" he asked.

"Yeah, I was kind of in the area. What time does the show start? I'm definitely hungry as hell."

"We have about an hour and a half to kill. Want to stop and get something to eat?"

"Cool. What do you have a taste for?"

"I'm going to be honest. I couldn't care less. If you want to get something fast, that's cool with me, or if you want to sit down at a restaurant, I'm game."

"Okay, so you threw the ball back in my court. Now don't be complaining when we get there," I teased.

"I promise I won't, but let me grab my keys and I'll meet you at the car."

As I headed back to my ride, I couldn't help but think about how good Brandon was looking. He didn't fit the typical mold I was led to believe gay men were supposed to fit. I was shocked at his level of maturity and definitely captured by his masculinity. I climbed into my car to wait for B and scanned my CD collection for a suitable one to play. Finding one I thought would set the mood, I threw it into the dashboard's CD changer. I skipped tracks until I heard Raheem DeVaughn's voice emanating through my sound system. As the chorus began, Brandon climbed into the passenger seat and we made our way out of his complex's parking lot toward Gladys and Ron's Chicken & Waffles located on Peachtree Street in downtown Atlanta.

"Who is this singing?" Brandon asked, breaking the silence between us.

"This is Raheem DeVaughn's latest joint."

"No lie? I must've slept on this CD."

"Mos' def. It's one of his best but, of course, not better than the first. That was my all-time favorite."

"Yeah, that was one of those CDs I could listen all the way through without having to skip a track."

"So true."

"So where are we headed?"

"You'll see. We're almost there."

"I don't know why you got to be all secretive. We're just going out to eat."

"I'm not being secretive…I'm simply remaining in control of the situation."

"Nah, I'm only letting you think that you're in control," he jokingly countered. After a moment of silence, he finally decided to ask what was on both our minds. "Does this feel awkward to you?"

"What?" I questioned, knowing fully well what he was referring to.

"This. I mean us. You know, you being on a date with another guy."

"Is that what this is? I thought we were just homeys chilling."

"Okay," he replied, looking out of the window, pretending not to be bothered with my statement.

"Seriously, I feel a little different about kicking it with you, even as two homeys chilling. When I usually chill with one of my boys, I'm not typically attracted to them." I noticed Brandon trying to suppress a smile as he turned to face me. I quickly turned my eyes back toward the road as if I were completely focused on it.

"Now, I know you felt awkward saying that."

"Please believe," I said, turning my head back toward him.

As I drove down the highway, I had an urge to touch him. The moment I had seen him when he'd opened the door, I was instantly enthralled in his aura, which left me mesmerized and in a daze. Some sort of attraction pulling me closer to him. Hesitantly, I placed my right hand on his thigh. As he jumped at the contact of my hand, I quickly withdrew it, but he stopped me by grabbing my wrist and placing it back on the spot. Interlocking his fingers with mine, we rode in silence the rest of the way to the restaurant.

smiled as I rode alongside Tyrone. The evening was turning out better than I expected. Sitting beside him, I couldn't stop myself from stealing a few looks at him as he concentrated on the road. The focused stare plastered across his face made me smile. When I'd opened my apartment door earlier and he'd stood before me, I had to catch my breath. It felt as if I'd had the wind knocked out of me.

Tyrone was the epitome of what I wanted my ideal mate to look like. Between six-two and six-three with a chocolate complexion and dark brown eyes, whose depth left me mesmerized, his boyish innocence drew me in. His physical perfection almost made me feel like the most unattractive person in the world, but the fact that we were vibing let me know that wasn't true.

I relaxed in the passenger seat and attempted to clear my mind before the south decided to rise in my pants. I didn't want Tyrone to know that he had me open so soon. I wondered where he was taking me to eat, although it truly didn't matter. It could have been McDonald's as long as I was with him. Closing my eyes, I let the ballad flowing from the car's speakers put me at ease until I felt Tyrone's fingers sliding from in between mine. I liked his touch and wasn't quite ready for him to let go. So, I quickly reaffirmed my grip. He didn't seem surprised by my gesture; he actually seemed rather pleased.

As we continued to drive, a part of me began to wonder if I was being played. Tyrone certainly didn't act like a man that had never been with another man before. I thought back to when I first fully came into the lifestyle and everything to me felt awkward. I can't remember how long it took me to show another man any type of affection; even if it was something as small as holding hands. But Tyrone seemed rather "with it" for a newcomer.

As we turned down Peachtree Street, I had a good idea of where Tyrone was taking me. I was hoping that it was either Justin's in Buckhead or Gladys & Ron's Chicken & Waffles. I was hoping for the latter since the taste for some BBQ turkey wings had already begun to make my mouth water. I couldn't suppress the smile that crept across my face as Tyrone pulled into Gladys and Ron's adjacent parking lot.

"Why are you smiling like that?" Tyrone asked after noticing my huge grin.

"I could ask you the same thing."

"Well, you were silent for most of the ride, and then all of a sudden, I look over and you have this big old smile plastered across your face. What's up with that?"

"Because I knew where we were headed."

"Oh you knew, huh? And how exactly did you know this when I never mentioned it to you?"

"I can read minds," I teased, climbing out of the car.

He followed my lead as I headed into the restaurant to grab a table. Although it was early, it was packed and we were told it would be a thirty-minute wait. I excused myself to the restroom to release the tension building in my bladder that was partly due to how nervous Tyrone had made me.

As I exited the restroom, I felt myself growing upset as I saw Tyrone flirting with the hostess. I really had no right to be jealous since we *technically* weren't together and *technically* not on a date, but I was offended nonetheless. Tyrone was losing points, and the night had barely begun. He began to win them back though when the hostess led us to a booth in the back of the restaurant.

"What's wrong?" Tyrone asked as I climbed into the booth. I was obviously wearing my emotions on my face again.

"Nothing," I replied. Part of me wanted to be upset but the other part of me was elated to realize Tyrone was simply running game on the hostess so she'd move us to the front of the line. "Why are you grinning like that?" I asked, noticing his huge smile.

"Because..."

"Because what?"

"'Cause you're jealous."

Jealous? How was he going to accuse me of being *jealous?* He didn't know me like that—even though he was right. I didn't know I was that transparent and quickly tried to find a way to mask my true feelings.

"Why would I be jealous? This isn't a date, right?" I replied in defense.

"Okay, then I was wrong," he said and brushed his foot against mine, the smirk still plastered across his face.

We were interrupted as our waiter approached the table, and he was one helluva good-looking brother; a redbone with a slim build and beautiful hazel eyes that sparkled every time he smiled my way. He almost pulled me in with his charm and big beautiful dimples. Brother was definitely the epitome of a pretty boy, and he was showing me more attention than was required. It made me hope I hadn't become "clockable."

As the waiter walked away, I noticed a look of displeasure on Tyrone's face. "What's wrong?" I questioned, knowing fully well what was on his mind.

"Nothing," he lied.

I laughed to myself. A part of me liked Tyrone being jealous. In a way, it made me feel like he was claiming me as his own.

"I know you aren't getting jealous?" I ribbed him back.

"Why would I be jealous when this isn't a date, *remember?*"

"Okay, cool. So if brother was to ask for my digits or if I were to ask for his, then you would be cool with that?"

"It's whatever, yo'," he replied nonchalantly.

"Let me ask you this, Tyrone. Why is it okay for you to get your flirt on with the hostess but when someone comes to get their flirt on with me you get upset?"

Silence followed my question as he apparently attempted to come up with an answer. Finally, a smile crossed his face as he came to the realization that he was in fact jealous and that he didn't have a good answer.

"But my flirting got us seated earlier."

"And if I play nice, *my* flirting may get us a huge discount," I rebutted.

"True, but if you flirt back with whatever his name is, then you might hurt my feelings," he replied, brushing his leg against mine once more, sending shivers down my spine.

The rest of our dinner was drama free as we enjoyed one another's company and got to know each other better. We discovered we had a lot more in common than just our passion for writing. He told me a little about a book he was working on, and I listened intently. I could directly relate to his level of excitement. It was the same excitement I'd felt after hearing Uniyah croon a song I'd written for her. I checked my watch and saw a smile creep across Tyrone's face.

"What's wrong?" I inquired.

"It's nothing. I was just admiring your watch. I have that same Kenneth Cole. He's one of my favorite designers when it comes to watch designers."

I smiled. I had a plethora of watches from the Kenneth Cole collection. His casual men's line was also one that I favored. Half of my closet was filled with his casual collection. "It appears we have something else in common," I replied.

"What's that?"

"You're wearing my favorite cologne."

"Really? You like Armani's cologne?" he asked excitedly.

"Yeah, I'm wearing it now."

"Damn, I thought I had just sprayed too much on when I smelled it in the car."

When the waiter placed the check on the table, Tyrone reached for his wallet as I informed our waiter that the service and dinner were fine. The waiter smiled, thanked us, and informed us he'd be back later to collect our payment.

"How did he know we didn't want separate checks?" Tyrone grumbled, displeased at the waiter's assumption.

"Could it be he sensed your jealousy or the way you spoke to him every time he smiled at me?"

"Nah, that wasn't it. I just think he's a bad waiter."

"No, he's not. He was very attentive and he wasn't as intrusive or overbearing as some waiters and waitresses can be," I replied while picking up the check. "And don't worry about it. I got it."

"Nah, shawty, I got it."

"It's all good. Let me treat you. Remember I invited you out."

"I appreciate that, but I asked you to dinner so I want to be the one treating you."

It was going to be a losing battle so I relented and allowed Tyrone to take care of the bill while I agreed to leave the tip. Besides, we couldn't waste any more time arguing if we were going to make it to Club Speak!

I left six dollars on the table, and Tyrone and I exited the restaurant and headed toward the parking lot. When we approached the car, he looked around to make sure we were alone and quickly grabbed my butt. With that, I was convinced I wasn't the first guy he had been with, but I planned to address that when the time was right. Right then, all I wanted to do was get to the poetry cipher and listen to some of my favorite poets recite their pieces.

Fourteen
MARKUS

Almost two weeks had passed since the night I heard Uniyah sing at the club. I was still daydreaming about how she had rocked the stage and blew all of her competition away. Many nights since then, lustful thoughts had invaded my mind as I attempted to sleep, but the weird thing was that, in reality, I wanted more than just the physical with her. I wanted to know what made her laugh and cry; what made her happy and sad. I wanted to know her in her entirety.

I had frequented the nightclub three times since then, hoping to run into her, but my visits yielded no success. I entered the club accompanied with hope and left filled with disappointment. But if it were meant for us to meet, fate would make it so.

When I wasn't fantasizing about Uniyah, my childhood nightmares would revisit my peaceful slumber. I did my best to wade in the water and wait until the storm passed, but it seemed the storm that was my past would never leave me. At times, I felt it weakening and then instantaneously it would strengthen with the force of a category five hurricane wreaking havoc on my mind, body, and soul.

There were nights when I turned to the bottle to help me escape and then there were times when I went through my regular routine of club hopping and freaking to wash away the pain. I was playing with fire, but I didn't really care. Alicia Keys' lyrics from her song "Karma" ran through my head: "What goes around comes around; what goes up must come down." I secretly hoped I wouldn't have to live those words.

I couldn't help but question if the events that were occurring in my life were due to something I did. I wondered if it were Karma that made me endure some of the shit I had endured. One thing was for certain: I still remained lonely at night and desired companionship.

It had been so long since I had been in a committed relationship I didn't even know if I really knew what one was. But with the nightmares, I thought I would be better equipped to handle them if I at least had someone I could talk to and confide in. Sometimes I just needed to hear someone say that things were going to be okay. It's funny how that one little phrase could have such an exorbitant impact on one's emotions and psyche.

My run was over, and I climbed down from the machine and removed the earphones from my ears as I raised my head to take a swig from my water bottle. It was another Saturday night, and I didn't quite know how I was going to spend it. Jay had become involved with a new female, so he didn't want to frequent the clubs with the same intensity that he had done when he was single. And I couldn't blame him. If I had someone to come home to, someone to call on a regular, and some type of consistency in my life, I wouldn't want to spend time in the clubs either.

I pushed my thoughts to the side as I lay on the weight bench to begin lifting. My legs were still sore from the rigorous workout they had endured the day before, and the run on the treadmill didn't really help matters much. I was elated that tomorrow was my rest day so my muscles could have a chance to recoup.

I put my upper body through a forty-five-minute workout and afterward headed toward the locker rooms to sit in the sauna and get some of the tension out of my body. I entered the locker room, pried off the sweat-soaked clothes that were clinging to my body, and wrapped a towel around my waist. Then I headed into the sauna and claimed a corner where I leaned back, closed my eyes, and tried to escape.

I debated over whether I would give the nightclub one more chance in hopes of running into Uniyah. I wasn't sure if I was using her as an excuse to frequent the nightclub or not. Truth be told, I had to admit to myself that I truly enjoyed the laid-back atmosphere that I found there. The club was one of the few places when all eyes could be on me if I wanted, or I could slip into the background if I wasn't in the mood to be noticed.

After what seemed like hours, but was probably no more than twenty-minutes, I climbed from the sauna and proceeded to hit the showers so I could get the hell up out of the gym. I had some errands I needed to run and my body was screaming for some sleep.

Three hours later, I had finished the miscellaneous shopping I had put off, gotten a haircut, had the car washed and detailed, and grabbed a quick bite to eat. I was exhausted from my productive day and I couldn't be happier than I was when I pulled up in front of my crib.

After I headed inside, I didn't want to do anything other than melt into my pillow top mattress and wrap myself in my feathered down comforter. Before I realized it, I was sound asleep in a slumber so deep nothing external could disturb my peace. Yet something internal would.

I tossed and turned all night. My inability to sleep was partially due to the unexpected appearance of my cousin who was on leave from the military. I thought that my days of "playing" with my "favorite" cousin had ended when he decided to enlist in the Army. I was somewhat uneasy due to my little brother spending the night at his friend's house and my mother leaving to work her overnight part-time job. I hoped that I'd be left alone for the two days that my cousin was in town because I was no longer the innocent, naïve, juvenile seven-year-old he used to molest. I was older, wiser, and, not to mention, stronger than I used to be. I now knew that what my cousin did to me was wrong and if he attempted to molest me now that I was fourteen, he'd definitely be in for a shock.

I turned over and glanced at my alarm clock and saw it was three in the morning. My cousin had come stumbling home two hours prior, drunk as a skunk and also smelling like one. He'd stumbled into the house and had gone straight to his old room, which was now my little brother's. I could tell he didn't have a good night since he seemed to be a little agitated, but I could not have cared less as long as he stayed the hell away from me. I rolled over on my stomach and closed my eyes. It seemed like as soon as my body began to relax and I was at peace, the storm began to brew.

I smelt my cousin before I felt him gently shaking me awake. He smelled like he had just climbed out of the shower and the scent of Irish Spring perforated my room. He sat on my bed and shook my shoulder again while whispering my name. I pretended not to hear him and acted as if I were in a deep sleep. But then he shook me roughly to let me know that he wasn't in the mood for my games. The shower and the few hours of sleep had helped him sober up but had left him horny.

Groggily, I turned over and noticed my cousin sitting on my bed, nude. What caught my attention was the protrusion of his manhood between his legs. For the first time, I felt afraid. When I was younger, my cousin had only resorted to penetrating me with his fingers and I feared that now that my body had matured, he would attempt to penetrate me with his manhood instead. I hated him with a passion like no other. I didn't know why he thought that I was some sissy that liked messing with guys. I swore if I had the opportunity, I'd kill him.

My cousin pulled the covers back and climbed into bed next to me.

"What are you doing?" I asked him. I could feel him rubbing his manhood against me and it was turning my stomach upside down.

"Come on, Markus, don't play games. I want to do like we used to do. I missed ya."

"Get out of my bed!" I angrily demanded, not knowing where I'd gotten the courage to stand up to my cousin.

"Markus, don't fuck with me. Take your clothes off."

"Get the hell out of my bed!" I yelled and began pushing him away from me. Before I realized it, we were wrestling and then, with all the strength in my adolescent body, I swung at him and hit him in the eye. He screamed out in pain and fell back onto the floor. The moonlight that seeped through the window allowed me to see the frustration mixed with anger plastered across his face. It was a look of sickness and perversion.

"Markus, you think I'm fucking with you tonight?" he yelled.

I sat upright and watched him feel underneath the bed and pull out a bottle. He squeezed the bottle and lathered whatever the contents were onto his penis. Wiping his hands on my sheets, he got up and headed toward me.

We began wrestling again and my fear strengthened me to keep him off of me. As I struggled with my cousin, I pleaded with God to let it be a dream, but it was indeed reality. I felt the tears building up in my eyes, and I did my best to hold them back. There was no way I was going to let him see me cry.

I felt my strength fleeting from the exhaustion. I wasn't going to be able to fight him off much longer. Regardless of how hard I fought and screamed, my cousin was bigger and stronger. He no longer was the scrawny teenager I had known. The military had helped strengthen him. Finally my cousin gained the upper hand and pinned me down on my stomach. With one hand holding my neck from behind, he used the other hand to pry my shorts off. With the aid of his knees, he forced my legs apart. I continued to struggle with him but it was to no avail.

My cousin separated my legs and before I knew it, I felt the most unbearable pain I'd ever felt as he penetrated my body with his penis. I let out a scream that I was sure the whole block heard. My cousin pushed my head into the pillow to stifle my cries and tried to pacify me by telling me if I stopped struggling, then the pain would subside. I had no desire to stop struggling; I just wanted him out of me. I struggled more as my cousin began to gyrate against my body. To punish me more, he pulled his penis partially out of me, and then slammed it inside again. I screamed louder but he pushed my face further into the mattress where nobody could hear my cries; where nobody could come to my rescue.

I bolted upright in bed, soaking with sweat. It took

me a minute to regain focus of my surroundings and realize that I was having another nightmare. Everything felt so real; especially the pain. I remembered that night like it had happened moments ago. It was the last time my cousin ever attacked me.

That night, as the pain perforated my body, I managed to swing my arm into my cousin's face, causing him to pull himself from out of me and protect his eyes. He screamed obscenities at me as I jumped from the bed, grabbed the cordless phone, and ran into the bathroom. After my cousin gathered his composure, he began to pound on the bathroom door. When he noticed that his yelling wasn't going to get me to open it, he began to sob and tell me how sorry he was. He kept begging for me not to call my mother or to tell anyone because he didn't want to go to jail. He kept apologizing and, for a moment, I felt sorry for him. Then I realized how confused I was for even feeling sympathy for him. He was sick and needed help.

I instructed him to leave. His flight didn't leave for another eight hours and I didn't care. I wanted him gone! I told him that if he didn't leave, then I was going to call the police, but if he left, I'd keep my mouth shut. Ten minutes later, I heard the front door slam shut. I ran out of the bathroom and watched as my cousin's rental car backed out of the driveway.

I went into the kitchen and grabbed all the ice trays and headed back into the bathroom. I ran a cold bath and allowed the tub to fill with water, and then dumped the ice into it. I climbed into the tub and allowed the coldness to numb me as I was still in a state of shock from the violation that my body had undergone.

I lay in the tub for almost two hours and, when I finally rose from it, the water was no longer clear but instead a deep pink. For the next two weeks, I had to take cold baths to stop the swelling, which made defecating almost unbearable. I should have been grateful that my cousin wasn't a hung man, because I'm sure he'd have sent me to the emergency room that night.

I remembered how I cleaned up my room and washed my sheets so that my mother wouldn't see the blood on them. I don't know why I covered for my cousin. I hated him more than I thought was possible. I loathed him and wanted to kill him, but I think I covered for him because I was ashamed. I didn't want anyone to know what he had done to me, and I didn't want anyone to think I was a sissy.

In some way my discretion gave my cousin the illusion that I cared for him. He always went out of his way to send me birthday cards filled with money or some expensive gift that I would end up giving to my brother or to a friend. He began writing me letters, apologizing for hurting me, and tried to get me to believe that he was truly in love with me. This was his sad attempt of explaining why he had done what he did. I didn't want to hear it, nor was I buying it. The night my cousin left was the last time I had seen him and if I were to see him now, I'd probably kill him.

I sat on the edge of my bed and stared at the wall as the last thoughts of my cousin faded away. The nightmares had once again claimed my peace and if I went back to sleep, they would only return. I climbed from my bed and headed toward the bathroom to wash the sweat from my body. The only thing I realized was that I had to get out. I had to escape. And I knew exactly where I was headed.

s Janelle and I pulled up to the club in her "souped-up" Maxima, I couldn't help but notice all the heads turning our way, trying their best to see who was about to step out of the mirror-tinted indigo blue Nissan with the Euro lights sitting on dubs. Janelle had invested just as much time, money, and energy into her ride as she invested in her wardrobe. Her dedication to her craft was part of the reason why she was one of the more popular up-and-coming designers in the ATL.

I was sure most of the ladies would be disappointed when we stepped out of the ride, and they realized we weren't a couple of brothers they could flaunt their "goods" for. The brothers, on the other hand, were definitely going to be in for a treat because Janelle and I were definitely dressed to kill. As usual, we were both sporting one of Janelle's original designs that showed just enough to grab a man's attention but definitely not enough for them to think we were "easy lays."

As we made our way to the club's entrance, we could

hear its "signature" song blasting from behind its doors and Janelle began to sing along to its lyrics:

Back it up shawty
Dip it down low
You know ya' a hottie
Ya' body is on fiyah
Wanna see you split the floor
Just shake it a lil more
Act like you working a pole

I couldn't help but laugh as Janelle struggled to bounce to the song in her heels.

As Janelle and I made our way to the front of the line, I could hear some of the other women whispering to their girlfriends while questioning out loud where the hell we thought we were going and who the hell we thought we were. Little did they know, Janelle had dated the owner of the club back in her college days. We stopped to show the bouncer some love, and then headed into the club where the DJ was now spinning a hip-hop track that I didn't recognize. As much as I hated the club, there was no better place to keep up with the latest music and dance moves; especially if you were an aspiring entertainer. I had to make sure that I could compete with the J.Los, Janets, and Beyoncés. In the music business, I learned it's all about the full package and not necessarily how good one can sing.

Once inside, I parted ways with Janelle and headed to the opposite side of the club to do my own thing. I could tell Janelle was in one of her moods to get her freak on. She was seeking out her on-again-off-again boo, Kareem.

I definitely wasn't trying to get all up in her mix so I made my way to the bar. Out of the corner of my eye, I scoped a brother that looked familiar. My eyes locked with his and I quickly turned away so he wouldn't know I was checking him out; I hoped darting my attention away from him didn't seem like a lack of interest. I turned to the bartender to order my drink and continued to ponder where I'd seen the brother before.

I took my drink from the bartender and handed her my money when she told me that it was already taken care of. Now I was looking good in my Prada boots and original custom-designed ensemble that Janelle had conjured up, but I didn't know I was looking *that* good. The bartender pointed her hand in a direction behind me to let me know who I owed my "thanks" to; and when my eyes connected with his, I couldn't help but smile. It was the guy I had locked eyes with earlier. I definitely was going to have to thank the gentleman personally for his kind gesture.

Doing my best to strut as seductively as I could in my stiletto boots, I made my way over toward him while praying I wouldn't fall. As I stood directly in front of him, I felt myself become tongue-tied while the words forming in my head struggled to come out of my mouth. I had never approached a guy in my life and my awkwardness must have been showing. Sensing that I was in distress, he decided to break the ice instead.

"After that sexy walk, I just knew you were going to say something profound." He laughed.

I couldn't help but join in his laughter; my silence after my great "presentation" had to be a big disappointment.

"I'm sorry. My aggressive diva persona fell a bit short," I joked. "I can stick with my day job."

"Right," he jokingly affirmed.

"So, to what do I owe this free drink?"

A moment passed before he answered and I figured he was looking for a cheesy pickup line to throw at me. "Let's just say it was something to get your attention and to get you to talk with me. Let's call it an icebreaker." A puzzled look appeared on his face when I laughed. With one eyebrow raised, he questioned, "What's so funny?"

"Well, I expected you to throw me some weak line that would've made me cringe."

"At my age, I think honesty is always the best policy and you're somebody I honestly want to get to know," he quickly countered.

The brother's charm had me mesmerized, and I couldn't shake the feeling that we had met before. As I looked into his deep brown eyes, I couldn't help but be engulfed in his rugged handsomeness. There was something about this guy that had my undivided attention and at the same time made me nervous. His deep melodic voice gave me a sense of security. When he spoke, a flash of warmth raced through my body. It was as if his voice exuberated authority and respect. He cut my analyzing short when he asked me to join him on the dance floor.

I allowed him to lead me through the crowd of sweaty dancers to the middle of the dance floor and hoped he had some skills. The drink he had bought me had begun to loosen my body and mood. Allowing the music to take over, I began to lose myself under the thumping bass and flashing lights.

I opened my eyes to see if my dance partner had been able to keep up or if I had lost him in the crowd. I was amazed as I watched him seductively maneuver his body along to the beat of the song. I couldn't take my eyes off his gyrating hips or his twisting torso. Saying that the brother could simply dance was an understatement. He actually took dancing to another level and it seemed I wasn't the only one in the room that had my eyes locked on him. As I looked around, I noticed other women staring in our direction and checking out his moves. This was all I needed to be set free.

As the speakers blared an upbeat song and the alcohol took its effect on me, I was like a caged bird set free after years of captivity. My training in dance mixed with my performing instincts took center stage and before I knew it, I was grooving to the beat. I threw it to the left and then pulled it back and threw it to the right, backed up, and dropped it like it was hot. I don't know what came over me. I usually was more reserved on the dance floor but something about this brother brought out a hidden sensuality in me that I couldn't contain.

After a few more cuts, we decided to take a break and unwind on the patio where we could cool down and catch our breath. Leaning against the patio's wooden fence, I casually checked him out from head to toe. He was well over six feet, which definitely was a plus, and from what I could feel on the dance floor, underneath his garments he had a well-maintained body.

I could also tell from our grinding session on the floor that the brother was definitely packing in that department, too, not that it mattered. Hell, who was I kidding? It definitely mattered. But aside from his body, what I loved most was his cocoa complexion and his dark brown eyes. He had a million-dollar smile, and something about it and his beautiful almond-shaped eyes left me wanting to know more about him. It was like there was a hidden story that resided within them.

I saw Janelle walking toward us, and from the look in her eyes, I already knew what she was coming to tell me. "'Sup, girl? Can I talk to you for a second?"

I turned to the brother and excused myself, asking him if I could get him something to drink while I headed to the bar for a minute. He declined and, instead, directed me to stay outside on the patio with Janelle while he went in to freshen up my drink. As he walked away, Janelle and I remained silent, choosing to enjoy his assets from behind until he was out of earshot.

"Mmm, Uniyah, you definitely pulled one hell of a catch!"

"You ain't lying. Anybody that can't see that brother is *fine* must be blind as hell. But what's up, girl?"

"Like you don't already know what I'm about to say," Janelle teased.

"Yeah, I know. You about to tell me you're going to bounce so you and Kareem can make up for some lost time. Don't put a hurting on him."

"Nah." Janelle laughed. "It's more like him putting a hurting on *me*. I swear he has more energy than that damn Energizer bunny. But you want me to drive you back to the crib, or do you want to take my keys and drive yourself home?"

Before I could answer Janelle's question, the brother—who had returned sooner than I expected—volunteered his services. I looked him up and down, decided to throw caution to the wind, and hoped I wouldn't live to regret it. Sensing my hesitation, he offered Janelle his driver's license number and full name. And Janelle, being the person she is, took both.

After Janelle had collected his information, we embraced and said our goodbyes with me promising to leave her a voice message when I arrived home. I watched Janelle head back into the club, where Kareem was impatiently waiting, and then turned my attention toward the brother whose name I had scooped from his driver's license when Janelle was writing down his information.

"All right, Mr. Greene, I'm all yours for the remainder of the evening."

Smiling like a child at Christmas, I saw his eyes twinkle. "Please believe I'll do my best to keep you entertained, Miss Uniyah."

I was taken aback. I was certain that I hadn't divulged my name to him and Janelle hadn't either. "How do you know my name?" I quizzically asked.

"I'm psychic," he teased, but seeing the concerned look on my face, he opted for the truth. "Seriously, I saw you perform Whitney's song at the club about two weeks ago, and I thought you were wonderful. But before I had the opportunity to introduce myself to you, you were gone."

I was a little more at ease, knowing that the brother hadn't been stalking me or checking around the club for some information on me. "Well, Mr. Greene, can I get a first name or would you like me to call you Mr. Greene for the remainder of the evening?"

"You can call me Markus and, if you don't mind, I want to get back out on that dance floor and see you work that banging body of yours some more."

I grabbed Markus' arm and led him back onto the dance floor. My plan was to keep him dancing until his legs were sore, and it just so happened that the DJ was cranking another of my favorite jams. I was definitely going to make him regret his request.

Reciprocate

Emails
Phone calls
Thinking-of-you cards
Voicemails
Messages
Notes just because
Specially made CDs
Candy
Sentimental gifts
All from the heart
My heart

A shoulder to lean on
An ear to hear your problems
Asking you how your day went
Enduring your false accusations
Not giving in to the temptations
Offering you a hand when you stumbled in life
Helping you to find your bearings
Leading you through those troubled times

Bringing you up when you were down
Having your back
Keeping your focus on track
Resting your head in my lap
Helping you to face your fears
Drying the tears when you cried
Betcha don't remember any of those times

All this
Must be I care
Not everyone receives my undying dedication
Yet you don't do the same
Instead you only play games
Breaking me down
Fucking with my emotions
What exactly are your intentions
What do I have to do to get some type of reciprocation
Is this what love is about
If so, then I want out
It seems like the more I give
Smiling in my face
The more you take
Damn, how much more of this must I take
The more, at our relationship I work
The more you hurt
Wondering if this all was just a mistake
Seems like you purposely bring on the heartache
Why is it my heart you trying to break

When is it my turn to smile
Bring me up when I'm down
Have a bad day
Have you tell me everything is going to be okay
Shed a tear
And without a doubt know you'll be there
Can I receive some appreciation
Just a little recognition
Damn, I'm begging for some reciprocation

Prioritize
For once put me first
Hear me
Feel me
What do I have to do to get you to love me
The war is over
Sound the horns
Throw up the white flags
I give up
The battle is lost
Victory is yours

Would've died for you
That's right, given up my life
Given you anything
Loved you unconditionally
I would've lived for you
Stayed faithful

Kept my intentions true
All I required
Even if I received it for one day
Was for you to reciprocate in some way

Clean your ears
Expand your mind
Try to hear what I say
I'm not asking you to change
Not really asking for you to go above and beyond
What I'm asking is really basic
All I want is a little reciprocation

I listened intensely to Brandon reciting his piece in front of the room of strangers. I absorbed every word he spoke, and admired his cadence and ability to recite such an emotional piece. As I watched him perform his piece with his head slightly bowed and his eyes fixated on the ground, I couldn't help but feel my own remorse. I thought of all the women that had done the same things for me; those who had gone out of their way to win and keep my attention and affection. I thought of how I would ignore or take their actions for granted. Hearing Brandon speak opened my eyes and my mind. It helped me to see that Brandon was a passionate individual that required attention, acknowledgment and, most importantly, reciprocation.

As Brandon finished reciting his piece, the room erupted in applause and finger snaps. I admired the way Brandon paused at the right places, emphasized the right words, let the emotions take form on his face. All of it gave the poem the needed dramatic effect it required.

Brandon shyly thanked the crowd and headed back to the table where I was seated. As he sat across from me, I couldn't help but see him in a different light. I heard the pain hidden within his poem and I heard his silent cry to be loved as he uttered each word. It made me wonder if I could actually love a man as intensely as he spoke of.

We listened to a few more poets perform their work—some without music and some with. By the time the last poet finished, I felt completely fulfilled by the whole experience and couldn't wait to see if these same people would accept my words whenever I gathered the courage to get up on stage and recite them.

Brandon pulled me from my thoughts as he tapped me on my shoulder to ask me if I were ready to bounce. I nodded, even though I wasn't quite ready for the night to end. I was truly enjoying my time with him.

I followed Brandon's lead as he made his way toward the exit of the club through the standing crowd that blocked it. I noticed a couple of people throwing looks his way—both men and women—and I couldn't deny that I felt somewhat jealous. I wanted to pull him back and wrap my arm around his waist to let everyone know he was with me. Although this was only our second date, I was already wanting to claim him.

Finally making our way to my ride, we climbed in and

I asked Brandon if he was ready to go home. I was a little disappointed when he told me that he was. I did my best to hide my disappointment. I definitely didn't want to alter the mood or ruin the night. I was appreciative of the time that I had already spent with him.

"So what did you think of *my piece?*" Brandon asked.

I paused for a second and hesitated before I answered. "Honestly, I loved the piece you wrote. It was as if you were wearing your heart on your sleeve for all to see."

"What do you mean, I was wearing my heart out on my sleeve for all to see?"

"I mean exactly that. I believe the quote is actually from one of Shakespeare's plays—*Othello*, I think. Basically, I'm saying your emotions were easily readable as you read that poem. I only recently met you and I already know so much about what kind of person, man, and lover you are."

"Is that a good or bad thing?"

"Well, I think it's a good thing. If you're the passionate brother that I pegged you as, then I'm definitely interested."

"Interested in what?" he quizzically asked.

I remained silent as I collected my thoughts. I didn't actually know what it was that I was interested in so I didn't quite know how to answer his question. "Let's just say that I'd be interested in getting to know you on a deeper level. You seem like the type of lover that everyone wants; the kind that would go out of his way to let his significant other know that he's loved. You know the type of person that a guy could come home to and, even though the world has dogged him out and everything seems to be going wrong, you'd make him feel better."

"Yeah, but if things keep going the way they have been, then I'm going to be nothing more than damaged goods."

"Damaged goods?"

"You know, almost like picking up a canned good and dropping it on the floor? Eventually that can is going to have dings and dents all over it due to all the abuse. It's usually the can that gets left on the shelf. That's sort of where I'm heading; except my heart is the canned good."

"Wow, I've never heard anyone explain heartbreak that way. That was a good metaphor. How can you be so close to becoming damaged goods when you're so young?"

"The gay lifestyle is like dog years compared to regular years. Even though it seems that I've been in this life for such a short time, I'm actually a true veteran when it comes to dealing with bullshit."

"So, why do you continue to pursue men? You've dated women, right?"

"Yes, I've dated women, but I choose not to ride the fence. I told myself a while ago that I was going to either date women, or men, but definitely not both. Sometimes, when I'm on the train riding home or to school, I look around and see women earnestly trying to complete the book in their hands, which is usually a story about a brother on the 'down low,' all in hopes of having a better understanding of the signs of a man that plays on both sides. I have too much respect for my sisters and the last thing I want to do is throw any more pain their way. I think they deal with enough bullshit already. Dealing with a confused lover is the last thing they need to have added to their lives."

I was definitely feeling what Brandon was saying and a lot of it hit home, especially since I was a brother "riding the fence." I don't know why I had such a strong desire to be with men and an equal desire to be with women. This was part of the reason why I was so confused. I didn't want to intentionally hurt anyone. I simply wanted to be happy and, at this time in my life, being with a man and a woman equally appeased me.

"You know I'm not judging you, right?" Brandon inquired.

"Yeah, I know, but I'm feeling what you're saying and I wish I could say I have the self-will to choose who it is that I am going to fall in love or be with but, emotionally, I just can't. I have desires for both men and women and, at this point, I can't say that I can be solely with one and not the other as well."

"So you are saying that if you and me, hypothetically, took things to the next level, I couldn't expect monogamy from you?"

I glanced at Brandon from the corner of my eye and thought long and hard about how I was going to answer his question. I didn't want our second date to be our last, but he was asking me a question that required the truth and I didn't want our foundation to be built on a lie. "Brandon, I can't honestly say that I'd only want to be with you, and I can't say if I were to be with a woman that I'd only want to be with her. I'm currently at a crossroads with my sexuality, and that's why I'm not promising anyone anything at this point until I am sure as to what it is that I want."

Silence permeated the car as the CD ended and the next began to load. I wished that I had lied to Brandon and told him what it was that he wanted to hear because then I'd at least have the opportunity to be in his presence a little longer. I glanced over at Brandon and his attention was focused out of the passenger's window as if he were pondering what his next move would be.

"What are you thinking, B?"

Brandon sighed before he began. "I really like you and would like the opportunity to get to know you as a friend, and maybe more than a friend, but I don't want to be hurt. I'm so tired of being hurt."

"B, I can't promise you what it is that you want. But I know one thing for sure: I won't lie to you. If something was to pop off between the two of us and I began developing feelings for someone else, I'd inform you." I reached over and grabbed Brandon's hand and was surprised when he didn't recoil from my touch.

"That's fair," he said, turning to look at me. "And I promise to do the same."

awoke to the sound of the house phone ringing and was shocked when I realized the pillow I thought I'd been holding all night had really been Uniyah. This was the third evening we'd spent with one another. I decided for something a little more relaxed this time. The first night we met was at the club, and then our first *official* date was the traditional dinner and a movie.

Last night, I decided to treat her to an evening at the Apache Café to hear some spoken word and afterward we circled around Atlanta's perimeter. To end the evening, I suggested we come to my crib to chill for a minute.

The two of us spent the remaining of the evening talking and really getting to know one another better. I couldn't believe that she, too, was a writer, an aspiring singer, and a dancer. It all began to come together. When we were on the dance floor, it was as if Uniyah was performing for an audience rather than merely being free. As she danced, she constantly scanned the room, making sure all eyes were on her. If she saw someone doing something that she liked, she'd attempt to imitate it. Nonetheless the girl had skills, and even though I didn't agree with her decision to put her college education on hold while she pursued her dreams full-time, it was her life to live and not mine.

I asked her to sing me something a cappella and was shocked when she began to belt out Minnie Riperton's "Lovin' You," hitting every note in the right key. She definitely had talent, but in today's hip-hop driven industry, talent alone didn't mean much. In fact, singing didn't mean much if you didn't have some rapper on your track adding some flava to it.

We enjoyed a bottle of wine and watched some late-night BET videos before falling asleep on the couch in our clothes. I hoped that I didn't poke her in the back all night with my dick because I had awakened with a serious hard-on. I pulled myself free from Uniyah, doing my best not to wake her, and raced to the phone. Peeping the caller ID, a smile ran across my face as I realized that it was Moms calling to check up on me.

"Hello," I whispered into the phone, heading into the bedroom so I wouldn't wake Uniyah.

"It took you long enough to answer. I was preparing to leave you a message."

"Sorry about that, Ma. I was still sleeping." I instantly regretted saying that. I braced for the lecture that she was about to deliver.

"Sleeping? I know it's a weekend, but it's almost noon and the day is almost over. Let me guess. You were out drinking and partying all night?"

As she went through her routine of questioning, I zoned out. My mom cared for me but I was a grown-ass man and if I decided to stay out every night and party, that was my business and mine alone.

"Markus, do you hear me talking to you?"

I must have forgotten to throw in the occasional *uh-huh*. "Yeah, Ma, I'm listening to you," I lied.

"No, you're not, boy! You're tuning me out, just like your brother does," she teased. "How are you doing, baby?"

"I'm good, Ma. Work has been killing me so that's why, on the weekends, I go out and do whatever I got to do to relax—legally, that is."

"I know. I'm just messing with you. But don't let work get the best of you, baby."

I listened to my moms for another ten minutes, updating me about the family and what was going on with her and my stepfather. I was elated to learn that my stepfather had finally talked my mother into taking a cruise to the Bahamas. I knew how badly she had always wanted to go, but she was afraid to fly and definitely afraid to sail. So this was going to be a big step for the both of them.

All that I remembered of the two since they married when I was a junior in high school, was them constantly working. Always trying to make sure that my brother and I had everything that we needed and that there was money in the bank for our college educations. As I prepared to say goodbye, my mother said something that turned a pleasant conversation into an instantly dreaded one.

"You know your cousin is coming into town."

All these years and I still had never told my mother about what had happened between my cousin and me. She always questioned me as to why we were no longer as close as we used to be, and I lied and told her that we both grew up and changed. It was simple as that—or so I made it seem.

I feigned interest so that my mother wouldn't begin to give me the fifth degree. "What's bringing him to town?"

"His enlistment is over with the military, and I don't think that he's going to re-enlist; especially with all that's going on in Afghanistan and this war on terrorism. I'm shocked that they're not postponing his discharge, like they did to one of my coworkers' boys."

"Well, that's good. Hey, Ma, I'm getting another call. Can I hit you back?" I lied to cut the call short. Discussing him was the last thing I wanted to do now, if ever.

I headed back into the living room just as Uniyah stretched her long slender body across my couch. When she looked at me doe-eyed, I felt my erection instantly return. I was grateful that I was wearing form-fitting boxer briefs under a baggy pair of lounge pants so she couldn't tell. I simply couldn't help myself. She looked beautiful; even with her hair in disarray and most of her makeup gone.

Forcing myself to calm down, I headed toward her,

sat down and put her feet in my lap so I could massage them. I was not into feet in the least, but Uniyah definitely had some pretty toes, which was a pure contradiction for what is said about dancers and their ugly feet.

"One of your little girls calling you?" she teased, referring to my phone call with my mother.

I laughed along with her. "I wish I had it like that, but I don't," I informed her, which was the God's honest truth. What man wouldn't wish he had it like that?

"Whatever. I took a peep at you and the way you were smiling on the phone and, not to mention, how your voice changed in pitch. You were definitely talking to a girl."

"I didn't say that I wasn't talking to a female. I just said that it wasn't one of my 'little girls,' as you insinuated."

"Uh-huh."

"That's cute."

"What?"

"You're jealous and the cute part is that it was my moms that I was talking to."

"Tell me anything." She pouted.

I slid Uniyah's legs off my lap, grabbed the cordless phone, and handed it to her. I told her to hit the redial button and when she declined, I did it for her.

"Hey, Ma, it's me. I know we just hung up, but I got someone over here that thinks you're one of my many little honeys. I'll let you talk to her and, by the way, her name is Uniyah."

I turned to Uniyah, whose face was beginning to change

shades from embarrassment. I tried to get her to take the phone, but she pushed it away. I told Moms to hold on and went to put her on speakerphone.

"Okay, Ma, I got you on the speakerphone."

"This is Markus' mother," my mother replied, doing her best to sound stern.

I couldn't help but laugh, and decided to go to the bathroom while my mother and Uniyah talked. When I came back into the room, Uniyah had the phone cradled to her ear and was laughing at something that my mother was saying on the other end. I grabbed her from behind and began nibbling on her neck, making her squirm and causing her breathing to change. She hurriedly got off the phone and playfully pushed me away.

"All right, Ma, we'll talk to you later," I said, after taking the phone from Uniyah. After I ended the call I tossed the phone onto the couch.

"I can't believe you had me talk to her!" she gasped.

"You were calling me a liar," I teased. "And I wanted you to know that I am a man of my word. Plus, it seems like you and Moms were getting along pretty well."

"Yeah, she's probably thinking that I'm some loose chickenhead."

"Nah, my mom isn't like that. Plus, this will buy me some time and get her to stop asking about when I plan on finding someone to settle down with so I can give her some grandbabies." I pulled Uniyah back against me and began to grind my pelvis against her backside.

"So, are you going to help me with that?" I whispered.

"From the way you were poking me all night, I thought you were already trying to make some. Your shit almost pushed me off the sofa and onto the floor."

"Whatever. That was probably my hand or something."

"Nah, it definitely wasn't," she replied, after turning around and grabbing my hand, and then placing her other hand on my penis and squeezing it. "Yeah, it felt more like that," she said and headed into the bathroom with her purse.

I watched her backside as she headed down the hall and closed the door behind her. I was hoping my aggressiveness didn't fuck up any chance of getting to know her. I headed into the bedroom to put on some clothes so that I could take her out to breakfast, and then drop her off. By the end of the day, I'd need to hit the gym for a few hours to work off some of my built-up sexual tension.

Uniyah bobbed her head along to the track as I watched her through the recording booth's window. She sang along softly to the melody and tickled the air with her fingers like a pianist working the "ivories." Physically, I was at the studio, but mentally I was elsewhere. My last "date," or whatever the hell it was, that I'd had with Tyrone still lingered on my mind. Even though I had enjoyed kicking it with him, I was wondering if I was setting myself up to be hurt. I was the type of person that eagerly jumped into relationships without taking the time to fully evaluate the pros and cons. I wanted this to be different. Yet and still, a part of me wanted to step out on faith and trust my heart. I was truly at war with myself.

"Brandon, how was that?" Uniyah asked, interrupting my thoughts.

"Umm...it was good, Uniyah," I lied. Truthfully, I had zoned out as soon as she began singing the lead vocals. I'd have to replay it at home and give her my honest opinion when I was less distracted.

"Brandon, I know you aren't sitting here telling me a lie! I could tell halfway through the song you weren't paying any attention. That's why I began singing whatever came to mind. Play the track back," she commanded.

I did as Uniyah instructed and discovered that, although the first half of the track was pretty good, the rest was a total mess. I looked up and saw the disapproving glare painted across her face. Even with the glass between the two of us, I could feel her anger emanating from the booth and into the engineering room. She didn't need to utter any words for me to determine what she was thinking.

"Uniyah, I'm sorry," I apologized. "I've got some things on my mind."

"I can tell but, like you always tell me, 'either leave it out of the studio or put it in a song.' Right now, we really need to have something completed so we can begin soliciting record labels. My plan is to have this demo completed within the next two months. But if tonight is a prelude to what future nights are going to be like, then I don't see us meeting that goal," Uniyah argued.

I listened to Uniyah lecture me and absorbed every word without interrupting. There was nothing I could say. She was right. A lot had been going on in her world, but she still managed to come into the studio and uphold her part ninety-eight percent of the time. Lately, however, she had been edgy and moody, with her personal deadline approaching. But I understood. This was her life and her dream, and Uniyah never believed in defeat or falling short. She was as determined to make a name for herself as a singer as I was as a music writer. She was holding up her end of the bargain, but I wasn't.

I glanced down at my watch, took a deep breath, and cleared my mind. "Okay, Uniyah, we have almost an hour left before our time's up, so let's try this one more time."

I keyed the track and told her to watch her pitch. I decided to devote all of my attention to getting the song done. Forty-five minutes later, we had our finished product.

"Uniyah, I think that this is the best track you've ever recorded," I said as we sat on the couch, with her legs resting on mine.

"I think you're right. Whatever the hell was on your mind when you came up with the leads and music definitely affected you in a good way! Damn, the intensity in the keyboards alone makes the song come alive. Brandon, no doubt, this track is tight!"

There was nothing like being able to sit down and listen to your finished product and to not have one negative thing to say about it. If there was such a thing as perfection, then this was the epitome of it.

"Uniyah, I got an idea!" I excitedly exclaimed as I pulled her up and onto her feet. Dragging her into the recording booth, I told her to sit on one of the stools while I pulled up another. I went back into the engineering room and grabbed my guitar, and then turned the microphones on. Uniyah stared at me in confusion. I took a seat beside her and looked her in the eyes.

"Niyah, are you really ready for your dream to come true?" I asked.

"Without a doubt," she uttered without hesitation. "I eat, sleep, dream, breathe, and live music. It's my life."

As she finished her statement, I began stroking my guitar and instructed her to sing along as I played. I covered everything from Anita Baker, Oleta Adams, Donny Hathaway, and Stevie Wonder. As I played, Uniyah sang each song but made each one of them her own. She added in her own ad-libs and runs, and I provided the choruses. I stopped playing and asked her again if she was really ready. She looked me in the eyes and told me to play whatever came to mind, and I did as I was told.

After the first couple of bars, Uniyah, with her eyes closed, began free-styling. She started off with some spoken word, which led into song. I continued to play as she bounced between the two. Here and there, I added in some ad-libs. Deciding to push Uniyah to her limit, I changed tempo and began playing something more upbeat. After a slight hesitation, Uniyah gained the flow of the music and began singing whatever came to mind. When she finished, she turned to me with her eyes glazed like someone high or buzzed.

"Brandon, are *you* ready?" she asked.

"Without a doubt."

"Brandon, I really don't think you're ready," she retorted.

"Test me," I stated with confidence.

"Feel me then."

In her soft alto voice, Uniyah did a run that led into a ballad. Her passion emanated throughout the song and motivated my playing. As she sang about wanting someone that didn't know she existed, the room began to blur as I began to enter into my zone. Closing my eyes, all I heard was Uniyah's voice as I played. Before I knew it, I had begun to sing and we were both on our feet, passionately singing to the fictitious lover we had created in our minds. As we came down from our high, our surroundings began to come back into focus and I realized we had a small audience forming in the engineering room.

The next group who had booked the studio was waiting for us to vacate but enjoying our impromptu "concert" nonetheless. As Uniyah dropped her final note, she opened her eyes and observed the audience that had formed. She smiled shyly, and then glanced at her watch before apologizing to the group and grabbing her belongings. As we walked out of the recording booth, the small audience, which included the rap group Real Deal, erupted with applause.

"Mos' def, you two definitely got some skills," one of the rappers from the group commented. "We'd like to work with both of ya'll. I got this fire song that needs a female on the hook, and we got another club banger that needs a brother on the hook. Can you flow, too?"

"Yeah, I do a lil' sumthin'," I admitted. "I ain't gansta though."

"That's cool. Our shit ain't all about the streets and thuggin'," another of the rappers stated. "We just tryna make people dance and bob their heads to some good hip-hop. Ya' feel me?"

"I feel you. Well, let us know when you want to do this and it's a done deal."

"I got you," the rapper replied.

Before Uniyah and I rolled out, I exchanged numbers with Real Deal's manager. This was definitely something to look forward to. Hopefully, we'd come up with something that Uniyah could add to her demo to show her versatility as an artist.

I stuffed the CDs with our recent recordings on it into my backpack and walked Uniyah to her car. She offered me a ride home but I declined and gave her a hug instead. I made my way to the train station and couldn't wait to get on board to resume my thoughts of Tyrone. I'd put them aside in the studio, but now they were back full force and I had to give them the attention they were demanding.

Nineteen
UNIYAH

I had no idea what was troubling Brandon at the beginning of our studio session, but he was beginning to piss me off. Here I was spending my hard-earned money, trying to put together a demo, and he was bringing his personal drama to the studio. I was being somewhat insensitive, but I'd invested a great amount of money, time, and energy on this project and I would be damned if I let my dream slip away when I was so close to grasping it.

Deep down I wasn't mad with Brandon, but more upset with myself. I had set out to score a record deal almost three years ago and put my college education on hold after my senior year to devote my time and energy to completing something that was marketable to a record company. Whenever it appeared that a door would open for me, it would just as easily close.

I'd had my share of false hope, working with independent labels that ended up closing their doors within months of promising me a deal, not to mention getting with agents who would only tell me that they knew that

I'd make it one day but, at the moment, it would be a conflict of interest representing me since they were already working with artists appealing to the same target market. I didn't think I could take having another door opened for me and then slammed in my face.

I hadn't talked to my mother in weeks. During our last conversation, she and my father had tried to convince me to put this "pipe dream" aside and go back to school to finish my degree. That angered me more than anything. If I didn't have my family in my corner to support my dream, who did I have? It was times like these that made me want to throw in the towel and quit. But then something would happen to let me know a Higher Power was on my side. Tonight was one of those nights.

I don't know what came over me toward the end of my recording session, but I felt something that I had never felt before. I felt pain intertwined with happiness. I felt high but not the kind of high you get from smoking a joint or drinking. It was something different. It was a feeling like nothing else I'd ever felt; a feeling I didn't want to end. I relished moments like that and it made me really pause and thank Him for bringing Brandon into my life.

Checking my watch as I pulled up to my apartment building, I was relieved that I was finally home and that I could soak in the tub. I had called Markus on my drive home so that he'd know there was an interest in him on my end. I had to admit that I was sort of feeling him. He made me feel like a high school girl and something about his eyes made me want to explore everything about him. When I looked into them, I saw a happiness masking something deeper. I don't quite know what that was, but if he gave me the opportunity to kick it with him on the regular, I was going to make it my mission to find out.

I was shocked as hell when David appeared from the shadows of the parking lot and approached me as I made my way to my door. "Damn, David, you scared the hell out of me!" I screamed. Since my talk with Janelle, I realized that what I was doing was wrong. Separated or not, David wasn't mine. He belonged at home with his wife and kids.

"Sorry, baby. I wanted to surprise you."

Damn, why did I even bother putting up with his trifling behind? I deserved better, but I had to admit that it was hard to find a man that knew how to lay the pipe and bring a sister to that point of ecstasy like he did. I thought I recognized an orgasm before I met David but realized that those *"faux-gasms"* weren't anything close to the real thing. I allowed David to wrap his arms around me and as he attempted to kiss me on the mouth, I turned my head so he would catch my cheek instead.

I don't know what the hell he thought he was doing. He knew he was in violation of the rules. We agreed from the beginning that there would be no kissing. That showed

a sign of intimacy and caring. And I thought he understood that an unannounced drop-by was definitely out
of the question. Shit, what if I had someone over? He
would have really disrupted my flow. That was probably
his plan. Like I had told Janelle, the brother was beginning to catch feelings and I truly had to put an end to
them. I figured this would be as good a night as any, but
I wanted a quickie for the road first.

I led David into my apartment and ignored his incessant rambling about me not returning his phone calls.
When I felt like he was done venting, I told him to have
a seat in the living room while I went to take a shower.
I entered my room, closed the door, and locked it
behind me. The last thing I needed was David up in my
space unattended, rummaging through my shit.

I hurriedly stripped from head to toe and jumped into
the shower, not even allowing the water to get hot. I
wanted to hurry up and get me some, but definitely
didn't want him at my place all night. Lately, I wasn't
feeling David like I was before. I'd always been a relationship type of girl and this no-commitment fling I was
having with him was getting old and very mundane. My
body and heart were telling me that I needed a man to
myself; I needed something more. My perspective on
love and relationships were taking a turn for the better.
I was now believing that I could find happiness.

I stepped out of the shower, wrapped a towel around
my hair, and patted my body down with another. I

headed toward my dresser to select a matching bra and panty set, then pried the towel off of my head and combed my hair out. When I entered my living room, David's full attention was on a basketball game. It looked like he had helped himself to my alcohol. I hated when people went through my stuff without asking me.

When he finally realized I was in the room, he turned the television off and walked toward me to wrap me in his arms. Again he attempted to kiss me in the mouth, which I again successfully avoided. I allowed him to lead me into the bedroom while he applied soft kisses to my neck down to my breasts.

Lying on the bed, he went to work prying off my panties and, before I knew it, my back was arching and my hands were pushing his face deeper between my legs. Pushing my pelvis against his face, I tried my best to suffocate him. The shit felt so good, I didn't want it to end. Sensing that I was close to an orgasm, he stopped and pulled down his pants and boxers and stood there waiting for me to service him. When I brought my face closer to his penis, something didn't seem quite right. It was wet!

David's penis had a colored discharge on its tip. I tried my best to remember if I had ever known David to pre-cum. The few times he did it was only during me giving him head. I rose to my feet, pushed David away from me, and turned on all the lights. Something wasn't right, and I'd be damned if I let him give me an STD.

"What's wrong, baby?" he inquired as if he didn't know.

I dropped to my knees and began eyeing his penis from base to tip. "David, why are you pre-cumming?"

"Oh shit, baby! You got me horny as hell; that's all!"

"Okay, so what's that smell?"

"Shit, I've been running around all day. It's nothing but some sweat. You want me to go take a shower?"

I couldn't believe he was trying to take me for stupid. I rose to my knees; I had to check him before he made the mistake of trying to play me for the fool. I put my robe back on and took a deep breath. I wanted to remain as calm as possible. "David, pull up your damn pants!"

"What?"

"I said, pull up your goddamn pants! I can't believe your ass is sitting up here in my face, telling me all these fucking lies."

"But I—," he retorted.

"Shut up!" I yelled before he could continue. "For one, you don't ever come to my crib without showering first. Secondly, pre-cum isn't yellow and thick like egg yolk, and third, nigga, did you forget I was a pre-med biology major? You got some type of STD or bacterial infection, and you want me to put my mouth on that diseased shit? You must've lost all of your senses!" I screamed.

I turned my back to him and began to head toward my bathroom. To add salt to his wound, I made sure to let him know his services were no longer needed. "By the way, David, I was going to wait until we were done, but I wanted to let you know that this thing that we've been having is over!"

"Oh, so you saying that you ain't trying to kick it with me anymore?" he asked, flabbergasted.

"*Mothafucka*, did I stutter?" I answered back with as much attitude as I could muster. I spun on my heels and again proceeded to head toward my bathroom to clean myself up. But before I reached the door, I felt him grab a fistful of my hair and fling me to the floor. Blackness engulfed me as my head made contact with the floor.

I thought back over the time I'd spent with Brandon and reflected on how much I enjoyed myself. But ever since our second date, I'd been questioning if that was what I really wanted from love. I was attracted to Brandon, but I had to admit I was still also attracted to women. Now I was toiling over which I was most attracted to. I wasn't totally ready to abandon one gender completely for the other. Night and day, day and night, my sexuality was constantly on my mind.

I turned over in bed and pulled the sheets off of me. I ran my hand up and down my chest and washboard stomach muscles, which were already sore from that afternoon's workout. I lay there for nearly an hour before deciding to get up and surf the Internet. Two o' fucking clock in the morning, and I couldn't sleep for the world. But I knew why: I really wanted to pick up the phone and call Brandon. Part of me wanted to hear his voice, but I didn't want to disrespect him by calling so early in the morning.

I teetered with the idea of calling him as my desktop

powered on from its sleep mode. Deciding against it, I quickly logged onto my Yahoo! Instant Messenger to see if Brandon was online, but he wasn't and I decided to log on to my AOL account. I began looking up the latest in sports and entertainment news instead. Half an hour later, I found myself in a chat room similar to the one that I had met Brandon in.

I searched through the profiles, skimming past the obvious playas, the "too-good-to-be-true" playas, and the wannabe playas; but paused when I ran across the profile of someone with "ATL" in their username. I proceeded to read it.

His profile stated he was five-nine, weighed 140 pounds, had a medium brown complexion, and was into working out. Besides his stats, his profile told me that we shared some of the same interests as well. Going against my better judgment, I decided to begin a private chat with "AtlBabyBoy."

Ty-N-Atl: Wassup yo?

AtlBabyBoy: Not a damn thing.

AtlBabyBoy: Can't sleep for the world.

The rest of my conversation with AtlBabyBoy had me asking and answering those routine questions: How old are you? Where are you from? What do you like to do for fun? I looked over at the clock and realized an hour had already passed. I was growing bored with the idle chit-chat until my new chat buddy revived me with a proposition.

AtlBabyBoy: You wanna come over?

I was both taken aback and intrigued at the same time. Brandon was the only guy that I had ever met off of the Internet and part of me was curious if I could have feelings for another guy as well. Now that AtlBabyBoy—who was now comfortable enough to tell me his name was Nicholas—had gained my attention with his invite, I began to inquire about him more and, most importantly, what he had in mind for me in the middle of the night.

AtlBabyBoy: Are you going to give me the fifth degree over the internet or are you going to come over and chill with ya boy?

I hesitated before I agreed to meet him but not at his crib. I told him that I wanted to meet somewhere neutral. After getting his cell phone number and arranging to meet within an hour at the Kroger grocery store on Cascade down the street from his apartment complex, I signed off of AOL and Yahoo! Instant Messenger.

Leaning back in my desk chair, I wondered if I was doing the right thing by going out to meet a stranger in the middle of the night. I was really feeling Brandon but, then again, we weren't actually dating or exclusive. I convinced myself there was no harm in a casual meet 'n' greet and headed into my bathroom to freshen up and put on some clothes.

I jogged out of my complex in the brisk wind, quickly got into my car, and turned on the heat; although it would be a while before it warmed to a comfortable temperature. Once my windows were defrosted, I headed for the interstate, eager to see what this encounter would bring.

With V-103's "Quiet Storm" soothing me, I rode down the nearly deserted I-75 to I-285. As I approached our agreed upon meeting spot, I pulled out my cell phone and began to dial Nicholas' number to let him know I was almost there, but decided to wait until I arrived.

I pulled into a parking space near Kroger's front door, quickly turned off the ignition, and sprinted from my car into the warmth of the twenty-four-hour grocery store. I picked up a hand basket to get a few items I needed for breakfast, and then proceeded to dial Nicholas' number.

"Hey, wassup? Is this Nicholas?" I asked, trying to sound cool and collected.

"The one and only. So what's the deal? Where are you?"

"Still getting dressed. I have to throw on some shoes, and I'll be on my way," I fabricated.

"All right, cool."

"So what you wearing?" I inquired.

"Hold on for a minute. I got someone on the other line."

"Did he just put me on hold?" I asked out loud.

I could already tell that I wasn't going to vibe with this brother. I hated being put on hold for more than thirty seconds. I'd rather someone tell me that they'd give me a call back in the next few minutes instead of leaving me hanging on the other end. I also noticed that homey sounded like he was a little soft, but I knew better than to judge him on that. My own voice didn't deepen until my senior year of college.

"Hey! Are you there?" Nicholas screamed into the phone almost three minutes later.

"Yeah, I'm here. Why the hell you put me on hold for so long? You could've told me that you'd call me back when you were done with your call," I chastised.

"I'm sorry. I was trying to tell my mom that I'd call her back but she kept talking and talking," he attempted to explain.

There was no way he was on the phone with his mother this time of the morning, but all I could do was to give him the benefit of the doubt. After all, I didn't know this guy and wasn't going to let some stranger rattle my nerves.

"It's all good. So what you got on?" I asked again.

"I got dark gray sweatpants on, some Nike flip-flops, and a black windbreaker."

"Cool. I'll meet you in the produce section."

"Hey, wait. How will I know it's you?"

"I'll have on some blue jeans, black boots, and a black pea jacket. Oh, I'll also have on a black hat," I lied. I decided if I didn't like what I saw when he arrived, I was going to bounce and leave homey hanging.

I walked around the store and picked up a few more

items I needed. After fifteen minutes, I decided to give Nicholas a call to see if he had arrived.

"You made it yet?" I asked when he answered.

"Yeah, I'm over by the watermelons. Where are you?"

"I'm getting off the exit. I should be there in about five minutes," I continued to lie as I made my way over to the produce section. Rounding the curve, I scanned the almost empty produce section and couldn't believe what I saw. I gasped, eased back around the corner, and collected my thoughts while replaying Nicholas' stats in my head: five-nine, 140 pounds, medium brown complexion, and into working out. I peeped back around the corner and saw everything *but* what he described. There stood a 200-pound, dark-skinnned, permed hair mother-fucker busting out the seams of a black sweatsuit that had *faded* to gray. His Nike flip-flops were a little too worn and his windbreaker a size too small as well. He stood with his hands on his hips, looking from side to side and occasionally glancing at his watch.

I couldn't *believe* this fat-ass sissy thought I'd be into him. I told him on the phone that I liked guys that looked and acted like men. Shit, a blind man could tell he was gay. I started to go over to homey and cuss his ass out but maintained my cool as I headed toward him.

I stopped a couple of feet next to him, in front of the peaches that were right next to the watermelons. I noticed him glancing my way. For a moment our eyes locked and a smile ran across his face. Just as he began to speak, I cut him off.

"What the fuck you looking at, sissy?" I yelled and headed to the checkout line without looking back. After I paid for my groceries, I hopped in my ride; pissed.

I began aimlessly driving without a destination in mind. I wasn't tired so I thought a late night-early morning drive would help to clear my thoughts. Before I knew it, I was over near Brandon's side of town. I looked at the time on my dash and noticed that it was close to sunrise. Against my better judgment, I pulled my cell phone out and dialed Brandon's number from memory. I prayed he wouldn't curse me out.

"Hello," he answered after a couple of rings. I loved the tone of his voice and that he was the type of brother I could kick it with on the regular.

"Wassup, B? Were you sleeping?" I inquired sheepishly.

"Nah, I was up late, working on a song for my recording session with my girl tomorrow evening."

"Can I ask you something?"

"You just did," he teased.

"Okay, smart ass. Can I ask you two more questions?"

"That's one. What's the other?" he continued to joke.

"You got to say 'yes' first," I replied through the Kool-Aid smile that was plastered across my face.

"How about I say 'yes' for now, but if I don't want to answer, can I still change my mind?"

"All right, that's fine."

"Well?"

"Can I come over?"

Brandon hesitated before he answered and the brief moment felt like an hour. "Sure, why not. I'm done messing with this song for the night."

"Will you do one more thing for me?" I asked.

"You are full of requests tonight. What is it?"

"Will you open the door and let me in?"

I had been sitting outside Brandon's apartment building for the latter part of the phone conversation. If he had said "no," I would have felt like a real ass. I didn't know what made me drop by unannounced because if someone had done that shit to me, I'd be pissed as hell. But I just had to see him.

When Brandon opened the door wearing only a pair of gym shorts, I momentarily lost my breath. Before I could stop or control my actions, I did something I had only fantasized about: I quickly grabbed him by the waist and passionately kissed him as I backed him inside of his apartment, closing the door with my left foot. I wanted there to be no doubt in Brandon's mind that I was feeling him. Whether he realized it or not, he was mine.

Twenty One
MARKUS

was still thinking about the time I had spent with Uniyah a few nights prior. I decided to skip the gym so I could hang with Jay. I pulled out my cell phone and quickly punched in his number; not sure whether he'd answer or not. Ever since he had been spending so much time with his new love interest, he always seemed to be unavailable to hang out. The only time we got time to talk was on the job, and even then we both were so busy with projects.

"Hello," Jay groggily spoke into the phone. I could still hear the sleep in his voice.

"What's good, playa?" I shouted into my Benz' wireless microphone.

"Damn, why you gotta be so loud?"

"Aww, be quiet, man. Are you available for a game of one-on-one? If you are, I'm about ten minutes from your crib."

"Damn, dawg, how you know I ain't got company?"

That was a good question—to which I didn't have a good answer. To be honest, I didn't really care. "You need to tell that girl to let you come up for some air. She'll be all right for a few hours."

I wasn't sure I liked my homeboy having a steady girlfriend. It appeared as if our friendship was being put on the back burner. I needed my one day out of the month where we could hook up and talk shit. But that was slowly changing.

"Well, *do* you have company?" I disappointedly asked.

"Nah, she already left this morning to go get her hair done, or some shit like that. Why the hell you sounding like a sad little boy?"

"Whatever, man. You're the one that's all ghost now, just 'cause you got a new thang going on," I joked.

"Whatever. I already get to see your ass forty-something hours a week. You forgot I work for you, *boss* man." Jay and I had an unusual friendship. Professionally he oversaw all of the firm's account executives reporting directly to me, and personally he was a close confidant that I ran the streets with.

"Yeah, I ain't complaining about work; I'm complaining about our *kickin' it* time. You know I can't make a move without talking to you first," I joked. "On the real, I want to get your input on this honey that I've been feeling."

"*You* feeling a sista? Now you know my ass got to get the fuck up because I don't ever remember hearing them words coming out of your mouth. Someone tell me that the King of Playas ain't got his nose wide open for one woman!"

See this is exactly what I needed from Jay. I needed his humor to ground me but, most importantly, I needed his honest opinion. I definitely needed my boy's thoughts and Jay was my closest friend. There wasn't much that I kept from him; I trusted him more than I trusted my own brother.

"Well, get yo' ass up, and I'll give you the details," I taunted.

"Say no more, man."

I quickly made my way over to Jay's side of town in less than fifteen minutes. Rapping loudly on his front door, I waited for his lazy ass to come and let me in. I heard movement within the house and saw a contorted figure heading toward me through the opaque glass portion of the front door.

"Aww come on, Jay, you could've put some clothes on by now," I teased as I shielded my eyes from his body that was wrapped in a small towel.

"Shit, you lucky I bothered to put this damn thing on." He moved to the side of the door so I could enter. "Why didn't you use your key?"

"You know I only use that for emergencies. Plus, I didn't want to pop in and catch your ass doing something crazy."

"Whatever, dawg. I'm almost ready. Turn on the TV," Jay replied and headed to his back bedroom.

I made my way to the living room and flipped on the TV, surfing through several channels before stopping on CNN. I listened as they reported on how the president was vigorously lobbying to have his national health-care plan enacted. As they moved to the next story, I shook my head as they reported on the unemployment rate reaching the double digits in some states. There was no denying that Obama certainly would have his hands full, trying to clean up after the Bush administration.

After channel-surfing for another thirty minutes, Jay finally emerged in his Nike basketball warm-ups and his beat-up "lucky" pair of shoes. I don't know why he called them lucky. Whenever we played one-on-one I often won and the *few* times he did win, it was only by a basket or two.

"I hope you're ready to buy breakfast this morning?" he heckled. "I've been working on my jump shot and perfecting my infamous crossover. I'm going to give you the beating of a lifetime!"

I laughed out loud. This was the same line that Jay threw at me before we started every game.

"Bring it on," I said, standing chest to chest with him.

"Consider it brought," Jay retorted before slapping me on the back.

An hour later we were heavily into our first game of 21, trash talking to one another, and trying our best to get into the other's head. I was leading by one point and it was a close game, but Jay was making me work for this win. For the first time in months, his six-foot-four height was working to his advantage and he blocked my jump shot not even a second after it left my hands. No matter. I ran midcourt and rebounded my own ball, hit a three-pointer, and yelled, "Game!"

"You mean, 'luck!'" Jay yelled before we both burst into laughter. "Nah, yo, good game. But next time…"

"Yeah, yeah," I replied.

Jay and I headed over to the court's worn bench and sat down to catch our breath while swigging on our bottled waters.

"So, man, tell me about this new lady you're supposedly feeling?" Jay asked.

I spent the next half-hour explaining to Jay how I had met Uniyah and about the way I was feeling. I barely knew her but I felt an instant chemistry whenever I was in her presence. The nights that she'd spent the evening lying in my arms, it felt so good. Those were some of the most peaceful nights I've had.

"So, Markus, if you got strong feelings for homegirl, what's the problem? You've done the club thing for a minute now and that's gotten you nowhere. Why not actually take the time out and get to know her? If you think it's going to materialize into something serious, you can take things to the next level. If things don't pop off, what's the damage done? Worst case is you have a girl you can hang with from time to time."

Jay was right. I'd take the time out and get to know Uniyah. To not complicate things, I wouldn't be sexual with her until we had a chance to spend some quality time with one another. Of course, this didn't include foreplay—a man did have needs. I thanked Jay and gave him some dap.

Jay decided to take a rain check on breakfast. I dropped him off at his spot so I could get home and take a hot shower and a nap. I jumped in my ride, cranked the music up, and hit the highway. It wasn't long after my shower that I fell deep asleep in the comfort of my bed.

I didn't know what time it was when I groggily answered the cordless phone resting next to my head, but I could see that it was pitch black outside. I didn't even bother looking at the caller ID display since I could barely read it in the darkness anyway.

"Hello," I yawned into the phone.

I was instantly jolted out of my restful state when I heard Uniyah sobbing on the other end begging me to come over to her place. I was able to calm her down enough so she could give me the address to her crib in Sandy Springs, the suburbs of Atlanta. I'd use my car's built-in GPS system to navigate me to her place. I didn't even bother to ask what was wrong with her. If she answered, I would not have been able to understand her through all the sobbing. My girl was in distress, and I needed to get to her ASAP!

oments after David threw me to the ground, reality set in. He had physically attacked me. I couldn't believe he'd actually put his hands on me. I clumsily attempted to pull myself to my feet but was knocked down again when David kicked me from behind. I struggled to roll over and moved out of the way just in time to see him bringing his foot down to stomp on me again.

I scrambled to my feet and lunged at him, knocking him into the wall. I wasn't the typical fragile female that most people pegged me to be. I could always hold my own in a fight with another woman, but I'd never had to protect myself against a man. Yet I was willing to go toe-to-toe with him with all my might.

I balled my hand into a tight fist and brought it across David's nose, forcing him to stumble back again, more in shock than pain, I suspected. Stupidly, I began to talk shit instead of grabbing the phone and calling the police.

"Nigga, have you lost your goddamned mind?" I yelled. "I know you didn't think that your ass was going to come up in my crib and disrespect me by putting your fucking hands on me like I'm one of your tricks. How many times do I have to tell your ass that I'm not one of your tricks?!"

"Shut the fuck up, ho," he countered, running toward me and knocking me down again. My body hit the floor with a loud thud, and I was starting to realize my mistake. I became frightened when I saw the look of hate in his eyes. I scrambled toward the bedroom door to get away from him but was stopped short when he grabbed my right ankle.

"Where you going, bitch?!" he bellowed. "You want to talk shit like you somebody, so why the fuck you trying to run now?"

I needed to get a hold of something I could protect myself with. Something deep inside told me that my life depended on it.

"I left my damn wife tonight so that we could be together. I turned my back on my own fucking kids because I wanted to be with you, and now you talking about we're through? Bitch, we ain't ever going to be through. We're going to be together until death does one of us part!"

David twisted my ankle as I struggled to get free and I yelled out in pain. I knew something was wrong from the sharp pinch I felt and the throbbing sensation that followed. I didn't try to stand; I couldn't even if I wanted to. David grabbed the back of my head and dragged me to my feet by my hair. I frantically searched the room for something—anything—then grabbed my nightstand lamp, spun around with all my might, and struck him on the left side of his face.

"Uniy—" he stuttered, staggering toward me.

"Shut the fuck up!" I yelled.

He lunged toward me and, in fear, I swung the lamp at his head again but harder. Blood gushed from David's nose before he dropped to his knees and fell to the floor. His eyes rolled back in his head and all was silent.

Panicking, I limped toward David's unconscious body, kneeled down, and shook him. He groaned but didn't awaken. He was still breathing so he wasn't dead—at least not yet. I slowly backed away and reached for the phone. Instead of calling the police, Janelle, or Brandon, I called Markus.

As soon as he answered his phone, tears erupted from my eyes and I began sobbing uncontrollably as I tried to explain what happened. I wasn't making sense but he managed to calm me down enough so he could get directions to my apartment. He told me that he lived nearby and was on his way. I quickly hung up the phone and went into the bathroom, confused as to what to do next. My ankle was hurting even more, but it wasn't broken. It was definitely sprained though. I peeled off my lingerie—scared of what both Markus and the police would think—and put on some clothes.

I was sure one of my nosy neighbors heard all the

commotion and yelling, and had called the "Po Po" by now. It would only be a matter of time before they arrived, but I hoped Markus would beat them here. As I waited, I kept my eyes on my bedroom door, in fear that David would regain consciousness and attempt to attack me again. When I heard pounding at the front door, I nearly jumped out of my skin.

I winced as I hobbled over to the door and was surprised to see that it wasn't Markus or the police, but Janelle holding a shopping bag in her left hand. Immediately upon me opening the door, she invited herself in and began rambling about something that had upset her at work. A minute into her conversation, she finally looked at me and realized something wasn't quite right. "Oh my God, Uniyah, what the hell happened to your face?"

Before I could begin to explain, I heard a gentle tapping at the door. I walked back to it and let out a sigh of relief when I saw Markus through the peephole. I opened the door and, instantly, tears began to erupt from my eyes as he clutched me by the shoulders and held me in a tight embrace.

"It's gonna be okay," he whispered as he guided me to the loveseat. Markus greeted Janelle before he took a seat next to her on the couch. Both waited for me to say something as I struggled with how to begin. Instead, I simply pointed down the hall.

Markus took the lead and headed toward my bedroom as Janelle followed closely behind him. I watched them before heading into the kitchen and getting some ice for my face that I could feel swelling. I was too afraid to actually look in a mirror, but the reflection I caught of myself in the toaster explained why Janelle looked so shocked when she saw me.

Not a minute after proceeding down the hallway, the two of them came rushing back into the living room like they had seen a ghost.

"Uniyah, what the fuck happened?" Janelle demanded with a mixture of anger and concern.

"I was attacked," I replied emotionlessly before sitting back on the loveseat.

"Did you know him? Did you call the police yet?" This time it was Markus doing the questioning.

"Is he dead?" Janelle added with tears beginning to form in her eyes.

"Hold up, hold up. Uniyah, just tell us what happened so we can know to proceed," Markus calmly directed.

I removed the ice pack from my lip and began to explain as best I could. "Well, I came home from the studio not too long ago and when I got here, David was waiting for me." I silently noted the look of recognition that came across Janelle's face at the mention of David's name. "I told him a couple of weeks ago that I wasn't comfortable being involved with a man that was married. He asked me if he could come in for a minute just to talk, and I relented and allowed him in. He began to plead for me to give him a chance to end things with his wife so that we could be together, and I told him that I wasn't interested anymore. I explained to him that I'd always be in constant fear that he'd also cheat on me down the line. The more he pleaded, the more desperate he became. It got to a point where we began yelling at one another and me telling him to get the hell out, and that's when it got violent."

I saw Markus' brow furrow but I continued anyway.

"When I turned my back on him to open the front door, he grabbed my hair and swung me to the ground. Then we started fighting. I ran into the bedroom, and he knocked me down; twisted my ankle. I was scrambling; it just got crazy. As soon as I could get on my feet, I grabbed what was closest to me and hit him with the lamp. Then I panicked and called Markus," I concluded as they sat, staring in shock.

"Did anyone call the police?" they both asked almost in unison.

"I didn't, and I don't think the neighbors did either. They would've arrived by now."

"So what the hell are you waiting for?" Janelle asked, searching for my phone.

"No! I don't want to involve any more people in this. I need some help, getting David out of here."

"You got to be kidding!" Markus angrily stated. "He attacked you, and we need to call the police."

"Please, Markus. Will you please let me handle things

my way? I want to get David up and out of my life. I need to get him the hell out of here and back home to his wife. David is her problem, not mine. Calling the police is only going make the situation worse," I exclaimed. "First they're going to want to do a report, and I'm going to have to give a statement. Then there's court, and the list goes on and on. In the end, the only ones that'll lose are his wife and kids. I'm not denying that part of this isn't my fault for dealing with David, even after I found out he was married. I tried to right my wrong by ending things with him. I didn't think it would turn out like *this!*"

I turned on the waterworks and continued sobbing. I truly was putting on a performance that could give Halle a run for her money. I walked toward Markus and embraced him as he gently rubbed his hands down my spine, releasing some of the tension I had pent up inside of me. Reluctantly, he agreed to allow me to handle the situation my way, and I thanked him with a passionate kiss on the lips. Now I had to figure out the hardest part of all—how to actually get David out of my place.

Twenty Three
BRANDON

I was surprised as hell to get the unexpected phone call I received from Tyrone a few nights prior. I was even more taken aback when he asked, if not pleaded, to come and see me. A part of me was saying "no"; another part of me wanted to grant his request. By doing the latter I was setting myself up to catch feelings for him and I wasn't sure if that was something I was ready to do so soon. Especially after the way my last relationship went down.

After my breakup with Danté eight months ago, I swore that I was through with men altogether and that I was going to strictly focus my attention on my education, my friendships, and my music. Up until Tyrone, I had done all of that with little or no deviation. I was content with satisfying my sexual desires myself, but lately masturbation was beginning to become mundane and unexciting. Tyrone would be just what I needed to break up the monotony.

I contemplated a bit more but was forced to make a decision when Tyrone told me to let him in. I thought he was joking until I heard the faint knocking at the door. I sprang from my bed—thankful I had already showered and brushed my teeth—then sprinted to the front room to let him in. I only had on my gym shorts when I answered the door, and Tyrone affectionately grabbed me and held me in a warm embrace while kissing me. I always wondered what our first kiss would be like and part of me always imagined it being nothing more than an awkward peck. I never expected it to be a *true* kiss. It was one of the reasons I had a hard time believing he had never been involved with a man before. Some of his actions were just too...*natural*.

I had pulled away from Tyrone, taking a moment to catch my breath and to look into his eyes. I was surprised at the sadness and the hurt they contained as they unflinchingly stared back at me. I had no idea what I was about to get myself into, but I didn't back down. I moved aside and nervously extended an invitation for him to come inside. Without faltering, he accepted. I took the bag of groceries from him and placed them in the kitchen.

As he brushed past me, I couldn't contain the growing protrusion emanating from my gym shorts. Luckily, with the exception of a small amount of light peeking in from the window, it was dark. I was beyond embarrassment, and I didn't want Tyrone to see me in my weakened state. Usually, when we were together, I was so much more in control; that night I was feeling vulnerable.

Tyrone had stirred feelings within me that I didn't

know existed. Many nights I lay in bed, thinking about a moment like this one, and it finally happened. Tyrone had pulled me in for another long embrace, and I couldn't stop grinning from ear to ear. I loved hearing his expressions of affection, and he was saying all the right things.

There was something about Tyrone that brought out a jovial side in me that I wasn't used to expressing but enjoyed doing. "I want to hear you sing me a song?" he had stated.

His request had caught me off guard because I hated to share my voice with people I didn't know. But that night something took over me. It was as if I was another person and, slightly nervous, I led Tyrone to my office where my Korg synthesizer sat.

Tyrone had sat in my leather executive chair, and I began to play a chord while I rummaged my brain for something appropriate to sing. Deciding to replicate that night with Uniyah in the studio, I opted to just sing with little thought. I had begun to croon from my heart.

Could you really be the one

Tell me

Could you really be in love

With me

Could your touch heal all the hurt

Tell me

Could love this time actually work

I sang the lyrics with all of the emotion I could muster.

I didn't concern myself with pitch or tone. I just wanted to express my feelings through song. With my eyes closed, I continued to allow my fingers to run across the keyboard as I belted out the rest of the song.

Been looking
Searching
I need that one to call my own
Hoping
Praying
That you are that special one
I know I can't endure any more heartache

I continued to allow my fingers to help me find the words to sing. I had briefly opened my eyes and looked Tyrone directly in his, took a deep breath, and continued.

No more running away
This time I want love to stay
Look into my eyes
See the hurt that therein lies
Come and love me
Give me your all unconditionally
And baby I promise
Baby I promise you in return
Mine you'll receive faithfully

I broke into an instrumental riff and continued to play the harmony of the song as the B-flats and G-sharps resonated throughout my apartment. With my eyes still closed, I had felt Tyrone's presence next to me but continued to play until I heard a soft tenor voice begin to sing.

Baby I'm afraid
Afraid of feeling this way
Scared of the hurt
Baby I've never felt so unsure
Could you really be
Someone tell me
I got to know
Are you the one?

When he finished singing, I stopped playing and turned to face him. All of the awkwardness I should have felt was gone and I boldly drew Tyrone's face toward mine and passionately kissed him. I didn't know what had come over me, but I didn't want that feeling to end; I didn't want that *night* to end. It felt like a dream. Everything seemed so perfect, and it worried me because afterward was usually when the storm began. Experience had showed me so and made me a skeptic, yet I couldn't help myself.

"Baby, I'm feeling you like crazy," Tyrone had uttered. "I know that you've been hurt in the past and I don't want to add to that pain, but I want to help you heal and love you like you've never been loved."

As I lie in bed now replaying that night's events and Tyrone's words, I wondered if I was setting myself up for another heartbreak. My body and soul were telling me I deserved one more chance at finding true love, and if I didn't take the chance, I'd never know if the latter could be true. I decided right then that Tyrone was worth finding out if it could be.

Twenty Four

It seemed like hours had passed before I successfully convinced both Janelle *and* Markus to help me drag David out of my apartment so I could take him home. After practically begging them not to call the police, they both relented and helped me carry him from my apartment to my car. When we neared my ride, Markus suddenly stopped.

"Uniyah, you aren't planning on driving alone with him in your car, are you?"

"No, I was planning on Janelle riding along with me." I looked at Janelle for some support, and the look that was plastered across her face mirrored Markus'.

"Girl, are you crazy? Have you looked at your face? There's no way I'm getting into a car with this crazy fool. I mean, what if he regains consciousness?"

"Uniyah, Janelle's right. Let's place him in my ride, and I can follow the two of you to homeboy's crib."

I was so damn tired of arguing, I simply agreed. "Whatever," I muttered and helped them carry David to Markus' car instead.

After placing him in the car, we sped down I-75 toward the south side of Atlanta to David's address I had lifted from his driver's license. I cranked my music up because I didn't want to talk to Janelle at the moment. I didn't need to hear chastising or anything else. The night had been long enough already. Out of the corner of my eye, I saw Janelle reaching to turn the volume down.

"Uniyah, we need to talk," she stated.

I exhaled and decided to get it over with. "Go ahead. I'm listening."

"I want to know what the fuck really happened back there. I didn't believe a damn thing you said back at the apartment. I realize part of it was for Markus' benefit, but now I want to know what really happened."

God only knew that I didn't feel like explaining the events to Janelle, but when I glanced over and saw the look of worry on her face and the tears forming in her eyes, her concern was genuine so I told her everything.

After I finished giving her the facts, Janelle placed her hand on my free one. "Damn, Uniyah, I'm sorry this went down the way it did. I'm glad that you were trying to end things with David, but if what you've been telling me is true about the way you put it down in the bedroom, I can see why he tripped out," she joked in an attempt to lighten the mood.

I couldn't help but laugh. She was always good at making a bad situation funny. I don't know why I thought she wouldn't understand or that she would be judgmental, but I did feel much better after I told her.

"So, if you didn't believe the story I told you back at the apartment, you think Markus knows I was lying?"

"You didn't lie. You just didn't state all the facts. And I was with you until you mentioned David's name. You never mentioned to me before that you had truly called it quits with him, so I knew that there was more to the story. In all honesty, I think that Markus will be okay. But if push comes to shove, you can always play the 'we aren't officially together' card."

"So true," I replied and pulled off the exit, after glancing at the directions I had printed off of the Internet. I glanced back in the rearview mirror and saw that Markus was still following closely behind me.

"Uniyah, I think that's your turn," Janelle stated.

I followed her directions and made a right turn. Slowing down as I continued to read the house numbers that we passed, my heart skipped a beat when I finally found the one I was looking for. I'm not sure if it skipped a beat because in moments I would be rid of David for once and for all or if it skipped a beat because I was going to have to face the woman whose husband I had been sleeping with.

Opting to not pull in the driveway, I pulled up in front of David's home instead and couldn't help but marvel at the beautiful ranch-style home with the manicured lawn and nicely trimmed shrubs. I couldn't understand why David would want to throw all of this away for me or anyone else. It made me sad for myself and also for his unsuspecting wife, who probably thought what she had *in* her house was just as perfect *as* her house.

I slowly climbed out of the car and made my way to the driveway while Janelle went to assist Markus with a semi-conscious David. I could hear him muttering and could swear it sounded like he was babbling about being in love with me. For a brief second, I felt my heart go out to him but quickly dismissed the feeling. We had come to the end of the road—literally and figura- tively; I wasn't about to turn back now.

I climbed the last stair to the front door and hesitated before ringing the doorbell. Moments later someone turned on the porch light and opened the door. I gasped as I noticed the handsome little boy that stood before me. He was the spitting image of David. He couldn't have been older than six and standing there looking at him caused a wave of nausea to run over me.

"Yes, ma'am?" he asked.

"Good evening. Is your mother home?"

"Hold on, please," he replied and ran back inside the house.

I felt my stomach ball up in knots as the slapping of house shoes hitting the hardwood floors echoed from a distant room but grew louder as they came in my direction. The door swung open wider, and there she stood: David's wife. David's very *pregnant* wife. Question after question quickly flooded my mind: Why would David want to cheat on her? Was it because she was pregnant? Would my telling her about David be dangerous to her health?

"May I help you?" she asked with attitude, interrupting the many rhetorical questions running through my mind.

"Uh, yes, uh, are you David's wife?"

"Yes. Why?"

"Well, I—," I began.

"What?" she replied, cutting me off. "Let me guess. You decided that you didn't want his sorry ass *after* bringing all this drama into my home?" She looked me up and down as if I was trash, and I then realized she already knew about David and me. "I don't know what the fuck he was thinking by trying to leave me for a little girl like you, but he must've been out of his damned mind!"

I turned my back, hoping that Markus and Janelle were close, but they were still at the bottom of the driveway helping to walk a somewhat erect but still semi-unconscious David up the driveway.

"David Jr. and Keisha, come here!" she yelled back into the house.

After her two children came to the door, she directed them to go get their father and bring him into the house. The two kids ran out of the house and the woman took one last look at me and began to turn away when the screams of her children caused her to spin back around. She pushed me aside as she walked as fast as she could down the driveway to see what the commotion was all about.

"David!" she screamed after seeing his face that was covered in both our blood.

I quickly hobbled past her and made my way back to my car, where Janelle was already waiting and Markus was in his own.

"What the hell did you do, bitch?" David's wife screamed after me.

"Look at *my* face and ask him what happened when his abusive ass wakes up!" I shouted back. "And if you don't want your children to grow up without their father around, I suggest you don't involve the police in this matter!"

"I oughta whip your ass, bitch," she retorted.

"Whatever," I replied and got in the car. I put the gear in drive and proceeded to pull off when I hit the brakes, rolled down the window, and gave her a last bit of advice: "Oh, you might want to get yourself checked 'cause whatever disease he's got, he's trying to spread it around, stupid!"

With that, I pulled away from the curb and tried to leave the situation and my affair with David where it belonged—behind me!

"What the fuck? What do you mean, dude was on the floor unconscious?" Jay questioned.

As soon as I followed Uniyah to David's house and then back to her crib, I tried to stay and comfort her but she told me that she needed to be alone for the night. Against my better judgment, I left her alone and came back to my crib to dial my boy, Jay, to give him the four-one-one.

"Exactly what I said, man! When I got to her crib, homey was knocked out with his drawers 'round his feet. She said he was an ex-boyfriend and when she found out that he was married she ended it, but he decided that it wasn't over until he said it was over. She said when she got to her crib that night, he was standing outside her door. She let him in so he wouldn't cause a scene and that's when he came in and attacked her."

"I don't know. Something doesn't seem right, Markus," Jay interjected before I could continue.

"Nah, yo. You should've seen how she looked when I got there. She was 'tore up from the floor up,' as her girl put it. Her hair was a mess, face all swollen, and her clothes all torn. Her bedroom looked like Floyd Mayweather, Jr. had been up in there fightin', so I believe ol' boy did attack her."

"I'm not disputing he attacked her. I just guess from experience, I know that women will tell you only what they think you should know. I think homegirl left some details out of her story, but I'm not the one that has to believe her. Anyway, you ain't tell me why homeboy was unconscious."

I was growing agitated with Jay, but I wasn't sure if it was because he doubted Uniyah's story or if, in some small way, I did, too. "Playa, if you let me finish without interrupting, I'll tell you how homey got knocked the fuck out," I continued.

"My bad. Go 'head then," Jay replied.

"Anyway, they were fighting, he knocked baby girl to the floor, and scrambling to get away, she grabbed a lamp, and basically went Jackie Robinson on his ass."

"That broad sounds crazy, if you ask me."

"Well, nobody asked your ass. And you're going to stop disrespecting my girl by calling her out of her name. Her name is Uniyah."

"Shit that name is u-fugly," Jay joked. "Seriously, I didn't know that you and her was down like that. I guess I'm the last to know."

"Well, you the one that's been missing in action. And after that game of ball we had, you ain't want to hang out like we used to 'cause your girl let you sniff the *poon tang* once."

"Stop hating."

"Nah, never that. I'm saying, don't get mad when you the last to know 'cause you too busy walking around with your nose wide open."

"Whatever, dawg. So why are you on the phone with me when you should be with your girl?" Jay inquired.

"I tried, but she told me she wanted to be alone tonight. I thought that was weird, but I don't like sweating a sister so I let her have her space."

"Damn, sounds like a brush-off. But with everything that happened tonight, I can understand her not wanting to be crowded. Give her a little time. She'll be cool."

I was glad that I decided to call Jay to get his feedback on the situation. After Uniyah gave the "I just want to be alone" speech, I really didn't know what to think. I was still a bit surprised at the feelings I was catching for her, but I kinda liked how it felt.

After finishing my conversation with Jay and making plans to get together after work on Tuesday, I sprawled across my bed, and kicked off my shoes and socks. I turned over on my stomach and let my thoughts rest on Uniyah and the night's events until I fell into a deep slumber.

"Markus, I got something for you." I continued to play with my Sega Genesis video game, hoping that my cousin would leave me alone. It was three days after my eighth birthday,

and my cousin had moved out but was continuing to spend the night on the weekends. Moms had stopped working as much, and she was now home more often. I was grateful because the more she was home, the less my cousin was here. For the first time in a long time, I felt God had answered my prayers. But I wasn't sure how long His grace would last.

"Markus, I got your birthday gift in the room. Come on, let me show you," my cousin coaxed. I reluctantly put the game on pause while I headed in the back room, with my cousin in tow. Passing my mother's bedroom, my cousin peeped his head in the door and could hear my mom lightly snoring. She was exhausted; especially since she had taken on an administrative position at the nursing home and was working more regular hours than before. However, the pay must have been good because she temporarily quit the overnight gig.

I entered my bedroom and waited with my arms folded across my chest for my cousin to give me my birthday gift. "Where's my gift?"

My cousin closed the door to my bedroom and went over to his overnight bag. I was relieved when I realized that he wasn't lying about a present. He pulled out a small gift-wrapped box and handed it to me. I quickly grabbed it and tore the wrapping paper off. My eyes widened and my mouth dropped open when I held the new Nintendo Gameboy in my hands. I loved video games!

My cousin saw the excitement in my eyes and smiled. "I thought you'd like that. I got you some games, too."

"Where?" I inquired with excitement.

"There in my bag, but you got to earn those."

"How?" I cautiously asked.

"I want us to play like we used to play and you can't tell anyone."

"No! I don't want to play with you!" I shouted.

It'd been months since my cousin had forced me to "play" with him. I thought that he was scared that we'd get caught; especially after the last time. The day after that last incident, my mom asked my brother and me what we had learned at school. I stated we had learned if someone was touching us inappropriately or making us do things that we didn't want to do, then we should tell an adult. Later that evening when I was going to bed, my cousin threatened to kill me as usual if I ever told. But for some reason, that threat no longer scared me. Maybe because I started to think that death would be better than the emotional and physical pain that he was inflicting upon me, or maybe because I had just given up. All I know is that my cousin didn't attempt to touch me again until now.

"Markus, if you don't want to play with me, it's cool. I'll go see if Jalen wants to play."

When I heard my little brother's name fall from his lips, the blood raced from my face and I stood motionless. I loved my little brother, and I would do anything to protect him; especially from my cousin. I didn't want him to have to go through the hurt that I had to go through, and I didn't want him to have to lie to Mama. Regretfully, I realized what I had to do. "Okay, I'll play with you," I relented, pushing back the tears that were forming in my eyes.

A sadistic smile formed across my cousin's face. I don't think I'd ever comprehend how my own blood could take pleasure in hurting me. Without him telling me to, I took the initiative and began to undress. I wanted it to be over as soon as possible. I lay across the bed as my cousin began touching my body. He started with my nipples and then moved to my genitals. His hands were soon replaced by his mouth, and I squirmed as he orally fondled my penis.

He continued to give me oral sex while he masturbated. I don't know what he expected because he kept looking at my penis as if it were supposed to do something. He wanted it to swell like his. As he continued to play with me, I began thinking about playing with my Sega Genesis again. I no longer bothered to pray. There was no point. I no longer cried or begged for my cousin to stop. It wasn't that I enjoyed what he was doing; in fact, I hated it with everything in me. There was no point in fighting. I didn't know I could hate something and someone as much as I did, but I hated my cousin with everything I had in me.

My cousin began to moan. He removed his mouth from my penis and rapidly began to move his hand back and forth over his own. He closed his eyes and his body began twitching. When this happened, I always knew that playtime was almost over. He ejaculated over my torso and then collapsed on top of me, breathing heavy. I managed to pry myself from underneath him and grabbed his T-shirt to wipe the mess from my stomach and my chest. Without so much as a muttered word, I pulled my clothes back on before my mother could wake up *and catch us. Although the act now left me emotionless, the shame was always there.*

As I turned to walk out the door, my cousin called me back. "Markus, you forgot your Gameboy and games."

Incredulously, I looked at my cousin. I couldn't believe that he thought that I would've wanted to play with his gift after what he had forced me to do. "I don't want them," I told him and walked out of the room without looking back.

I lay on my back and stared around the room. Focusing on the little light that struggled to seep through the blinds, I became lost in thought. I was trying to make sense of my experience with Brandon days before.

I rolled over on my right side and thought about the passionate kiss we had shared in front of his keyboard before I allowed him to lead me to the bedroom. He had felt so good in my arms, and I didn't want to let him go for the world. For some strange reason, holding him in my arms that morning just felt right. It felt natural, even though everything I was ever taught said that it was wrong. I couldn't believe how rapidly things had progressed from that one simple kiss. It was like a fire had been ignited within me and something deep down within my soul had been stirred.

As I kissed Brandon, allowing my tongue to flicker in and out of his mouth, my hands had begun to roam all over his body. I had allowed my fingers to explore his muscular curves, and the mere contact of his skin caused all of my senses to go haywire. I had initiated all of the morning's events. I was the one that had practically invited myself to Brandon's crib. I was the one that had made the request for him to sing to me. I was the one that had approached him and kissed him passionately.

After exchanging passionate kisses, we retired well into the morning with him resting his head on my bare chest. Later that morning, when I stirred, Brandon also awoke with a smile plastered across his face as he looked up at me, staring down at his nude body. I couldn't help but admire the beauty of his physique. His stomach held a perfect six-pack of abs, his arms were strong, and his legs slightly bowed. The latter had turned me on immensely.

As I marveled at him resting, I wasn't sure if I was prepared to take that step and completely cross over. I still liked women but something about Brandon had intrigued the hell out of me. I wanted to find out what it was. Whatever it was kept me awake at night and daydreaming at work, when I should have been focused on other things.

Brandon must have sensed my apprehension and he slowly pulled away from me and climbed out of the bed. I had watched in anticipation as he walked across the room to his iPod docking station and turned on the iPod. If he were a woman, I would have been running the show. Yet, in this situation, I let him lead.

Brandon had made his way across the room, pulling out candles and lighting them so that there was some light in his heavily dimmed room due to the curtains being closed. Tamia softly crooned "make tonight beautiful" in the background. Intrigued, I continued to watch him. It was hard not to compare his actions to a woman. It was only women that I'd ever been with. When a woman knew that a man was watching her, she often put on a show: an extra shake in her step to emphasize the twist of her ass; a batting of the eyelashes; a seductive smile. Yet, Brandon did none of that.

Everything he had done was natural, masculine, and sexy. He didn't try to be something he wasn't. There was no dramatic show put on for my benefit. He was comfortable in his skin; far more comfortable than I had felt. As he had lit the final candle he looked up at me, and our eyes made contact. He had smiled and, nervously, I returned the gesture.

I regained my composure and made my way over to where he was standing, gently placing my hands around his waist. Our lips connected and our tongues became intertwined. He had taken a slight step back to observe my physique and, apparently impressed by my features, he had brought his lips back to mine, then to my neck, and used his tongue to trail down to my left areola.

He had gently suckled my nipple and added a little pressure. I tried to suppress my pleasure as his teeth gently bit down, but I couldn't stop the moan that had erupted from my throat. I had pulled him down on the bed and closed my eyes as I tried not to concentrate on the act itself but on how good it made me feel.

Brandon had traced his tongue all over my body, including every ripple in my stomach. I lay back and watched him trace his way down to the thin line of pubic hair directly under my belly button. I was harder than a rock and more turned on than I had ever been. My penis pointed toward the ceiling and the air's coolness tickled it until Brandon hovered over it with his warm breath. He had held my penis in his hand, running it over the length before taking as much of me as he could into his mouth. My eyes rolled to the back of my head, and my toes curled.

Not wanting this euphoric feeling to end, I pushed Brandon's head away. Psyching myself to believe that making love to him would be no different than making love to a woman, I gently pulled his body up until his ass hovered above my dick.

"Hold on," he cooed. Reaching into his nightstand, he grabbed a bottle of lubricant and a condom. I was glad that Brandon practiced safe sex.

Placing the condom onto my penis, he then squirted some of the liquid lubricant onto my shaft. Teasing the head of my penis with his buttocks, he leaned forward and began tracing his tongue up and down my torso before reaching my mouth. I gently parted his buttocks and leaned back before slowly lowering him onto my penis. Letting out a grunt, I saw the pain-filled look on his face. This was probably due to the girth and the slight curvature of my penis.

Taking his time to adjust, that pained look on his face

dissipated. Looking me in the eyes, he slowly gyrated his hips against my pelvis. The candlelight that lit the room cast his shadow on the wall. His manhood was fully erect and bobbed up and down, slapping against his stomach. Increasing his rhythm, with one hand, he took his penis in his hand and began stroking it. He felt so good and so tight. I wanted to change positions, but I wasn't sure if I would hurt him by impaling my nine-and-a-half-inch penis deeper inside of him.

I had tried to hold back, but I wasn't going to be able to contain the mounting sensation building up inside of me. Brandon leaned his head back, and I could see that he was in a world of his own. Not nearly fifteen minutes after he'd straddled me, his thighs clenched around mine and his seed erupted onto my chest.

Seeing him reach his climax pushed me to do the same. With a loud groan, I pushed myself deeper inside of him and leaned forward to wrap my arms around his body as my seed erupted from the tip of my penis, filling up the condom. Brandon sat up and smiled as he watched me breathing heavily. My body continued to pulsate from the intensity of our lovemaking and the orgasmic rush. I took several deep breaths trying to get a grip on the sensation that was still running through my body.

Slowly dismounting me, Brandon went to the bathroom to get a washcloth. Minutes later, he returned with a warm cloth, and he wiped me down before nestling next to me. We lay there motionless as we listened to the iPod proceed to play Chanté Moore and Kenny Lattimore's rendition of Keith Sweat's "Make It Last Forever."

"Why are you smiling like that?" Brandon had asked, breaking the silence that had begun to engulf the room.

"Like what?"

"I don't know. There was a weird smirk on your face."

"I don't know. I was just enjoying the moment," I had replied, which was partly true.

"Oh, well, that's good to know. Happy I could, uh, make you smile like that then," Brandon had replied before pulling me in close to him.

❖❖❖

I replayed that morning over and over again in my head. The part I didn't tell him that night was that my smirk was a result of how much I was "digging'" him. I couldn't believe that I had kissed, had foreplay, received oral sex, and had sex with dude. I couldn't help but wonder what the hell I had just done. *Did I just make the biggest mistake of my life?* It would be a question I would ask myself for days—maybe even weeks—to come.

THREE MONTHS LATER...

Twenty Seven
UNIYAH

I couldn't believe that three months had come and gone since I'd performed my rendition of Whitney's "All the Man That I Need" at Club Chillax in midtown. When I wasn't in the studio recording tracks with Brandon or, rather, re-recording them, I was spending the rest of my spare time with Markus. Things between the two of us had really taken off since he'd come to my rescue the night David had attacked me. I'd realized then that I would give Markus my undivided attention and had yet to renege on my decision.

It seemed like we were made for one another. I couldn't remember a time when I sat at home crying because he had done me wrong, or because we had a bad argument. It seemed that the only time we did argue was when we wanted an excuse to make up. I couldn't wait until we actually got completely physical.

I continued applying makeup to my face as I prepared to head down to Club Chillax to meet with the owner. He said he needed to brief me on what to expect during the final competition, and I wanted to hear what he had to say. I was hoping he was going to give me a tip on what my other competition was like because I was tired of my singing aspirations being nothing more than a pipe dream.

Honestly, a part of me was feeling a little guilty about running out to meet with the owner, but as much as I loved Brandon and respected his writing, producing and support, I was having second thoughts about him being able to take me to the next level. I spent a lot of time thinking about our chemistry, which was uncanny. But I did wonder if it would be enough to garner the attention of a record company. I mean, when a record executive heard that a renowned producer had penned a track for an aspiring singer, I was certain that they'd take more notice rather than hearing that the track was penned by two nobodies. I loved Brandon with all of my heart, and if I was able to acquire a record deal, there was no doubt that I'd bring him along so that he could establish a name for himself as well.

I grabbed my keys and headed out the door. Jumping in my ride, I surfed the music channels of my satellite radio for something good to listen to as my car warmed up from the cold. I couldn't believe it was in the forties, and it was only the middle of October. Hell, I couldn't believe that spring had come and gone as fast as it did and now summer was about to do the same. I settled on Heart & Soul and listened to the latest from Mariah, envying every bit of her success—budding career, everlasting success and a husband that adored her like she was the last woman on earth.

Half-an-hour later, I pulled into the club's parking lot and noticed the only other car there was a champagne-colored Acura. I couldn't wait for the day when MTV or BET did a feature on my crib and showed all my rides parked out in my driveway or in my private garage. "One day, girl, one day," I muttered to myself as I walked into the club.

"Hello," I bellowed to the empty room, my voice bouncing off the walls and echoing in the empty space. I slowed my stroll as I began to look around the club for any sign of Keno, the owner. I called out into the room once more and, to my surprise, my call was answered.

"Hold on, baby girl. I'm just finishing this call," a baritone voice replied.

I took a seat at the bar and positioned myself on a barstool. As I waited for Keno to finish his call, I debated on which song I would sing on Saturday. I wasn't sure what type of crowd it was going to be and that made my song choice that much harder. If the room was predominately filled with women, I didn't want to come out singing a song about how sexy I was. I would need to rock one of those "take no more shit from men" anthems that made Mary J. famous and women loved. And Fantasia's "Two Weeks Notice" definitely had me crooning in the car and in the shower. That was the type of song a female audience would appreciate, and I made a mental note of that.

"Damn, girl, I forgot how fine you are!" Keno exclaimed, after resting his hands on my shoulders and breaking me from my thoughts.

I spun around on the barstool and gave him a quick, professional hug: no body-to-body contact but more shoulder-to-shoulder with a pat on the back. Keno smirked at the gesture but didn't release my hand he had voluntarily taken into his own. I cocked my head to the side and curled the corner of my lip to let him know I was hip to his moves but not encouraging them. I didn't want him to waste any more of my time spitting game at me that would get him nowhere. Besides, I wanted to hurry and get back home so I could cook dinner for Markus. I had to be having feelings for him to be thinking about cooking.

Keno could obviously tell his game was getting him nowhere and proceeded to get down to business. "Look, Uniyah, I'm not going to waste any more of your time, so why don't we just get right down to it."

"I'm listening," I replied.

"I think you're the most talented singer who's performed in this club, but I'm afraid that you're going to receive a lot of hate from the ladies. That alone may keep you from winning Saturday night's competition. And to be honest, between you and me, one of the female judges really has it in for you. It's like she's jealous or something, but she's hell-bent on not crowning you the winner; regardless of how good you are."

"Hold on, I thought that the winner was decided by the audience. When did judges become a part of this process?"

"In the past, this was how it was decided; but then contestants would pack the room with their family and friends and the contest became nothing but a popularity contest. This year, I revamped the process. The audience picks the winners in the preliminaries; but then we have a panel of judges to decide from those who make it to the final."

"Okay, so, uh, what? Are you suggesting that I drop out?"

"Well, what if I were to tell you that I could persuade the other female judge to vote in your favor so you'd have three of the four votes needed to win?"

Now he had my interest. I was determined to walk away the winner on Saturday night. "And how do you plan to do that?"

"Don't worry about that. Just know that I'll come through and, if push comes to shove, it's my damn club. I'll declare you the winner; regardless of what the other judges have to say. Remember they are paid by me."

"Cool. So why are you so willing to help me?" I asked with curiosity.

"I have something you want, and you have something I want," he replied with a devilish grin.

"And what would *that* be?" I asked, hoping he meant he wanted a chance to hook up with my girl, Janelle. He had tried in the past to come at me, but something about him just rubbed me the wrong way.

Keno glanced down at his watch and looked over his shoulder. "Hey, why don't we go back to my office before one of the staff comes in and hears us talking? I don't want any rumors going around that I rigged the competition."

"True, true," I agreed and followed Keno across the dance floor and down the hall to his private office. After entering the room, he closed the door behind me and locked it. I became alarmed but continued to keep my cool. I needed him to hurry up and finish talking about the details of Saturday and what he needed me to do to guarantee my win so I could get out of there. Call me naïve, but I was desperate to win; and apparently my desperation was plastered across my face.

"Okay, so what is it you wanted?" I asked.

Keno walked past me as if he were heading to his desk, slowly spun around, and grabbed my ass.

"This," he replied.

I pushed his hand away with fury. At six-one, with a medium-built athletic frame, sexy bald head, and the dreamiest hazel eyes I had ever seen, it was no surprise that he usually "got" every woman he went after. But I was not any woman, and I would be damned if he thought he was going to proposition me like I was some trick. Keno had always been the flirty type, but he was taking things to a whole 'nother level.

"So, you telling me if I let you fuck me up in here like some ho, then you'll guarantee my win?" I asked disgustedly.

Keno rounded his desk, pulled out his executive chair, took a seat, and lit one of the cigars that rested inside the mahogany humidor that sat on his desk. "First, lower your damn voice," he reprimanded after blowing a puff of smoke out the corner of his mouth. "And secondly, I ain't trying to treat you like no ho. It's like I said, I have something you want and you have something I want. All I'm suggesting is a 'trade,' so to speak, and we both walk away satisfied."

"Keno, this ain't even going down like this. You've known me for years, and you're stepping to me like *this*? You must really think I'm stupid!" I shouted, not caring about my voice level anymore. "Yeah, you promise that I'll win if I sleep with you and if I don't, I can't say shit about it 'cause I'd be just as guilty as you for going along with your little plan. Please, run that game on someone else."

"Look, Uniyah, you know I've always had a thing for you. I've been steppin' to you for a minute, so don't try to act like my interest is coming as a surprise. I see this as, well, the right time to make things happen for the both of us, if you know what I mean," Keno replied, stamping out his barely smoked cigar. "Are you trying to tell me you'd throw away a chance of a lifetime to take your career to the next level because of 'a little lovin'? Come on, girl, think about it. You're making it bigger than it is."

I stared at Keno and couldn't believe what he was saying to me. Even more, I couldn't believe what I was about to do. I needed this opportunity more than anything, and he was right: I had given "it" up for much less. Why was I being so "selective" now when it could cost me my future? I took a deep breath and ran my hands through my hair. Without a word, I made my way over to Keno—knowing deep down inside I was going to regret everything I was about to do—and fell to my knees.

I pulled the covers off me and dragged myself out of bed. All night I had tossed and turned until finally falling into a restless sleep around three a.m. Over the last few months, I had become so accustomed to Uniyah sleeping beside me that it was difficult for me to do so when she wasn't there. And now that she was spending more time recording her demo and preparing for her performance at Club Chillax, I was forced to sleep alone more and more. It didn't take me long to realize that holding my pillow tight was no substitute for holding Uniyah, but there was nothing I could do. I knew from the beginning how much singing meant to her, and I wasn't about to try and pry her away from her passion and her chance to score a development deal with a major record label.

As I headed to the bathroom to get dressed for work, I realized how tired my body was. Although Uniyah and I had decided to take things to the next level and date exclusively, I hadn't really been dating exclusively. I was still creeping on the low and seeing someone else on the side. I didn't realize how much energy it took to do so. As I splashed cold water on my face to wake myself up completely, I wondered to myself how long I was going to actually be able to keep up this game of charades. I knew how things played out in situations such as this and, ultimately, somebody would get hurt. I couldn't tell which one I was feeling more, but the time was going to come soon for me to make a decision.

I quickly did my normal routine of shitting, showering, and shaving as I prepped myself for my long day at work. I planned on spending a long evening at the office as I had been neglecting a few pressing matters in my attempt to juggle my social life. Plus, I had planned an eventful weekend for Uniyah and myself to congratulate her on her upcoming win at Club Chillax. After seeing her perform that night I first laid eyes on her and comparing that performance to the other contestants that had performed subsequent nights after her, none of them held a light to my baby's voice.

I had already planned a very romantic congratulatory evening at the W Hotel in downtown Atlanta for her. I had spent a fortune on the room and on making sure that everything would go smoothly. The more time I spent with Uniyah, the more I could see myself planning a future with her. But in order for me to be able to take things to the next level with her, the two of us were going to have to take things to a more intimate level.

I was hoping that the romantic evening would put an

end to all the teasing and that we'd finally be able to make love. I tried my best to respect Uniyah's wishes in regards to becoming intimate but, hell, it had been over three months since we'd been kicking it and a brother could only do so much fantasizing and "self-loving" before he'd have to have the real thing.

I checked myself once more in the mirror and admired my cotton, baby blue, button-down Kenneth Cole shirt, my polished black and gold Stacy Adams cufflinks, and my red power tie with the blue and black accents running throughout it. I placed my matching Stacy Adams tie pin on my tie and headed over to my dresser to apply some Burberry cologne before slipping into my dark blue pinstripe jacket. I always loved to make an impression when I walked into a room and, today, I would be sure to do just that.

I went outside, jumped into my Benz, and zoomed out of the complex. I had to make a thirty-minute drive in less than fifteen minutes. As I jumped onto the interstate, I prayed that I-85 South wasn't backed up because anyone who has visited the ATL knew that traffic during morning rush hour was horrendous.

As I pushed seventy miles per hour, I dialed Uniyah's number from the radio console on my car's dashboard and waited for her to answer. As I suspected, I got her voicemail but left a brief message, instructing her to call me at the office anyway. I found a convenient parking space at my office's garage, parked, grabbed my black and brown, two-tone leather briefcase, and made my way to the office.

I checked my watch and cussed myself for not making it on time; I couldn't stand being late. And even though I didn't have set office hours, I liked to be at the office by 8:30 a.m. I lived by the motto: To be early is to be on time; to be on time is to be late; to be late is unacceptable.

I walked through the revolving doors of my office building and greeted the concierge with a nod. I needed to be focused today on completing the marketing presentation that was due by Monday morning. I was nowhere close to being finished, so I really needed to keep my attention centered on completing it and having it on my director's desk by the close of business so I could devote my undivided attention to Uniyah.

I stepped on the elevator and pressed the button to the twenty-first floor. While it ascended, I thought about what my planned romantic evening with Uniyah could bring: a night of pure ecstasy. The thought was all the motivation I needed to knock this marketing project out and rush to her side. As the elevator door opened, I put on my "game" face and headed down the hall to my corner office. I had already decided the day was going to be a productive one. After all, the rewards to come just couldn't be beat.

Twenty Nine
UNIYAH

I pulled myself up from between Keno's legs as he lustily looked me over, his penis lying limp between his legs. I grabbed an empty coffee mug on his desk to dispose of his seed and wiped my mouth with the back of my hand in disgust. I wanted to get home and gargle as fast as I could, not to mention shower, since the act in itself had left me feeling completely dirty. With a lot less dignity than I had when I first entered the club, I hastily smoothed out my clothes and grabbed my purse to leave. But not before turning to Keno and letting him know I expected—demanded—that he keep our verbal agreement. He nodded before throwing a kiss my way, and I spun on my heels in disgust and stormed out of his office.

I expeditiously made my way out of the club and to my car so that I could be alone with my thoughts. I couldn't believe that I had allowed Keno to get the best of me; that I actually allowed *myself* to "go down" on him. I swore to myself that if I didn't win the competition, I would make sure Keno paid for the humiliation he caused me. He'd be stupid to let my bourgeois demeanor fool him for an instant.

As I flew out of the club doors, I saw another female contestant approaching the club. I was hoping to leave unseen but there was no way that I could avoid Sonia since she was parked directly next to my car and heading in my direction. I tossed my hair to the side and faked the best smile I could.

"W'sup, Sonia?" I asked, tossing her an insincere grin.

"Hey, girl. You came to see Keno, too?"

"Yeah, *something* like that. What? Keno's calling all the contestants in before Saturday's contest?"

"Yeah, I think he is. Remember the last winner from two weekends ago?"

"Are you talking about the redbone sister who sung that Yolanda Adams gospel song?"

"Yeah, that's my girl. She said that Keno wants to see her later this evening, so he's making sure we're committed to the show's performance tomorrow and not bringing any surprises."

"Yeah, he wanted to know what songs I was performing and to tell me what I needed to know regarding sound check," I lied.

I was pissed as hell. There were only three women in the competition and if Keno had called us all in for a "private" session, then I had gotten played.

"I'm sorry, Sonia. I don't mean to rush you, but I have to get home and take care of some business."

"Oh, all right, girl. Go ahead and do you."

Without losing my composure, I made it to my car and got in. I cranked up the volume on the radio and screamed. I wasn't sure who to be more upset with: Keno or myself. I pulled away from the club as the tears fell from my eyes. This entire competition was too good to be true. As I made my way home, I dialed Markus' number and left him a message, telling him I had to cancel our get-together later due to some last-minute preparations I had to attend to.

After hanging up, I called Janelle. I needed her to calm me down before I did something stupid that could land my ass behind bars. Without going into too much detail, I quickly made arrangements for her to meet me at my crib.

I struggled to drive home as the thoughts of what had happened continued to swirl around in my head. I parked and practically ran inside the house. I needed a drink—a stiff one to calm my nerves and put me at-ease. What I really wanted was a joint but it had been almost three years since I had smoked one. With singing as my full-time focus, I didn't want to do anything that would affect my vocal cords.

After slamming the front door shut, I ran into the bathroom and quickly grabbed the Listerine off of the cabinet shelf. I took a swig and gargled a long time. I felt degraded, stupid, and used. But what I hated most was that I was to blame for the way I was feeling. Keno hadn't forced me to do anything; I should've just grabbed my belongings and headed out the door. I convinced myself that doing it would be worth winning the competition. I wasn't so sure anymore.

I heard Janelle knocking on my front door, and I rinsed my mouth for the fourth time before going to open it. When I saw Janelle, I couldn't keep the tears from erupting from my eyes. That *sonofabitch* had made a fool out of me and there was nothing I could do about it. Janelle grabbed me in her arms and attempted to comfort me and calm me down without actually knowing what it was that was bothering me. She led me over to the sofa and sat me down while she went into the kitchen to fix me a Bacardi 151 and Coke. After placing the drink in front of me, Janelle sat on the adjacent couch and waited for me to tell her what had happened.

I closed my eyes and took a long sip from my glass, allowing the liquor to slide down my throat and warm my chest before it settled in my stomach. I exhaled deeply, and then began to tell Janelle the entire sordid story of how I had allowed myself to be convinced into "trading sex for stardom."

Just like a best friend, Janelle listened intently to my account with Keno without judgment or opinion. I needed someone to listen, and she was doing a great job. I also told her how scared I was that Markus would somehow find out since he frequented Club Chillax and had talked to Keno a time or two. Contrary to popular belief, guys talked as much as women—if not more— and I definitely didn't need Markus to get an earful of this. And as angry as I was, I was also hoping that the other girls didn't fall for Keno's proposition as well. Knowing he'd played everybody would inflate his ego even more.

For the rest of the day, Janelle stayed with me and offered her words of comfort, convincing me that everything would be fine and that I had enough talent to blow away any competition; regardless of what "favors" had been performed. I agreed but, deep down inside, we both weren't sure.

Keno was holding everything in his hands, including my future. And I couldn't believe how stupid I could be to jeopardize the only true thing that had brought me happiness—my singing—and I was also risking losing the second most important thing that made me happy: Markus. I grabbed the almost empty Bacardi bottle and took it to the head. I couldn't erase what I had done but, at least for the night, I could try to make myself forget.

When Janelle departed, I picked up my iPhone and began making some much needed phone calls.

T hree months, six days, and ten hours had passed since Tyrone and I had shared that morning of intimacy. Five weeks, two days and seven hours was how long it had been since I'd last heard from him. I'd be lying if I said it didn't have me shaken. It wasn't often that I engaged in anything sexual, but that night I felt a connection with Tyrone; one that I wanted to pursue. He claimed that it was his first time being intimate with a man, and I feared that I had rushed things in an effort to keep him from losing interest in me.

The days not hearing from him felt long and lonely. I called and left messages, but they went unreturned. I tried emailing and catching him online, but he had canceled his account. I was confused and distraught. I thought I was at least owed a "Dear John" letter, but instead all I got were sleepless nights and mounting questions that wouldn't receive any answers.

I did my best to keep my mind off of Tyrone. I tried engrossing myself in my studies and writing. I even increased the amount of time I spent in the studio with

Uniyah. Just to keep from obsessing about him, I had begun recording songs of my own but nothing seemed to ease the pain or fill the void. I wish that I understood why men did the things they did. If he wasn't comfortable with what we did that night, why couldn't he have just said so? Then I'd at least have some clue as how to proceed.

I rode the train aimlessly with no focus on where I was supposed to be headed. I winded up missing my stop and having to double back. Exiting the train, I headed to transfer to my bus. I had been so deep in thought that I didn't even realize that it had begun to rain. I hopped on the bus and placed my earphones over my ears and closed my eyes as Uniyah's voice filled the tiny speakers.

She wasn't sure what song she wanted to perform for the competition, and I told her that I'd give her my decision in the morning. She had one Toni Braxton selection, two Fantasia songs, and a cut from Beyoncé to choose from. Of course, I was more in favor of the Fantasia song because of its emotion and range that Uniyah could do justice to. A true artist could take any song and make it their own, so I wasn't worried.

I grabbed my belongings and threw my iPod in my backpack as I headed toward the front of the bus to exit. I hopped off the bus and leisurely made my way to my apartment since the rain had now slowed to a steady drizzle. Ironically, I was roughly two blocks from my apartment, when the sky opened back up and the rain began to pour down on me.

I held my backpack over my head and jumped over the potholes filled with water. I miscalculated the length of the last pothole in front of my apartment and ended up jumping in it, slightly twisting my ankle. Now my stride had been reduced to a slow hobble as I entered my complex drenched from head to toe.

I made my way to my apartment and couldn't stop the tears that fell from my eyes. I don't know what I was crying about but something told me that I needed to let everything out. I was tired of falling for one guy after the next, only to be disappointed in the end. I led myself to believe that Tyrone was "The One"; even though all the signs were there that he wasn't. I don't know what it was about him that had intrigued me so, but he had entrapped me and now I couldn't get him out of my mind.

I needed to know why I had been dissed; why he had been ignoring me and not returning my messages. I desperately wanted to hear his voice. I wanted to hear him ask how my day had gone; ask what song I was currently writing; ask when he could see me again. I needed him to care.

It was ironic because Tyrone didn't owe me any of this, but I had become accustomed to him doing all that without me asking him to do so. Now I was left in need of some attention. Part of me wanted to get on the Internet and get into a chat room; to meet somebody new who could instantly replace Tyrone. But I didn't want to go through the rigors of getting to know someone else all over again or having to deal with all the "games."

I wasn't in the mood to go to the club or to any parties. I simply needed to be held by someone familiar.

As the realization came to me that I was indeed alone, the tears flowed more freely from my eyes and I was glad the rain that had fallen on my face was masking the truth. I couldn't remember the last time I had cried like this, but part of me felt relieved. It was like a heavy burden had been lifted off of my shoulders.

As I placed my key in the door, I felt a presence. It was like someone was watching me. I spun around to make sure I wasn't about to be attacked by an intruder. Not seeing anyone, I turned my attention back to entering my apartment until I heard something shifting in a dark corner opposite my doorway.

I dropped my keys as the figure stepped from the shadows and showed himself. After all of the thoughts, the unanswered questions, sleepless nights, self-doubts, tears, and pain, there he stood before me. Tyrone bent over and picked up my keys, and I angrily snatched them from his hands. I turned around and tried to hurry and hide in the safety of my apartment. I wasn't sure what emotion would pour from me if I started talking, but I didn't want him to witness what his distance had done to me. I couldn't steady my hand enough to get the key in the lock. Tyrone walked quietly toward me, placed one hand on the small of my back, and the other on my hand that held the key. He turned the lock, using my hand as his guide and pushed the door open.

We entered the apartment together in sync. His steps matched mine and I had to admit that part of me wanted to be mad while another part was saying, *"get over it; he's here now."* He closed the door and continued to embrace me from behind, placing his chin in the crook of my neck. I loved the way he smelt; the way he felt; the way he breathed. My heart was beating in rhythm with his and seemed to overpower the silence that lingered in the air. The last time when I took the initiative to make a "move" on him, he ran away. I didn't want to chance that happening again and decided I would follow his lead this time.

We embraced for almost ten minutes before he brought his mouth to my ear and whispered an apology for avoiding me. I wanted to ask him why he had disappeared but wasn't sure if I were ready for the answer he might give, so I declined. I thought back to the conversation we had when he admitted he was still attracted to—and dated—women. Part of me knew that was why he had been missing in action for so long, but I wasn't ready for him to confirm that.

My mind was telling me to push Tyrone away and send him home, but my heart was screaming, *"let him stay."* It had been so long since anyone had just held me, and I was enjoying the simple embrace and affection. I desperately needed to be held and didn't want to be alone, but being with Tyrone would only end in heartache. This was a warning I deliberately chose to ignore.

Instead, I chose to listen to my heart and not my mind.

After a few more passing minutes, Tyrone finally stepped back and turned me around so I could face him. I turned my face toward the wall because I didn't want him to see the tear stains that had trekked down my cheeks. He gently used his finger to turn my face back in his direction and softly brushed my lips with his own. A tremble ran through my body, and I felt weak in the knees. He kissed my eyelids and my cheeks. Then he moved his lips down to my neck. My head instinctively rolled back as his tongue made contact, and I gripped his shoulders tighter.

I let him walk me over to the sofa where he sat me down and slithered his tongue from my neck and into my mouth. I relished the pleasure he was bringing me and felt all the anger, sadness, and pain I had been carrying the past five weeks slowly diminish. I was back in his arms where I wanted to be, and the love that I had felt for him was once again ignited. Yet, I could only wonder how long it would be before I got "burnt" again. Like a moth to a flame, the allure was too strong for me to pull away. Once again, I was throwing caution—and my heart—to the wind for an opportunity to be loved.

Thirty One
MARKUS

I checked myself in the mirror to ensure that I was as debonair as humanly possible. Satisfied with what I saw, I grabbed my car keys as I headed out the door. I wanted to make it to Club Chillax before the competition began. I was anxious to see how Uniyah would do. From what I'd observed, she was the type that could perform well under pressure and, with all that was at stake, she'd definitely be under a lot of pressure. My romantic evening would be exactly what she needed to take the edge off afterward.

I was proud of myself for being able to withstand temptation and warding off all the advances from other women that tried to gain my attention. I was committed to making things work with Uniyah and, as hard as she was making it by not giving me a taste of the "goodies," I was certain that if I remained patient, it'd pay off in the end. The thought of holding her in my arms and making love to her all night caused me to become slightly aroused. I did my best to shake the thought as I pulled into the club's parking lot. Nobody else needed to "see" what I had on my mind.

I parked on the side of the club and observed the number of limousines parked in front as I made my way to the front door. I had heard some big-time producers were supposed to be in attendance, including some of Atlanta's own, and figured the stretched Lincolns and Hummers, and other luxury cars must have belonged to them. I was sure when Uniyah saw them, she'd be even more nervous.

With a smile plastered across my face, I entered the club, which had undergone a major "facelift." Keno had definitely put some serious cash into renovations and, for a moment, I thought I was in the wrong place. I glanced around the partly empty club and noticed that Keno was huddled over the bar, apparently giving some of his staff last-minute instructions to ensure that the night went smoothly.

I headed in his direction, waited for him to finish talking, and then pulled him in for a partial hug and handshake. Over the last few months, he and I had become better acquainted after he enlisted my expertise on how to market the evening's event. In fact, it was me that suggested he advertise the event on the radio, do some minor renovations, and personally send out invitations to some of the top recording labels. There was nothing that I loved more than a client that knew how to listen.

"W'sup?" Keno shouted.

"Not a damn thing. I wanted to holla at my girl before she performed," I replied.

"Good luck with that. She's definitely gone into *diva* mode. She's locked in my office in the back, prepping for her performance. I don't even know what it is that she's performing because at sound check, she asked me and the house band to leave the room while she and her own band rehearsed. You definitely have your hands full with that one," he jokingly teased.

"You don't have to tell me. But please believe, she's worth that little bit of 'drama.'"

"I'm sure she is," Keno replied, raising an eyebrow.

I wondered if he and Uniyah had some past history before I came into the picture. If they did, it was their business. That was the past, and I was definitely the present and the future.

"So, where are all the big-time producers that are supposed to be in the house?" I inquired, trying to ignore the sly look Keno gave me.

"Oh, they're here. Most of them are in *diva* and *divo* mode, too. Shit, the brothers are worse than the women, but you're more than welcome to mingle with them up in the V.I.P. section."

"Mos' def. I think I'll do that. Do I need a pass or something?"

"Yeah, I almost forgot. They demanded that I have some type of security system in place to filter out those who aren't 'stars.'" He laughed, handing me a plastic gold key card, and instructed me to show it to the bouncer at the top of the stairs.

Keno and I engaged in more small talk before I left

him to finish with his last-minute preparations. He seemed anxious and had stated that he was a little worried that if the affair wasn't a success, his books could be in the red. Even though he listened to me and dished out the funds to promote the event, he didn't seem to fully trust my expertise. Yet, I was confident that by the end of the night, he would know I was damn good at what I did.

I even told him to raise the admission by seven dollars and the drinks by two. It was to be expected that people would complain, but they'd finally break down and dish out the dough; especially to front like they could hang with the ballers. Nothing turned a sister off more than a brother that was too broke to buy her a drink.

Heading up to the V.I.P. section, I did as Keno instructed and showed the bouncer my gold key card. He stepped aside, allowing me into the private lounge where I commenced to scope the room to see who was in attendance. I was impressed that the room was packed not only with producers, but also signed artists. Everyone was trying to get the "up" on who might be the next hottest thing.

I headed toward the bar where I ordered my favorite drink, a Blue Motherfucker, to calm my mood. As I waited for the bartender to hook me up, I noticed a sister sitting on a barstool that looked like she'd rather be elsewhere.

"Wow, you're wearing that look of displeasure well," I shot at her, causing a subtle smile to spread across her face. I couldn't help but notice how attractive she was when she wasn't frowning.

"I'm not sure if that's a compliment, or a diss," she shot back.

"It was nothing more than an observation, but I see that it brought a smile to your face."

"Who says it was the comment that brought the smile?" she seductively asked.

It didn't take me long to realize that homegirl was hitting on me, and I decided to play the game. There was nothing wrong with a little harmless flirting. "So what forces you to be here tonight, Ms. …?"

"You can call me Imaní," she stated, extending her hand, which I shook. "And to answer your question, the president of the record label that I work for personally assigned me the task of checking out the new talent showcasing here tonight."

I took my drink and purchased one for her before inviting her to a nearby sofa to talk a little more, doing my best to ward off her strong sexual innuendos. I wasn't sure if I disliked her aggressiveness or if I was so caught up with Uniyah, that I simply didn't have interest in anyone else.

Minutes into our conversation, two gentlemen from two of the top urban production companies joined us. As we all got acquainted with one another, I disclosed that I was a partner in one of Atlanta's top advertising firms and had helped Keno promote the event. But more importantly, I let them know I was in attendance in support of my baby, Uniyah. I could see the look of disappointment cross Imaní's face at the mention of

Uniyah's name, but something told me that she truly didn't care if I was involved with someone or not.

I was happy when one of the producers mentioned he had been told that Uniyah was definitely someone to look out for. He offered me his business card to pass along to her; and the others, not wanting to miss out on the next big thing, offered theirs as well. Of course, Ms. Imaní's card had her cell and home numbers scrawled across the back. I noticed that she was located in New York. If Uniyah hadn't already had my heart, I would've been spitting game until she'd offered me an all-expense paid trip to the Big Apple. Not that I didn't have money of my own, but like the saying goes, "Why spend mine when I can spend yours?"

I departed from the group to do some more mingling and headed to the balcony that overlooked the lower level and the stage area. I was astounded at how quickly the club had filled to capacity. I hoped Keno had taken my advice and was counting the number of guests he allowed into the club. From the looks of things, the fire marshal would definitely be making a personal appearance.

I scanned the crowd and finally caught a glimpse of Uniyah in front of the stage in a conservative evening gown that accentuated all her right curves. I tossed back the rest of my drink but almost choked on it when my eyes saw what I didn't want to believe.

Perspiration began to form across my brow as I stepped back from the balcony. I kept telling myself that I was mistaken; that I hadn't seen what I thought I had. But my mind, or my eyes, weren't playing tricks on me. I stepped back toward the balcony and peered over it to get a better look. My heart raced faster and beads of sweat formed under my armpits as I confirmed what I now knew to be true.

Sitting in the front row of Club Chillax, I highly anticipated the night's performances. Uniyah and I had been putting in double time to ensure that she was at her best for the competition. All of our hard work was going to be put to the test, and I hoped that it would be the night we finally got some recognition. Sipping on my Hennessy and Coke, I waited patiently while the master of ceremony took the stage and pumped up the crowd.

I was glad the night wouldn't be filled with wannabe rappers spitting game about lives that they never lived. I was even more impressed that the club didn't allow the night's performers to use prerecorded tracks. There was nothing that I loved more than a performance with a live band.

I took another sip of my drink and glanced up into the balcony area, presumably the V.I.P. section. As I was hugging Uniyah earlier to wish her luck, I could've sworn that I'd seen Tyrone. But I was tripping. After all, Tyrone had left my place this morning to go visit his family in Florida. Brushing aside the feeling that Tyrone had lied to me and not gone out of town, I tried my best to focus my attention on the young performer that had now taken the stage.

The young entertainer had come out singing a neo-soul ballad with lyrics that were far too deep for the audience to vibe with. It was the type of song that required people to sit down alone with a glass of wine and totally open their mind to the words. It wasn't the right song to start a competition off with or perform in this type of setting. It was a good thing that Keno had amended the rules to give the performers two song selections instead of one. I hoped that the brother currently singing came strong with his next selection. It sure didn't seem like the crowd was feeling his first.

After listening to three more performers—two of whom were really good—it was finally Uniyah's turn. I was a little worried. One of the female performers that had previously performed had definitely brought her "A" game and was playing—or rather singing—for keeps.

Uniyah shocked me when she didn't perform any of the songs we had rehearsed or considered, but opened up with the ballad that put Mariah back on the top of the charts instead. I listened intently as Uniyah sang a rearranged version of "We Belong Together." I held my breath for the high notes she would have to hit. Although she had a five-octave vocal range, Uniyah was inconsistent when it came to hitting the notes in the higher register. To my surprise, so far she was holding her own; but she had yet to reach the end of the song where the highest notes and runs were "waiting" for her.

I was nervous because of all the moving Uniyah was doing onstage. Every time Mariah performed the song, she made sure to plant herself firmly and concentrate solely on her vocals. But Uniyah was on the verge of overexerting herself as she worked the stage from side to side.

I should've had more faith in Uniyah. Not only did she hit the note, but she showed her vocal range as well. Uniyah had really impressed the audience and received a standing ovation as a result. She exited the stage as the next performer headed to the microphone, and it looked like Uniyah was in the running for first place.

After the rest of the performers gave it all they had, there was a brief intermission as each one regrouped for the next performance. I went to the bar to get another drink, hoping to run into someone of importance so I could get some feedback from a professional regarding Uniyah's performance. I mingled with a few people that I recognized, assuming that they could direct me to where all the people of importance were. I frowned as I was informed that they all were up in the V.I.P. section and was dumbfounded as to why Uniyah didn't get me access to it where I could do a better job of selling her.

I headed back to my seat as the MC took to the stage to rev up the crowd once again. I took a sip of my drink and wondered what Uniyah would perform next. Before the first performer was re-introduced to the audience, the MC informed everyone that the artists would now perform original songs only. I wondered why Uniyah didn't inform me that she'd be performing one of our pieces. Nervous energy abounded me as I waited to see which one of our pieces—*my* pieces—she would sing.

After sitting through songs of all kind—some good; some bad; some darn near duplicates of existing songs—I braced myself when Uniyah took to the stage again. Her band adjusted their instruments, and then began playing a melody I didn't recognize. As the backup singers began singing the hooks, I realized that it wasn't one of our songs but either one of hers or one that someone else had written. After all of our days and nights of hard work, it felt like a slap in the face to see she didn't think any of the songs I wrote, or co-wrote, were good enough for her performance.

Regardless of the audience's wild applause, I was fuming. I was hurt and wanted to get up and leave, but I didn't have the nerve to walk out on a friend. I tried to convince myself that there was a valid reason why she had done what she did. In the end, I only hoped that her decision paid off. But for me it was a dose of reality. I could no longer count on Uniyah to bring me along as a writer or co-producer, if she did happen to get signed to a recording deal. It was time for me to start doing my own *thang* by finding other artists to work with.

I sat through the rest of the evening's competition

with my mind in another place. Before I realized it, the MC had taken the stage to announce that the judges would make their decision soon. While everyone left their seats to either refresh their drinks or mingle with the performers, I continued to sit where I was. I didn't want to speak to Uniyah at that moment. I didn't want my emotions to come out; I didn't want to end up saying something I'd regret later.

"Hey, boy, why are you looking so glum?" Janelle inquired as she bent down to give me a hug and a kiss on the cheek. From the lack of emotion on my face, she could tell that I wasn't pleased with what Uniyah had done. "Brandon, you know that Uniyah is going to do Uniyah. So, I don't know why this was a surprise to you."

"Damn, Janelle, you'd think she'd at least have the courtesy to tell me that she wasn't singing one of our songs. She had my ass in the studio day and night working with her to prepare for this performance and then she pulls some shit like this, and I'm supposed to brush it off like it's nothing?" I didn't mean to blow up at Janelle but I had to get my frustrations out and, unfortunately, she was the victim. "I'm sorry, Janelle, but I'm pissed. I don't mean to take it out on you."

"It's okay, baby boy. I understand where you're coming from. Make sure you save some of that tongue lashing you gave me for our girl after the show. I don't want to be the only one that gets chewed out," she teased.

Janelle always knew how to lighten the mood. I loved how she found the brighter side to everything and brought humor to any situation. I was still upset, but not as much as before. Uniyah would still hear about it, though.

Twenty minutes and a third drink later, the MC made his way to center stage to crown the night's winner. Janelle held my hand and squeezed it tightly as we waited. She wanted Uniyah to win as much as I did, and I was sure the winner would be a female. After all, they were the ones who'd sung their hearts out.

"Ladies and gentlemen, please congratulate our second-place winner…Keyshon!" the MC shouted.

I couldn't believe Mr. Neo-Soul had actually taken second place. He was an okay singer but definitely not one of the better performers. I wasn't trying to hate. I was only speaking the truth and, from some of the whispering in the audience, I could tell there were others that agreed with me.

"Now, ladies and gentlemen, it's time for what we've all been waiting for! Who will be walking away as the winner of tonight's competition? Remember the first-place winner will receive production and studio time to record a demo. And for those of you who haven't noticed yet, we have producers from some of the top urban production companies in the house tonight. The winner will have his or her choice of which producer they'd like to work with. So, without further ado, drum roll, please," the MC commanded. "And the winner is…"

Janelle squeezed my hand even harder and I could feel my leg start to shake.

"…Trenton Jones!"

The room exploded in thunderous applause as he raced to the stage to take his bow before being joined onstage by Keno, who congratulated him. Before Trenton could thank everyone for their support, everyone's attention was diverted as a scream erupted from the back of the club.

"Keno, man! Yo' car is on fire!" somebody shouted.

Chaos ensued and everyone followed Keno—who was yelling for someone to call the fire department—as he hastily made his way outside of the club. Keno stormed though the crowd, which had trickled outside, yelling expletives and demanding the perpetrator to "man up" and confess. The crowd mumbled but nobody came forward. Keno's cell phone rang and he listened intently to the caller on the other end. Suddenly, all of the blood rushed from his face and he put his hand on his forehead.

"What the fuck do you mean, my house is on fire?" he screamed into the phone.

The folks in the crowd began making their way to their own cars—some of who were obviously heading across town to see Keno's house go up in flames for themselves. Keno had taken much pride in the eight-bedroom mansion he was able to purchase from his club's success—plus a few other "hush hush" deals on the side. Now, his prized possessions were going up in smoke. Everybody knew that Keno would eventually get his. He had done enough dirt to warrant it. But nobody knew when, and nobody knew how. Now, someone was finally getting their revenge.

I watched as the firemen rushed to the club parking lot with their truck sirens blaring in an attempt to put out the orange and red balls of flames that used to be Keno's car. I had expected him not to hold up his end of the bargain, so I was prepared. After running into Sonia that afternoon, I had done a little research of my own and learned that Keno had propositioned the other two female performers as well. I never had a chance, whether I went along with his plan or not. None of us did.

I was playing my part well, pretending to be as shocked as the other patrons as I watched Keno storming around his car, yelling into the phone. He looked like he was about to break down in tears, and I felt myself gloating inside. The motherfucker should have been glad I didn't arrange for Club Chillax to "feel the heat" as well. I had sure thought about it.

I looked at the other two female winners standing by and couldn't help but wonder what they had to do for, or *to*, Keno to guarantee a win that never came. I wondered how they were feeling and if the looks of shock on their faces were about Keno's car, or the fact they they'd lost after selling their souls to him. I bet revenge was swirling in their thoughts as well. Fortunately, I had a friend who owed me a favor and had arranged to "take care" of Keno's car and crib without it being traceable to me. Keno had finally fucked with the wrong one.

As I turned to head back inside the club, I locked eyes with Brandon and could see the look of disappointment and betrayal etched across his face. He was upset that I had chosen not to use one of our songs, but I didn't want him to get hurt or caught up in all this drama. He didn't know what went down between Keno and me, and if I had performed one of his songs—and Keno did exactly what I thought he would do—Brandon would feel like *his* music wasn't good enough. I didn't want to put him through that emotional pain.

I looked away from Brandon and headed to the back to get my belongings. I simply didn't have the strength to face him at the moment. I'd lay everything out on the table later. Hopefully, he would understand.

After I entered the makeshift dressing room, I changed into some fitted jeans, a spaghetti-strap cotton shirt, and a leather mid-waist jacket. As I hastily gathered my clothes, I heard my cell phone chirping, notifying me that I had a message. I turned off the screen lock and read the message that Markus had left.

Baby I'm sorry you didn't win. I left to avoid all the ruckus. Meet me at my crib because I have a big surprise for you!

A smile spread across my face. After all the disappointment of tonight, I still had something to look forward to that would raise my spirits. I quickly saved the text message and started a new one addressed to Brandon. I told him that I'd explain everything to him soon. I exited the club and headed away from the lingering crowd. I was glad that I had chosen to park on the far end of the wall so leaving would not be a problem.

As I pulled away from the club, I slowed down and saw Keno talking to a police officer. Too bad the stupid motherfucker couldn't name any names without implicating himself. I'm pretty sure his longtime live-in girlfriend would love to hear all of her shit had been burned to the ground because her womanizing boyfriend decided to literally fuck with the wrong bitch. Then again, maybe she wouldn't be surprised at all. As much as we like to "play dumb," women know their men.

I cranked up my car radio and sang along to the Xscape track that blared from the stereo's speakers. As I sped down the interstate, I couldn't wait to get to Markus' place to show him that I wanted to devote my heart, my love, my undying affection, *and* my body to him. I couldn't remember the last time I had felt this way about a man, not even my ex-fiancé. I was scared to divulge to Markus that I was beginning to fall in love with him, in fear that he might run or, even worse, say that he didn't feel the same, so I chose to keep my feelings to myself.

I couldn't stop smiling as I thought about finally being able to make love to him. Despite all of the Keno drama, thoughts of being with Markus sat in the forefront of my thoughts. In fact, just to get through the little "deed" I had to perform on Keno, I forced myself to fantasize *about* Markus.

I wondered what surprise he had in store for me tonight. I was certain it wasn't any type of anniversary celebration yet, so I didn't know why he would want to surprise me. Allowing the suspense to get the best of me, I put my foot to the pedal and fumbled with my cell phone, trying to focus on the road and attempting to dial his number with my free hand. I listened as the phone rang three times, and then nearly lost my breath when I heard his masculine tenor voice fill my ears.

"Hello."

"Hey, boo. Are you waiting for me?" I asked, hoping that I didn't seem too anxious.

"Hey, baby! Yes! Where are you?" he asked in a softer tone.

He seemed elated that I had called him. Damn, he had no clue what he was doing to me.

"I'm on the expressway on my way to your place, and I wanted to hear your voice."

"Well, I appreciate you giving me a heads-up, so I can tell this chickenhead to get up and get out," he teased. "On the real, it wouldn't have mattered just as long as you came. Are you upset about not winning tonight?"

"To be honest, I'm not upset; more disappointed. I worked so hard and wanted to win so bad, it almost hurt when they announced the winners and I wasn't one of them. One thing I've learned is rejection and disappointment go hand in hand when it comes to singing. I can either stop singing or use this as a driving force to try and work harder."

"Damn, baby, I didn't expect you to take it this well. I have to give you your props. You definitely did your thing with that Mariah song. That's one of my favorites. The way you hit that note at the end made every hair on the back of my neck rise; along with something else. You had everyone in the V.I.P. section whispering and giving you props on that performance. You best believe I made sure to talk you up, and even got a couple of business cards from some producers. You were hot tonight, baby, and I'm not just talking about that dress you were wearing!"

I allowed Markus to continue complimenting me and never stopped to interject. Even if I'd wanted to, I couldn't; I was blushing too hard. I'd never had a man in my life that was as supportive as him or gave so many encouraging words that made me want to strive harder. Whatever surprise he had in store for me was going to be nowhere close to the one I was going to spring on him. I wanted to connect with Markus on every level possible. I hoped he was ready for what I was going to put on him.

Thirty Four
MARKUS

It was like a blessing from up above when Keno's car caught on fire. It gave me the opportune time to make my exit. I didn't want my cover to be blown by running into Uniyah, who would probably want to introduce me to Brandon. After all, he only knew me as Tyrone and that's exactly how I needed it to stay. I could only imagine the reaction Uniyah would've had after finding out that I was kicking it with her *and* her homeboy.

I was so nervous, it felt as if I were going to piss in my pants. I'd always known that eventually I'd have to make a choice and decide which life I was going to live. I just didn't think that this time would come so soon.

I can't say I'd never been attracted to a guy before Brandon. But it was only with Brandon that I'd chosen to explore those feelings and allow my curiosity to get the best of me. I had gone too far the night we had sex. I think that's what shocked me the most. I never thought I'd be able to go that far with a man. It freaked me out and had me thinking that maybe I was some kind of a weirdo.

After that night, I tried my best to focus all my attention on Uniyah and work, doing my best to avoid Brandon at all costs. I wined and dined Uniyah but never tried to push up on her sexually. I wanted to make sure that the feelings I had felt for Brandon were completely out of my system. I thought I had succeeded until the other night when I happened to stake out his crib. Brandon made me feel something that I couldn't even begin to explain. All I know is that what I felt for Brandon was completely different than what I felt when I was with a woman.

Those five weeks prior to that evening, when I was missing in action with Brandon, I did my best to live my life on the straight and narrow. It was hard not acknowledging the pent-up feelings that had been brought to the surface due to my encounters with Brandon. It was even harder looking Uniyah in the eyes and giving her a false promise of a future with me. Those five weeks I lived my life in complete denial, trying to elude my feelings for the same sex and, as hard as I tried, my true essence revisited me every time I looked in the mirror. It was time to finally come to terms and admit that one thing I was afraid to: I, Markus Tyrone Greene, was bisexual.

To most, I would be considered gay. But I still had strong sexual desires for women. That was the problem. With me, I was only sexually attracted to them and couldn't care less about gaining a mental, emotional, or spiritual connection with them. For the longest, I tried to pretend that I could feel those emotions with Uniyah but the more time we spent together, the more of just a close friend she became. Well, not necessarily just a friend, but a friend-with-benefits.

I loved holding her when she spent the night at my crib, or me at hers. I loved listening to her talk about her dreams and how she planned on changing the music industry one day; and I loved all the simple things that we did together. And that was the problem: I loved the *things* we did together; I just didn't love *her*. I had strong feelings for her, but they could never compare to those I had for Brandon. And as much as I wanted the traditional American family with the wife, kids, dog, and white-picket fence, deep down inside it wasn't going to happen.

I sped home to get as far away from the club as possible and to clear my mind. I kept hearing a voice in my head urging me to come clean with Uniyah so that I wouldn't hurt her. But another voice was telling me to let things fall into place on their own. I didn't really have anyone to turn to or anyone I could confide in. I had done such a good job at keeping my alter ego a secret.

I realized in the very beginning that Uniyah and Brandon were acquaintances. I didn't think that their bond existed outside of the recording studio. Never once did either of them talk about hanging out with the other, or doing anything that didn't pertain to recording. In all of my excitement for Uniyah, I hadn't thought about Brandon being in attendance at tonight's competition.

I desperately wanted to call Brandon and explain everything to him but was afraid that after he learned the other woman was his friend, I'd lose both of them forever. I had spent so many years being alone and I didn't want to go through all the trouble of having to go out on dates, go to clubs, and do the meet 'n' greet thing all over again. It was all so tiresome, and I didn't have the strength to begin that search again.

I tried to take my mind off of my drama and thought about Keno instead, and his fucked-up situation. I couldn't imagine who would be so deranged as to set his car on fire. It made me wonder if it had been a woman and, if so, what he could have done to push her over the edge like that. Thinking about Keno's situation only led me back to thinking about Uniyah. I wondered if pushed over the edge, could she be the type of woman to exact revenge on another. In my heart I doubted she could. My baby didn't seem like the type.

I arrived at my condo and raced to my door. For some reason, I sought the comfort of home. I felt as if I were in control there. I lay across my bed and proceeded to close my eyes when a thought popped into my head to contact Uniyah so she wouldn't feel as if I had abandoned her.

I texted her inviting her to come over for the romantic evening I had previously planned. When she came, I'd test the waters and see if she could deal with the truth, or if I would have to fade out of the relationship. I hated doing the latter. It was like dangling someone's emotions on a rope, with them hoping you'd eventually give them your heart. I had done the fade-out so many times that I couldn't even remember the exact number anymore.

One could say that I was a master of the practice. All I simply had to do was tell whomever I was kicking it with that I needed some space and that I'd call them when I had a chance to evaluate my emotions and feelings. From that point, I would drop from calling them every day to every two days and eventually the calls would cease. There'd be an email here; a text message there. In the end, I'd simply disappear.

It seemed like a coward's way out but sometimes the direct approach could be so emotional and confrontational that the person would end up making you feel bad, and you'd eventually take them back only to end up resenting them and the relationship. The fade-out gave both parties the opportunity to heal and nurture their own feelings so that maybe—with time—a friendship could emerge from the rubble of the unsuccessful relationship. But for me, the friendship thing never happened. The best I could hope for was that if we were to see each other in public, we could at least be cordial to one another. Laughing half-heartedly, I finished the text message to Uniyah, asking her to meet me at my crib.

I rolled over on my back and kicked off my shoes as I placed my hands behind my head and relaxed. I closed my eyes and tried to clear my mind. It was in these quiet spaces that I couldn't convince myself to break things off with Uniyah. I couldn't find a good reason why I should. She didn't know about Brandon, or that I was even kicking it with someone else, so why cause drama when I didn't have to? I'd play the same role with Brandon.

I loved that he was cool with my bisexuality and knew that I was still interested in women. Not having to explain it to at least one party made it somewhat easier. I'd just make sure that when I was with him, I'd make him the center of my attention and the same for when I was with Uniyah. My *playa* days weren't over, as I thought.

I drifted to sleep as I waited for Uniyah to arrive, resting up so that I could once again play the devoted and supportive boyfriend. I balled up into the fetal position and couldn't recall a time when I felt so at ease with myself or with a decision as important as the one that I had just made. In the end, I'd probably wind up losing both of them but, until that day came, I was going to enjoy all of the love I was getting—from both of them.

barely uttered more than four words during my ride home with Janelle. I kept asking myself if I were upset or happy that Uniyah didn't win. I hoped that Janelle knew me well enough to know that my silence wasn't a sign that I was angry with her, but more with the way things went down during the competition. I had never thought, in my wildest dreams, that Uniyah would pull the stunt that she had.

I was overwhelmed with emotions, and I wanted to go home, light a candle, and fall asleep while some soft music played in the background. I sincerely missed Tyrone and wished that he were around to hold me. Uniyah was my girl and I didn't want to wish any misfortune upon her, but I was a strong believer in karma and what went around, came around. When it did come back around, as usual, I'd be there to lend her a hand.

I closed my eyes and began to ponder what the text message she sent was supposed to mean. I couldn't understand how she was possibly going to explain her blatant backstabbing. I'd allow her the opportunity to say her peace, but doubted our friendship would be the same. I truly didn't want to lose Uniyah as a friend. She had definitely been there for me during some rough times. But right now, all I could feel was hurt and betrayal.

"Janelle, can you slide the new Alicia Keys CD in?" I asked while my eyes remained closed.

Janelle obliged and we rode the rest of the way in comfortable silence. As Janelle pulled up in front of my spot, I gave her a kiss on the cheek and thanked her for her generosity. I took my time getting to my apartment, still feeling a mild pain from having twisted my ankle earlier in the week. I couldn't wait to be in the comfort of my residence.

After I entered my apartment, I closed all the blinds, turned off all the lights, pulled out my favorite scented candle, and went to my keyboard.

I took a seat in front of it and turned on the built-in recorder. Closing my eyes and forcing myself to relax and play whatever came to mind, I allowed my fingertips to grace the ivory keys. My playing helped me to release all of the built-up anxiety, tension, disappointment, and hurt that I'd been holding in.

I began to play with fury. The more I played, the more emotional I became. I was in my musical zone. I continued playing and pounding out note after note. I wasn't playing any particular melody; simply expressing my feelings through music. As everything I felt left my body, my playing became calmer and more harmonious. I'd discovered that I did my best writing when I was upset or troubled. With how I was feeling, I should have churned out a masterpiece that night.

Feeling more at ease, I turned off my keyboard deciding to retire in my bedroom to check my email. Although he was out of town, I was hoping Tyrone had sent one. I really needed to hear from someone who could bring a smile to my face. I waited for my laptop to boot up and turned on the "Quiet Storm" on V-103. I relaxed on my bed, listening to the music playing and hoping that one day it'd be one of my songs.

I couldn't help but feel Uniyah was taking our friendship for granted. I was good enough for her when she couldn't find anyone else to write or produce for her. But now that she was tasting success a bit, it seemed like she was forgetting who was there with her from the beginning.

I pushed the thoughts away, not wanting to anger myself again, and signed into my email account. A smile spread across my face when I saw Tyrone's name in bold in my Inbox. The smile that had appeared on my face quickly vanished when I recognized the name of my ex-lover sitting below Tyrone's message: Kyon Benjamin Williams.

Kyon was the first male-to-male relationship I was ever involved in. He made me feel things emotionally that I thought I could never feel with another man and had awakened a side of me that I had kept secret for so long.

I was seventeen years old and he was twenty-five when we'd met one night as I was leaving my part-time job. He'd approached me and asked if he could call me some-time. Without a second thought, I gave him my cell number. We talked on the phone for almost two weeks before we actually went out on a date together. He was fully aware that I had never been with a guy, but I was interested and desired to see where my curiosity would lead.

Almost three months had passed before we'd even shared a kiss. He was very patient with me and didn't pressure me to have sex with him. On my eighteenth birthday before I left for college, *I'd* decided it was time that we took things to another level. That night I lost my virginity—not to one of the women that I'd dated throughout high school but to a man that I had fallen hopelessly in love with.

From that moment on, everything between us escalated. We were inseparable and anyone who was in the same room with us for more than five minutes could tell that we were deeply in love. But like the old saying goes, what goes up must eventually come down and that's exactly what happened. As my nineteenth birthday approached, we made big plans to celebrate. He was going to fly to Atlanta and we were going to spend the weekend celebrating. But four days before my birthday, Kyon suddenly changed.

From the day I'd met Kyon, we had talked on the phone at least five times a day. But that had become almost nonexistent in those four days leading up to my celebration. When I sent him an email, it went unreturned, along with my voicemails. I was at a loss as to what was going on, so I took it upon myself to get answers.

The evening before my birthday, I borrowed a friend's

ride and drove up to D.C. When I arrived at his apartment, I waited for a car to enter through the gates and followed in behind it. Then I parked in a shaded secluded area in the corner of the parking lot hidden under the shadows of the trees, waiting for him to come home. I didn't know what to expect but things between the two of us had changed, and I wanted to know why.

As ten o'clock approached, I saw Kyon creeping across the parking lot. I sprang to attention and jumped out of the car, prepared to confront him. When he recognized me and saw that I was angrily approaching him, he begged me to leave and promised that he'd call me in an hour. But he just wanted me to leave so he didn't have to answer my questions or explain his behavior.

As question after question poured from my mouth, he'd stood looking at me dumbfounded. I didn't know if he was in shock that I had the audacity to confront him or if he truly didn't have any answers as to why he had been treating me the way that he had been. Finally, after I'd stopped questioning him, he'd finally said the four-word sentence that tore my heart in two: I just need space. He went on to elaborate that he needed to evaluate his feelings, his life, and where things between the two of us were headed. But I knew what that meant. If the end hadn't already arrived, it was surely coming.

I was mystified and confused. Leaving him, I retreated to my parents' home, located in the suburbs of Maryland, in a state of shock. I didn't know what the hell "I just need space" meant. Was he not coming around anymore?

Was I not supposed to call or email him? Was I supposed to sit around and wait for him to call me and say that he wanted to be with me?

I asked my family and friends what they thought the statement meant and no one could answer. Of course they thought that I was talking about a female, but regardless of the sex of the individual inflicting the pain, the feelings were still real. I spent my nineteenth birthday at my parents' home holed up in my old room alone; and the one time I did leave my room to run to the store, I came back to see a UPS package sitting on my doorstep. In it was some of the small things I had left over his house—books I'd loaned him; a shirt; an overnight toiletry case. I was confused and I couldn't come to the realization that we were over.

I needed to know why he decided that he no longer wanted to be with me. Why he no longer wanted to be *in love* with me. I grabbed the bag and raced to his apartment again. I stood outside ringing the doorbell for almost twenty minutes before I started shouting. He didn't even have the decency to open the door. He shouted through the door that he'd call me and for me to leave.

I stood there for almost thirty minutes in a daze before I once again dragged my defeated body home. I was so hurt, I couldn't even cry. I didn't know how to function or how to go about my day-to-day activities. I had been so accustomed to spending my time and my life with him that I didn't know what I'd do without him. Now I was alone, and I didn't know why.

It had been more than three years since that painful night and now, here he was, sending me an email after I had finally moved on and begun to heal. What it was in regards to, I had no clue. Part of me was intrigued and another part—the bitter part—wanted to delete the email without even reading it. I hit the power button on my laptop, blew out all the candles, turned my radio off, and climbed back in bed.

I didn't know what I was going to do so I closed my eyes and called upon the Lord to give me direction. I had to read the email to finally be able to close that chapter in my life, and yet, part of me didn't want to end the chapter but for it to continue. How could I feel such passion and love for someone who had caused me nothing but pain? Although I pretended not to know, the answer was abundantly clear in my heart: It was because he was the first man I'd ever loved and probably always would. I definitely needed God's direction on this one. With a deep breath, I powered up my laptop again, logged into my account, clicked on the email, and proceeded to read it.

To: Brandon
From: Kyon Benjamin Williams
Subject: Flash from the past
W'Sup, Brandon? I hope everything is going well with you. I know that I am the last person that you'd want to hear from. I wanted to take a moment to clear the air with you—I know it only took me close to three years to do so. I want you to know that I

never stopped loving you and that our sudden and unexpected demise had nothing to do with you. I had really begun to fall in love with you and didn't know how to deal with my feelings so I pushed you away. I tried to live the perfect life and began dating women exclusively. I recently found out that I have been diagnosed with cancer and have been undergoing treatment. For the last year since being diagnosed I couldn't help but to think about what my life would have been like if I hadn't run away from you. I remember how supportive you always were. To this day I wonder what life would be like if I hadn't turned my back on us. I don't know why I'm writing you...maybe somewhere deep down I'm hoping you'll return my email and maybe we could give *us* another try. Either way I hope that you are living your dreams and ask that you keep me in your prayers.

The irony of the situation left me flabbergasted. Now, after finding out that he had been diagnosed with cancer, he wanted me back. The email had placed me on an emotional roller coaster. Part of me wanted to cry and another part was filled with anger. I wished that I had never read the email. Wiping away the single tear that had begun to slip from my eye, I deleted the message. I powered down my computer and climbed back into bed. Before closing my eyes for the night, I said a quick prayer for Kyon. He would always hold a special place in my heart, but I wasn't prepared to revisit the pain that he had caused me. I was determined to see if the grass would be greener with Tyrone.

I was pleasantly surprised when I arrived at Markus' crib, and he said he had a surprise for me. He told me there was no need for me to come inside but to meet him at his ride instead. I followed his instructions and waited patiently for him to come outside. I didn't even notice him creeping up as I bent down to check my hair in the side passenger mirror of his car.

"Damn, what you tryna do to me, girl?" he jokingly asked, staring at my protruding ass.

"Playa, please, you're not ready to take it there with me," I retorted with a devilish grin, daring him to take me up on my challenge.

"It's not me that's acting like I'm *skurred*, baby girl."

I allowed his statement to linger as my attention was diverted to the suitcase that was hanging by his side. Before I could begin to question where we were going, he put his finger to my mouth to quiet me.

"Just turn around, and let me handle this," he directed.

Always down for a surprise, I shrugged my shoulders and let a smile form across my face to let Markus know

I was down for whatever. Taking me gently by the shoulders, he turned me around and embraced me from behind. I gasped as I felt his growing manhood against my backside and moisture gathered between my legs. We never discussed the lack of intimacy that was missing in our relationship, but that was partially my fault.

I had been so busy with the studio, dance classes, vocal training, and whatever else that happened to pop up that I had totally neglected him in that area. Yet, I couldn't help but ponder why he had never pressured me to give him some ass. Was he truly content with just spending time with me, holding me, and being affectionate? Janelle teased me that he might be content with waiting because he was getting *his* elsewhere but something in my heart told me that this wasn't the case. I cocked my head back so that I could gaze into Markus' eyes, and I could tell by the sincerity and the love that was embedded within them that he deeply and truly cared for me.

A smile formed across his face and he pulled a handkerchief from his pocket. Now my curiosity was piqued. Again he motioned for me to remain silent as he tied the handkerchief around my eyes and then guided me into the passenger's seat of his car. I didn't know where we were headed but, at this point, it didn't matter. I was just elated to be sitting next to Markus and spending time with him.

As he drove to God only knows where, I couldn't help

but think about my actions through the course of our relationship. I hadn't been the perfect girlfriend, like he probably thought me to be. I wondered if I should tell him about my sexual fling with David and what had truly gone down that night he came by and found him unconscious on my floor. Then there was the situation with Keno. I should have been upfront and told Markus the truth about my acts of infidelity and given him the chance to decide if he wanted to continue to pursue our relationship after the truth was revealed. But there was no way in hell I could do that.

My thoughts were interrupted as I heard Markus turn up the radio. I could clearly hear the soft alto of Toni Braxton singing about the "game of love." I nestled into the comfort of the passenger's seat, recalling the many times I had acted the fool over something stupid. Silently, I vowed to keep my emotions in check going forward. I reached over and placed my hand on Markus' free hand. I needed to feel him and to connect with him. He welcomed my gesture openly and our fingers interlocked. Now fully relaxed and at ease, I allowed him to take charge of the evening.

Somewhere in the mix of my thinking, I must've drifted off to sleep. When I felt the car stop, I opened my eyes, forgetting about the blindfold that still remained across my eyes. I heard Markus' door slam shut and his footsteps coming around to the passenger side of the car. I heard him exchange words with someone, and then he opened my door so he could help me out and remove my blindfold.

As I took in my surroundings, I saw that we were in the front of a hotel and Markus had valet parked his car. He had just finished giving directions to a bellman, telling him to take his belongings from the trunk and to meet us at the front desk. Taking me by the hand, he led me into the lobby of the downtown W Hotel. I had never had the privilege of staying in a five-diamond luxury hotel and tonight it looked like I was going to get my chance.

Markus asked me to have a seat in the lobby as he checked us into our room. When he returned, he told me that we were leaving. A quizzical look came across my face, and I couldn't understand why we were all of a sudden leaving.

"Let's go," Markus commanded as he took me by the hand.

I walked back through the rotating door, confused. My confusion subsided upon our exit. Before us stood two white horses with a carriage attached. Markus looked at me and kissed me with more passion than he had ever done before. Whispering in my ear that he wanted me to feel like the true queen that I was, he proceeded to help me up into the carriage where chilled champagne waited.

I couldn't believe what Markus had done; especially since I'd only seen stuff like this on television and in the movies. At that moment I was more in love with Markus than I'd ever thought I'd be.

For over an hour we rode around downtown and midtown Atlanta, enjoying each other's company as we sipped on champagne. We stopped at Centennial Olympic Park, where we got out and walked around looking at the water fountains and the stars. We talked about everything and shared things that we had never shared before with one another. We talked about the upcoming Thanksgiving and Christmas holidays and where we were going to spend them. We talked about a future together.

As the moon shined brightly in the center of the sky, we headed back to the carriage so that we could retire for the rest of the evening. Even though I hadn't won the competition at the club, had betrayed a friend, and ruined a man's house and car, somehow the night had still turned out to be one of the most memorable nights of my life. It would definitely be one that I would never forget.

Thirty Seven
BRANDON

I rode the northbound train headed toward Buckhead's Lenox Square mall, where I was to meet Uniyah at California Pizza Kitchen. I don't know why I had agreed to meet her so soon because I was going to definitely need more than fourteen hours to get over her stunt at the club. It was a blatant act of betrayal and backstabbing, and I didn't know if I could forgive her for her actions easily. Curiosity alone was the reason I was riding the train on this gloomy afternoon.

I couldn't help but look into the sky as the train emerged from its covered tunnel, and I was greeted by a gray-colored sky where the sun was hidden behind the voluptuous clouds. The darkness that the clouds brought hinted that fall was just around the corner. I glanced at my watch, wondering why it seemed like it was taking longer than usual to get to the mall.

As I waited for the train operator's voice to announce that we had arrived at my stop, I couldn't help but think about Tyrone. I had become very much smitten by him, and I didn't think that I would fall so fast for someone that I barely knew. The more time we spent together, the more I was falling head over heels for him. I was more than ready to take things to the next level.

I wondered if Tyrone felt the same or if he was still struggling with his identity. I hadn't asked him if he was involved with a lady friend or not, but I figured that what I didn't know wouldn't hurt me. I wasn't a fan of men who decided to play on both sides of the field, especially at the same time, but I was almost certain that Tyrone didn't fit the mode of the typical bisexual brother. He seemed to be dealing with his gay feelings well, and I was confident that we were developing a connection with one another; one I hoped would lead to exclusivity and a one-on-one, full-fledged relationship.

Seeing people rising from their seats and heading for the exit doors, I pulled myself up and exited the train as well. I glanced at my watch and noticed I wasn't so late after all, so I slowed my pace. I needed to remain focused and remember that my interest was with Tyrone so there was no need to entertain any of the passing attractive faces that were brazenly trying to make eye contact with me. I was pretty much a one-on-one type of guy, which was one of the reasons why I hated coming to Lenox.

The influx of flamboyant gay men who gravitated to that mall caused me to stay away from it. Of course I didn't have any problems with gay men, or I'd have a problem with myself. My problem was that some gay men didn't care about the feelings of others and were outright inconsiderate to the general public.

Finally making my way to the restaurant, I could see Uniyah seated at a table talking incessantly to whomever was on the other end of her cell phone. The look on her face let me know that she wasn't pleased and that she was giving the person a piece of her mind. As I informed the hostess that I was with Uniyah, she gracefully walked me over to the table as Uniyah was slamming her phone down on the table. Even frustrated, she looked refreshed and relaxed. It had been a while since I had seen her with this look of contentment, but I was still mad at her and planned to let her know.

As I sat down at the table, I forced a frown on my face to let her know that I wasn't exactly pleased to be in her company. She took notice and, after the waiter took our drink orders and walked away, she reached across the table and clasped both of my hands with hers and a sincere look fell across her face. Momentarily it appeared that she was at a loss for words and didn't know exactly how to explain her actions the night before. After an awkward moment of silence that seemed to last for an eternity, she began to speak.

"Brandon, I owe you an explanation and an apology for what I did last night but, before I get into that, I want to let you know that I didn't want to hurt you and that's why I did what I did. I don't want you to think that I don't value you as a friend, or as a talented musician and songwriter, but please understand that I wasn't going to win; regardless of what song I had chosen to sing."

She was briefly interrupted as the waiter approached,

placing our drinks before us, and asking if we were ready to order. We both placed our orders and I hurriedly rushed the waiter away as I was anxious to hear the rest of Uniyah's explanation. With a look of embarrassment, she continued to tell her story of how the club owner had invited her to the club for a private one-on-one session before the competition and propositioned her for sex if she wanted to win. A look of disgust came across my face when she admitted that she partially complied with the request by performing oral sex.

Listening intently, I had a few questions but I allowed Uniyah to tell the rest of her story first. I couldn't believe that her level of desperation had caused her to throw away her dignity and pride to perform an act of intimacy on someone in exchange for a chance to win a competition. In my opinion, this was one stop short of prostitution. I did my best not to judge her but to fully hear her out. I had to admit that she was throwing more at me than I expected.

Uniyah took a sip of her water and continued to tell me how she had contacted all the female performers and, after a little prodding, got them to disclose that they also were propositioned for sex in exchange for a chance to be crowned the evening's winner. As the anger in Uniyah's eyes intensified, she told me how her anger escalated, causing her to arrange for Keno's car and house to go up in flames.

I sat flabbergasted as she confessed that she was the

one responsible for the acts of arson that brought the evening's events to an abrupt end. She wanted to win, but I didn't think that she'd go to those extremes. I didn't know whether to feel sorry for her or to sympathize with her. She had put a lot into her performance and refused to claim defeat, but she had done some things that could've caused her to go to jail and bring her singing career to an end.

I cleared my throat and thought out my next words before I opened my mouth to speak. I could see the tears that Uniyah was desperately trying to hold back. I had never seen Uniyah so close to losing her composure as she was about to at that moment.

"Niyah, I don't really know what to say. You've dropped a bomb on me and I wished you had disclosed this to me earlier, so that I could've been a friend and stopped you."

After putting my anger aside, I began questioning Uniyah about the fires. I had to make sure that she could not be tied to them in any way. I was impressed to see that she had gone over every possible scenario and, in the end, nothing could be tied back to her. I could see that she was waiting for me to say that I forgave her and as much as I wanted to, I decided I'd make her wait a little longer. So, instead, I changed the subject.

"Why are you glowing?" I asked with no discretion.

My question brought a smile to her face and she began to blush. "What are you talking about?"

"I'm not stupid. You got some," I replied.

"And if I did?"

"Well, it's about time. You've been out of commission for so long, I was wondering if the shit even worked anymore."

We teased each other for a while and before I knew it, we had finished our entrées, ordered, and eaten dessert. I told Uniyah that I wanted to finish talking about the night before, and she obliged. I informed her how much her actions hurt me, our friendship, and how I hoped that one day we could get our relationship back to where it had been.

I told her that, after much thinking, I'd decided that I needed to branch out musically and begin doing some things on my own as far as vocals and producing. I could see that she didn't like the new direction I was planning to take, but she understood that I needed to evolve as a musician and I couldn't do it by riding her coat tails. I promised her that our friendship wasn't over but that if she wanted to rebuild the bond we once shared, she'd need to be upfront and honest with me in the future.

She didn't like me encouraging her to work with other musicians and producers, but I was happy she trusted my judgment in that area. After we paid the tab and embraced before we parted ways, I reached into my pocket and pulled out my iPod so I could jam to some of my favorite music on the train ride back to my crib. Tyrone would be meeting me there later, and it would soon be my turn to blush and glow.

Thirty Eight
MARKUS

Things between Brandon and I had intensified into a full-fledged relationship, which was quite a task since I was simultaneously in a full-fledged relationship with Uniyah. No matter what I did, I couldn't separate my feelings from either and it was that much more difficult now that I realized that the two of them were the closest of friends and not mere associates.

After learning of their tight bond after the concert, I had nonchalantly questioned Brandon about how close they were. I feigned an interest in the work that he was doing in the studio, and that's when he opened up to me about their friendship. I don't know why I had never shown a great interest in Brandon's world outside of school until now. I now realized that my feelings reached beyond the infatuation stage, and I found myself wanting to know everything there was to know about him.

I took a great joy in asking him questions about his upbringing, things he liked, and the things he disliked. I loved hearing him go off on a tangent and completely open up to me. At times I felt compelled to do the same with him, and I wondered if there would ever come a time when I would be able to open up to him completely about my relationship with Uniyah. In a perfect world I would've loved it if he would've told me that he was willing to share me with her, but life wasn't perfect and we didn't always get the things or, in my case, the people that we wanted. The day would soon come when I'd have to make a decision and a choice between the two. I feared losing them both, but I'd continue to play with fire until *someone* got burnt.

Although I liked hearing about Brandon's world, there was indeed a downside to it, like him sharing all of Uniyah's secrets with me, including what had happened between her and Keno as well as the fire afterward. As much as I was shocked, I was somewhat intrigued. Luckily, my secret affair with Brandon would force me to never openly confront Uniyah about any of her actions.

As I lay back with Brandon reclining in my arms, he invited me to come to the studio to kick it with him for a session. He even offered to help me with my spoken word CD, but I didn't want to take any chances of running into Uniyah while we were there so I successfully "danced" around the invitation. I'd have to take him up on his offer one day because I'd soon run out of excuses but, until that day came, I'd continue to "dance."

With my back resting against the headboard, my eyes were fixated on the television screen. I really wasn't paying any mind to the show that was on. I was too deep in thought and enjoying sharing time with Brandon to actually care. I loved coming over and spending the evening with him, holding him as he slept. He looked innocent as he rested in my arms, and I loved how affectionate I became with him. Every time we were together, I couldn't help but scoop him up in an embrace.

I glanced at my watch, knowing that I'd have to leave him soon if I was to make it to Uniyah's crib later on that evening. The thought of her took me back to the night before when I decided to show her what she meant to me. The night Brandon thought I had flown down for a trip home to Florida to supposedly celebrate my mom and stepfather's anniversary.

❖❖❖

That evening, after Uniyah and I had returned from our carriage ride in Centennial Olympic Park, we headed back to the hotel room where she showered me with gratitude—verbally and physically. I was so grateful my plan had worked. I didn't know how long I'd be able to hold out before I insisted we take things to the next level.

Upon entering the room that night, tears flowed from Uniyah's eyes as she was surprised by the rose petals strewn over the white, plush carpet and the king-sized bed. I took her by the hand and led her to the bed. Removing her shoes one by one, I massaged her feet as we continued the in-depth conversation that we had begun earlier in the park as the candlelight danced on the walls.

I listened intently as she talked to me about her family, friends, and her past relationships. It seemed that after her last relationship when she was engaged, she became really apprehensive about falling back in love. She told me how her heart had turned cold when someone showed an interest in her or in taking things to a serious level. She told me how she had used sex as a way of escape and had embedded her feelings and passion into her music. Her desire to be heard caused her to strive to the next level and to apparently do whatever it took.

I learned that her parents had never showed any interest or support when she attempted to express herself artistically, whether through poetry or singing. I took great interest in hearing her speak of her estranged relationship with her parents who were not too proud of her decision to take time off from school to follow her singing aspirations and convinced her that becoming a singer was foolish. They attempted to discourage her from singing in the church choir, joining the school chorus, or participating in anything concerning the performing arts. But being the deviant that she was, she had chosen to follow her heart and her passions.

I also learned that she was able to maintain financially because her father had relented and agreed to support her for two years. However, he made her promise that if the singing thing didn't take off, she'd either have to go back to school or fend for herself. She told me that her father paid for all her studio time, dance lessons, and vocal coaching—all at her mother's displeasure. She was nearing this deadline, and was set on not proving her parents right.

As Uniyah wound down, I disappeared into the suite's bathroom to run a bath for her. I wanted everything to be perfect. I waited patiently as the Jacuzzi filled so I could turn the jets on. I lit the candles, which I had the hotel staff strategically place around the tub and the bathroom, and then I headed back out to Uniyah.

I stopped and stared at her as she lay on her side, looking deep in thought as she sipped on the glass of wine that I had poured for her earlier. I approached her and she smiled at my presence. I gently took the glass of wine from her hand and placed it on the coffee table, and then took her by both hands and pulled her from the bed. Passionately embracing her in my arms, I intensely kissed her, allowing my tongue to dance along with hers, tasting the red wine she had been sipping on. I loved the way Uniyah kissed. It was never sloppy or rushed. It was always meticulous, passionate, and tender.

As I continued to embrace her, I moved my hands under the bottom of her cotton shirt. I waited for any resistance and, when I didn't receive any, I slowly began to raise the shirt over her head. Next, I loosened her fitted jeans and helped her step out of them. She now stood before me in just her g-string and bra. I took a step back to admire her body. I loved how she was stacked with the legs of a dancer but with an ass that came out of nowhere and breasts full enough to give her serious back pains.

I twirled her around and admired the defined muscles in her back and shoulders. There was no denying she could give any model a run for her money. If she had pursued a modeling career, I'm sure that she would've easily acquired a contract without having to go through all the hassles that she was currently enduring.

I unclamped her bra and freed her breasts. Moving closer to Uniyah, I allowed my lips to graze the back of her neck, causing her to shudder but letting me know it was okay to continue. I continued to move my tongue down the small of her back until I reached the top of her g-string. In one swift movement, I allowed her to seductively step out of it. Smelling the scent of Uniyah almost made me lose my mind. With my dick fully erect and fighting against the restraints of my boxers and my pants, I calmed myself down and forced myself to wait before sampling her goodies.

I took her by the hand and led her to the bathroom where she was greeted by the fifty candles that surrounded the bathtub and countertops. I walked over and turned on the radio system, allowing Boyz II Men to croon about how "fifty candles burned bright" as I assisted Uniyah into the tub.

As she settled in and adjusted to the temperature, I

gave her a minute to relax and enjoy the jets massaging her body from all angles. As she relaxed, I took the opportunity to disrobe and jump in the adjoining shower. Exiting the shower, I quickly dried myself off. Now, dressed in some boxer briefs, I wrapped a terrycloth robe around my body. I leaned down and slowly engaged her in another kiss. I'd been yearning for her for so long and tonight it seemed that Uniyah was game with doing whatever I needed her to do. As the song ended and Alicia Keys' voice next filled the room, I reached for the liquid soap and a loofah, and gently washed her from head to toe, moving my hands in circular motions.

When I was finished, I took a moment to look into her eyes and the intensity in them entrapped me. She rose from the water and stepped from the tub where she grabbed both my hands and kissed me. I grabbed a towel and patted her dry. Before I could finish, she grabbed my hands again to kiss me. Releasing my hands, she reached for the robe and unloosened the tie. I tried to stop her because she was ruining the flow of my plans, but she silently let me know that she was now in control and I was to follow.

She leaned back to take me in from head to toe. I stepped back from her—to prolong the temptation— and then grabbed her face and kissed her again until she broke away and ran her tongue down my bare torso. On her way down toward my navel, she ran her tongue over every ripple until she reached the top of my boxer briefs.

Then she took hold of them, and pulled them down, exposing my fully erect manhood.

She led me to the bed and directed me to lie face down. Taking the massage oil that I'd bought to massage *her* from the nightstand, she moved to the base of the bed and began massaging my feet before applying the oil to my entire body. Slowly and deliberately, she worked her hands up my body before stopping at my neck. She kissed me gently on my earlobe, and then instructed me to turn over.

I closed my eyes, waiting for my full frontal oil massage, until I unexpectedly felt the warmth of her mouth on my penis. My toes curled as she moved her mouth up and down my shaft, twisting and twirling her tongue as she worked me over for almost a full twenty minutes. God, how I loved a woman who took her time! Finally, unable to hold back any longer, I exploded—partially on her, mostly on myself.

Uniyah got up and returned with a moist cloth in her hand and proceeded to wipe me down. She lay next to me looking content; however, I was determined to show her what content felt like. I rolled over and allowed my fingers to toy with her bush. No surprise, she was soaking wet. I slipped a finger inside her, and she let out a deep moan. I pulled it out, intent on teasing her a bit more before giving her all of me.

I gently took one of her voluptuous breasts in my hands and softly kneaded it with my fingers before doing the same with the other. I saw her close her eyes and, once she did, I leaned down and placed my mouth over the nipple and softly blew. Her back arched and her breast moved toward my mouth, but I didn't take the invitation. I allowed my tongue to slowly trace around her nipple before I finally took it in.

I moved down to her midsection and let my lips gently graze her neatly trimmed pubic hairs while inhaling the scent that was strongly permeating from between her thighs. I took both of her legs in my hands and gently pushed them in the direction of her head, and then plunged into her with my tongue. Passionately, I lapped up her juices while she moaned and bucked toward me.

I could tell that she was about to climax so I slowed my pace and then sped it up, slowed it down, and then sped it up again. Seconds later, she began bucking back in full orgasm. I continued to lick, suck, and tease, until she grabbed my head and pulled it deep into her juicy spot. When she finally calmed and caught her breath, she opened her eyes and saw that I was sporting a massive hard-on. I could tell from the look in her eyes that she was pleased and more than ready to take things a step further.

I lifted myself from the bed, got a lubricated condom, and placed it on my manhood. Coming back over to the bed, I climbed on top of Uniyah and kissed her passionately while teasing her gates with my penis. Several times she attempted to put it inside of her, but

I pulled back to relish the moment. When I could no longer fight the urge, I entered her body and let out a deep moan, indulging in the soft, wet, warmness of her that I had dreamt about for so long. I pulled in and out of her slowly and gently, giving her time to adjust to my size. Then I flipped her over and entered her from the back. After a few strokes she pushed back and pulled herself onto all fours.

With her ass in the air, I took to it and handled my business. I loved every moan and groan that she made. As I intensified my strokes, she fell to her elbows and grabbed tight to the bed sheets.

"Oh my God, I'm 'bout to cum! Baby, don't stop! Baby, please don't stop!" she shouted as her body began convulsing.

Slowing down and allowing her to enjoy her climax, I made my strokes long and deep, making sure I hit her spot. After I finally ejaculated for the second time, she collapsed and I nestled on top of her. We lay together breathing heavily, our breaths finding rhythm with each other, while the music blaring throughout the room continued to serenade us.

Mustering the last of my energy, I carried her into the shower. As we bathed, I teased her body with my soapy fingers. We relished the moment until the steam in the bathroom and the water turning cold forced us to call it quits. We dried off and crawled back into bed, where we cuddled for the remainder of the night, talking about whatever we could think of until drifting off to sleep.

❖❖❖

Brandon stirred and pulled me away from the thoughts of my night with Uniyah. Apparently he could feel my arousal as my manhood poked him in the back as we spooned. He turned over and smiled at me with a look that let me know he was ready to handle business. I smiled seductively at him in return. My reminiscing about Uniyah was about to become my reality with Brandon as well. I pulled his face close to mine and sucked his bottom lip while he slid his hands into my boxers. I closed my eyes and let nature take its course. I'd just have to be a little late to Uniyah's…

Thirty Nine
BRANDON

couldn't help but feel ecstatic when Tyrone asked me to attend a basketball game with him at Phillips Arena. I was a big basketball fan and even though we weren't going to see any of my favorite teams, I was happy nonetheless that he had extended the invitation to me. I raked through my closet for something purple and yellow to wear. The Hawks were playing the Magic, and I was more of a Magic fan than a Hawks one. Being that he was a fan of Dwight Howard, Tyrone would be reppin' similar colors as well.

I checked myself in the mirror and headed out the door. I was to meet Tyrone at the Georgia Dome train station because he didn't want to drive through all the traffic. I was shocked to see the train station practically empty on a Tuesday evening, but concurred that the extremely drab windy temperatures of this fall season caused everyone to head home early or to utilize their warm cars instead. I waited for the train to arrive and reflected on how good it felt to actually be with someone. It had been such a long time, I had almost forgotten how much I missed having someone call me to say the simple things like, "good morning" and "good night." I vowed to try and make this relationship with Tyrone work, so I'd never have to forget how that felt again.

Just as I made my way to the Five Points Transit Station, I felt a vibration on my hip. Instinct already told me who it was, and I couldn't stop the smile that crept across my face. I glanced down at the LCD and read Tyrone's name, and then instantly punched the TALK button.

"W'sup?" I asked, beaming.

"Why you got a smile on your face?"

"Why do you always think I'm smiling every time you call me?" I questioned, knowing full well he had me all figured out.

"Okay, I won't assume that you're always elated to hear my voice," he teased.

"Good. You shouldn't." I laughed.

"So where are you at, B?"

"I'm about to board the westbound train so I should be there in about five minutes. Why? Are you there already?"

"Yeah. I got here a few minutes ago, but I'm anxious to see you, boy. It's been nearly a week since we had an opportunity to spend some quality time with one another."

"When did you begin to count days?" I asked, relishing in the fact that for once I was the one being "clocked."

"B, you know that you're always wanted by me. I don't

know why you insist on playing with a brother. It's you that spends all your spare time in the studio, and when you're not there or studying, you're at the gym. I can't even get ya' to come and work out with a brother anymore because now you want to do your own thing. But it's all good. I understand you ain't got love for me anymore."

"Oh, is that so? So it's not you working all of those late hours, kicking it with your boy, Jay, and then when you have some free time, you're dividing it up between me and the gym?" I didn't mention that some of his time was probably spent with some female that was unsuspecting of his sexual preference.

"Nah, that's all in your imagination," he jokingly countered.

"Tell yourself that enough and eventually you'll begin to believe it," I teasingly retorted.

As the train approached, I waited for the departing passengers to exit before I boarded and attempted to find a seat to myself. I told Tyrone I would lose him in the tunnels and informed him that I'd call as soon as I got to the Dome/GWCC/Philips Arena/ CNN Transit Station.

As the train pulled off, I closed my eyes and realized for the first time I was truly in love. With past lovers, I had also experienced things beyond the physical but it wasn't on the level of what I was experiencing with Tyrone. A wave of fear ran over me because I didn't quite know how Tyrone felt about me. I debated with myself on whether or not to reveal my true feelings to him, or if I should keep them to myself for the time being. I recognized the pain of unrequited love and wasn't quite sure I wanted to go down that road again by putting my emotions out there so early.

Before I could reach a definitive solution, the train operator announced that my stop was next. I quickly cleared my thoughts and regained my composure. I didn't want my newfound resolution to disrupt the time I was about to spend with Tyrone. I'd deal with my feelings at some other time.

As the train came to an abrupt stop, I quickly exited and immediately saw Tyrone standing no more than ten feet away from me, looking as gorgeous as I last remembered. Yep, I was in love. He initially didn't see me but when he finally turned my way, our eyes met and the smile that spread across his face almost melted me. Physically he was everything that I wanted. I loved when his chocolate arms engulfed me when we were sleeping. His muscular frame provided just the right body heat when he lay next to me. I even loved when he snored lightly on the nights when he was extremely tired.

Playing it cool, I made my way over to him and attempted to make eye contact but couldn't look him in the face without a huge smile forming across my own. Tyrone leaned down to my ear and whispered how much he missed me. I could no longer contain the smile I was trying to hold back. Anyone that had ever been in love could tell that I was in heaven.

I was floating on air as we made our way from the transit station and into the arena. Tonight, regardless of the repercussions, I was going to confess my love to Tyrone. And if he shared similar feelings, then this would be the night we'd make love—something I had never experienced before with anyone, man or woman. I shared deep feelings for my past lovers but it was by no means love. And when we were intimate, that's all it came down to—intimacy—but never had we made love. Lately, my sexual encounters with Tyrone fell into that same category—just intimate.

I was anxious for Tyrone to get completely comfortable with me. Right now he was the "top" in our dealings. He was the one that did the penetration, and I was the "bottom," the one on the receiving end. I'd love for us to be equally versatile. The few times he attempted to reciprocate, I would not allow him because I wanted him to be a hundred percent certain that he was ready to make that move with me. The last thing I needed was for a grown man to have an emotional breakdown at my expense. Pushing these thoughts out of my mind, I began concentrating on when and how I'd inform Tyrone that even if he wasn't, I indeed was ready to take things to the ultimate level.

Forty
UNIYAH

"Damn, Niyah, tell me that you're exaggerating and things did *not* go down like that," Janelle enviously inquired.

"Janelle, things went down *exactly* how I described. It was like a fantasy."

I had just finished describing my romantic evening to Janelle, and she was squirming with envy. Just thinking about the love Markus and I made and the intimacy that we shared caused a heated sensation to grow between my legs. I was hoping my night with Markus would be the first of many to come. For the first time, it felt right to let my guard down and actually allow someone to enter my world. I never thought that I'd overcome all the heartache and drama I had to endure in the past so quickly or that I would completely trust a man again so soon, but I found myself doing that with Markus.

"Uniyah!" Janelle yelled into the receiver to get my attention.

"I'm sorry, girl, I was daydreaming," I replied after realizing I must have missed a few of Janelle's comments.

"I can't believe Markus has me open like this. After my ex-fiancé, Broderick, and all the shit that went down between the two of us, I thought that I'd never be able to love someone unconditionally like this. But it seems that God has blessed me with an angel sent straight from heaven to rebuild my trust and hope in men."

"Go on and preach it, sister girl. Now why don't you look out for ya girl and see if Markus has a brother, cousin, pretend cousin, hell, anybody, 'cause if I had a penny for all the losers that I've had to put up with in this dating world, I'd be a rich woman," Janelle joked before continuing. "Well, I wasn't going to tell you this but since you're my girl, I might as well spill it."

"Janelle, please tell me that you're not pregnant."

"Heifer, no! I'm only twenty-seven and I definitely don't have the patience for any crumb snatchers. I was trying to tell you that I've gotten so tired of going to the clubs to try and meet Mr. Right that I've finally resorted to cyber love."

"You mean you've resorted to the Net and chat rooms to get a date?"

"You don't have to say it like that," she joked. "But, yeah, I began to use the Internet to help out my social life. It saves me the time of going out with jerks and losers. This way, I get an opportunity to vibe and feel a brother out before making an effort to go out with him."

"I ain't mad at ya. I remember Brandon recently telling me that he resorted to the same thing, and I've never seen him as happy as he is now with this new guy. The only thing I know about this new guy is that his name is Tyrone. I think I might have to suggest that he introduce us to his newfound beau. Now talk to me, have you found anyone worthwhile in your search?"

"I have two prospective gentlemen in mind. I have dates lined up with both of them next weekend. I'm hoping that I'll be able to find someone that will take me out of this dating game because a sister is growing tired and beginning to lose faith in finding that special someone. Shit, if things don't begin turning around for me soon, I'm going to turn into a straight-up hoochie."

Janelle's last comment made me laugh hysterically. Her becoming a hoochie was as likely as a nun becoming a call girl. Janelle was a goodie-two-shoes. And even though she'd had a one-night stand or two, she always worked hard to make herself as well-rounded as possible and the ultimate triple-threat: pretty, smart, and fun. It made me realize that if Janelle had trouble finding a good man in a city like Atlanta, then that left little hope for the rest of the single women that were also in search of Mr. Right.

She was the epitome of what every man claimed to be seeking. She was beautiful, educated, financially stable, had a good head on her shoulders, and could definitely throw down in the kitchen. She was the type of woman that you could take home to mama but when you got her home she'd be your first-class freak—so she'd told me. She could go from a homegirl that threw back a beer watching a basketball game to the elegant diva you'd be proud to have on your arm at an NAACP gala. Yet, she was still single and looking for love like everybody else.

"Look, Niyah, I got to run but you make sure you stay in touch and, more importantly, do whatever you have to do to keep that man of yours satisfied!"

"I hear you, girl. You take care but, more importantly, keep the faith," I encouraged.

After I hung up with Janelle, I pulled myself out of bed and lazily walked into my master bathroom to draw myself a nice steamy bath. I dropped a few bath beads into the water and waited for the tub to fill. Slowly undressing, I admired my physique in the mirror. I had long legs that were perfect for dancing. My ample-size ass was firm but juicy and was the reason men often did a double-take when they passed me. My stomach was flat, and when I flexed, I could see a sexy but distinct outline of a six-pack. My breasts were firm and voluptuous. I was grateful that gravity hadn't taken its toll on them. I ran fingers across my chocolate nipples, which were currently erect.

Looking at my body in the steamed mirror got me hot and thoughts of Markus only heated me up more. I turned off the water and cautiously stepped into the bathtub, lowering myself gently in the heated liquid that caused the skin on my legs and buttocks to tingle as well as on my breasts and neck after I was fully submerged.

I placed a damp washcloth over my eyes and allowed the soft music I had turned on in the background to soothe me. It wasn't long before I found myself arching my back and slipping my fingers between my legs. I allowed a soft moan to escape from my mouth as I reminisced about the love that I'd made with Markus the night before. He knew when to be sensual and when to be aggressive without me having to tell him. That, in itself, was a turn-on. Thinking about the way his strong hands massaged me from head to toe before he dipped down and tasted my juices caused me to move my fingers more rapidly.

I slipped another finger inside of me, moving it in and out just as Markus had done with his long, deep strokes. The thought of making love to him brought me to the edge and, before I knew it, my body was convulsing in the water as I climaxed hard. I lay still in the water. The water's waves, caused by my body's vibration, floated over my breasts, covering, and then uncovering them in a constant motion.

I pulled myself up from the tub and entered my shower to really wash up, and then got out and wrapped myself in a soft, terrycloth robe. My legs were weak from the orgasm I'd given myself and the sensation afterward continued to throb between my legs. I thought of satisfying myself once more, but reached for the phone instead. I knew someone who could do it even better, and I decided I'd give him a call to see if he was up for the job.

Forty One
MARKUS

I lazily lay in bed debating on whether or not to drag my ass out of it. Since things were steadily progressing between Brandon, Uniyah, and me, I'd been going to great extremes to make sure that they never found out about the other's significant partner. True, I knew that they were acquaintances almost from the very beginning, but the more I spoke to both of them, the more I realized that their union extended beyond the studio. When I wasn't with one, I was with the other. Sometimes I forgot who I was supposed to be or which I was supposed to be into—guys or girls. So far I had been successful at not having a slip-up but if I didn't stay on top of things, I'd definitely fuck up.

I had spent the night before with Brandon at the basketball game and it was truly an experience that I'd never encountered before. After going to the box seats I had received from a client, Brandon had decided to get a little touchy-feely during the third quarter but I didn't complain. At first I was a little apprehensive about the public displays of affection, but I slowly warmed up to it. Brandon suggested we move to the sofa in the back of the corporate box suite to be more "comfortable." I obliged because there was a television in the back that was broadcasting the game so I wouldn't miss anything.

But what started as innocent cuddling turned into Brandon sticking his hand down my pants and stroking my growing manhood. I had never felt so nervous in my life. Yet, I was enjoying Brandon's spontaneity. Then a stir at the door caused me to jump.

"Calm down. The door is locked, remember? Besides, we're already into the third quarter," Brandon stated to ease my fears.

I heeded Brandon's advice and took him in my arms to continue what we had begun, when suddenly we heard someone pulling at the doorknob and proceeding to twist it. I nearly pissed in my pants as I jumped up, practically throwing Brandon to the floor. I hastily zipped up and began adjusting myself. Brandon regained his balance and did the same before heading to open the door, as I casually plopped onto the couch, doing my best to look nonchalant.

"Excuse me, gentlemen, it's against the arena's policy for you to lock the doors to the box," a female arena worker rudely informed us as she allowed five frustrated guys to enter the room.

I had never been so embarrassed in my life. I did my best to concentrate on the game as each guy crossed my path to get to the seats situated in front of the box. The looks in their eyes were screaming "fucking faggots," and I could feel their glares on me throughout the night. Brandon sat back down on the couch but on the opposite end, making sure there was plenty of room between the two of us. I noticed he, too, was just as embarrassed and could barely look at me. Silence emanated between the two of us for the remainder of the quarter.

"Are you mad at me?" Brandon asked after minutes of silence.

"Nah, I'm not mad."

"Do you mind if we leave?"

"Why? Are you mad at *me*?" I inquisitively asked.

"No, but I'm really uncomfortable now. We don't have to end the night. I just want to get out of here."

"You know they're going to be looking at us funny when we leave," I informed him, referring to the arena workers manning the check-in desk.

"I know, so let's go ahead and make this as quick as possible so that we can get it over and done with."

I allowed Brandon to take the lead as we made our exit. Just as I predicted, we got nothing but stares from the workers who were manning the reception booth. But as we exited the arena and headed for the train station, we both broke out in laughter.

"Well, what do you want to do now?" I asked.

"How 'bout we just head to your place and chill before it gets too late."

"Nah, let's head to your spot."

"Why can't we ever chill at your spot?" he asked. "Do you have a wife or a live-in girlfriend you didn't tell me about?"

I could tell that this was a question that had been on his mind for some time due to his tone. "No. If I had either, how would I be able to spend the night with you on the nights that I do, or spend as much time with you as I do?"

"Honestly, you really haven't spent that many nights at my spot and then there were times when you had to leave in the middle of the night or at the break of dawn and I didn't say anything."

"B, it doesn't make me any difference where we chill. I just thought it'd be easier for us to chill at your spot instead of us driving all the way out to my crib and then me having to drive all the way to your spot to drop you off, and then having to turn around and come home. Remember, it's a work night."

"Whatever," Brandon said dismissively.

"B, do you want to chill at my crib!" I angrily snapped. Being dismissed irritated me more than anything in the world.

"No, I'm good," he replied. "Maybe we should call it a night since you have work in the morning, and I have class."

"Okay. Why don't you allow me to take you home since I only parked one stop away?"

"That's okay. I'm used to the ride."

With his last words, I no longer saw the sparkle in his eyes or the smile that came across his face whenever our eyes met. And because it bothered me so, I realized, at that very moment, that I definitely shared feelings for Brandon that extended beyond infatuation. As hard as it was for me to admit it to him or to myself, I was falling in love with him.

"B, can I please give you a ride home?"

"If it's not out of your way," he replied, the brevity still in his voice.

"Cool," I replied.

The wait for the train was done in silence and from time to time I couldn't help but steal a glance at him. He was so handsome. There was no way that I could continue to play him, especially with his own friend. There was no way that I could live with myself if he found out that Uniyah and I were seeing one another. I didn't want to hurt him that way. I didn't want to be like one of those ex-lovers he'd told me about that had broken his heart and left him alone to pick up the pieces. I definitely didn't want to be categorized in the same group as them.

But I couldn't help but continue to ask myself if it was possible for two guys to love each other unconditionally. Better yet, was it possible for two *black* men to do that? I so wanted a future with Brandon, and I wanted to be able to unite with him and not be ridiculed by family, friends, or society. I didn't want our bond to be judged by the bitter and insensitive. With Uniyah I could have a future that was flawless. The only problem was that Uniyah was in love with me, and I simply liked her. And after the last night I spent with Brandon, I'd never be able to care for Uniyah the way I cared for him. Even though the sex with her was G-R-E-A-T!

❖❖❖

Two weeks after the basketball game with Brandon, I sat in silence in the privacy of my office. I was unable to focus on any of the tasks that needed completion. For the last few weeks, I had been burdened with my feelings for Brandon *and* Uniyah. I cared deeply for the both of them and did not want to bring harm or hurt to either, but I simply couldn't figure out how I'd be able to come out of the situation unscathed. I ran different scenarios through my head and, after all was said and done, none of them seemed feasible. There was no way that Brandon would continue to see me after learning that I also was intimately involved with his homegirl.

The sad reality is that I would have to continue my game of deception or risk losing them both. My only other option would be to lay things on the line with both Brandon and Uniyah and allow them to make their own decision in regards to where we stood. But after being intimate with both of them, feelings had already begun to develop on both ends and this would be easier said than done.

I glared at the glowing computer screen where numerous emails waited to be opened. The red flashing light on my phone notified me that I had several voicemails that required my attention. But I wasn't in the mood to read or talk to anyone. At the present, the two people that I was dating were both pressuring me to take our relationships to the next level. Recalling the night before, Brandon made his request quite clear after the basketball game.

That night we shared our first semi-argument over whose place to chill at. Relenting, I decided we'd chill at my place. I don't know why it had taken me so long to do so—maybe it was fear of Uniyah dropping by or Brandon finding something of hers that I didn't even realize was there. It could've possibly been that I feared the two of them talking and putting everything together—the condo's location, my car, my career, in one of their casual conversations.

After I had entered the apartment that night, I immediately embraced Brandon and apologized for my behavior. He quickly forgave me, and we spent the remainder of the evening talking. It was at the end of our conversation when Brandon asked me if I could define what we were doing. I danced around the question, attempting to buy myself some more time to think, but seeing he wanted an answer right then, I took a deep breath and did my best to explain where my head was.

"Look, B, when we met, I told you that I was bisexual and that I still dated women from time to time so, to answer your question, I have seen one other person since meeting you." I could see the look of disappointment on his face, and I immediately regretted my decision to answer him honestly.

"Yeah, I knew that you were attracted to men and women, so I can't get upset about it. Plus, we've never put any restrictions or boundaries on our dealings."

"So, if you feel this way, why is there a look of disappointment on your face?" I questioned.

"Because I have deep feelings for you and want to pursue something deeper."

I knew that this was coming. In fact, I felt the same way; but there was still the dilemma of U-N-I-Y-A-H. "So B, are you telling me that you aren't dating anyone else?"

"Honestly, I'm not. I don't have the time or desire to juggle more than one relationship. I have school, Uniyah, the studio, and you. The last thing I need is to add someone else into the mix."

"Well, what do you want me to do, now that you know that I'm dating someone of the opposite sex?"

"I don't know. Give me some background on this person. How long have you been dating, and how exactly do you feel in regard to her?"

I took a moment to clear my thoughts. The last thing I wanted to do was trip up and reveal to Brandon who it was that I was dating. I carefully ran my responses to his questions over in my head before finally spitting them out verbally. "Well, we met roughly around the time you and I met. As for how I feel about *her*, I can honestly say that I have strong feelings for her but they are truly different feelings than the ones I share for you. My feelings for you are really strong and the ones I have for her are more along the lines of what I feel for a good friend."

"I see," Brandon said with a smile.

"Do you?" I asked, simultaneously grabbing his chin and lifting up his head so that our eyes could meet. Before he had an opportunity to answer me, I bent down and gently kissed him on the lips.

"You didn't answer the other question," Brandon stated sternly.

"What question?"

"What are we doing? Can we define what it is that we're doing so that there won't be any gray areas?"

I struggled for an honest and sincere answer, and I decided to feel him out instead. "Well, why don't you tell me what you think we're doing," I countered to stall for time.

"Well, it's apparent that we're dating one another and that we share feelings for one another. I'd be lying to you if I told you that my feelings were nothing but a crush. Simply put, I'm totally in love with you. Everyone develops feelings at different levels and at different times but this is where I am—in love with you. I would like for us to concentrate on continuing to get to know one another but with more exclusivity."

Brandon's words were definitely not what I had expected. I never knew his feelings for me were so deep. Part of me was scared while another part of me was flattered. But I understood where he was coming from. After all, it had been close to five months since we'd met, and he deserved exclusivity.

But the thought of being in a real one-on-one relationship with a man still ran chills down my spine. Not chills of fear of being *involved* with a man but chills of fear of being totally *committed* to one. The thought of society's ridicule, my family's criticism, and my friends' perception all began to run through my mind. I never thought that I'd be at this point in my life where I was questioning who it was that *I* was. I truly picked a fine time at the eve of thirty to determine what my sexuality happened to be.

"B, man-on-man relations are truly new for me, so I can't honestly tell you that I can give you what you want. I only think it's fair that you give me a little time to truly evaluate my feelings and make a decision that isn't forced. Can you deal with that?"

"I have no choice but to deal with it. I appreciate you wanting to evaluate your feelings for me before making a decision."

As we lay in bed, with him between my legs and his back resting on my chest, I allowed the silence to wash over us for a while before saying anything else. "Yo, B, are you asleep?"

"No, I'm lying here enjoying myself and enjoying being in your company."

"I want you to know that I fell in love with you that very night we were at your place and you sang for me and played the keyboard," I openly confessed. "I know you didn't like my response to needing some time to evaluate things between us and the direction we are headed, but I promise you, if you can give me a few days to decipher things and get my priorities straight, then you'll have more of a solidified response."

"I can do that. Tell me, if you fell in love with me that night, why am I just now hearing about it?"

"Because I thought it was too soon to tell you how I felt. I didn't think you were ready," I teased.

"Me? Not ready?" he asked, cocking his head to one side and flashing the beautiful smile I had come to adore. "When it comes to you, I'm more than ready…"

Now as I sat in my office, totally discombobulated, with my time dwindling, I was nowhere closer to making a decision now as I was then. The worst part was that Brandon's birthday was in four days. The pressure of everything was eating me up inside. I had to take some time and clear my mind.

Grabbing my car keys, I headed out of my office after stopping to tell Jay that I had to make an emergency run. In some way, it was the truth. I needed the rest of the day to decide how to proceed with both Uniyah and Brandon. And if that wasn't urgent enough, I didn't know what was.

Things between Tyrone and me were moving much faster than I thought they would now that he'd made a decision. I couldn't believe that he had finally admitted he was falling in love with me. It had been two weeks since we sat down and put our feelings out in the open, and now everything seemed so surreal. Imagine my shock when he asked me if I could give *us* a chance. A part of me still didn't believe that two same-gender-loving men could really be blissfully united *and* committed—in Atlanta of all places.

Atlanta was known to be a mecca for black gay men and you'd find an array in the bustling metropolis. Unfortunately, it was a rarity to find black gay men *united*. And as much as I appreciated the Internet, I felt it was becoming the biggest thorn in black relationships, especially in the gay community. With so many ways to meet folks just to "hook up," monogamy was almost impossible. The Internet offered convenience and the ability to be as deceitful as you chose to be.

One would be amazed at how many men lied about

things such as their ages, HIV status, or marriage status. Sometimes as I browsed the "information superhighway," I wondered how so many attractive, black—effeminate, masculine, thugged-out, professional white collar, blue collar, thick, slim, mediocre, and breathtaking—men could be single. Some of them were not. But for the ones that truly were, I found us all to be looking for the same thing in one fashion or another: companionship. I certainly didn't enjoy sleeping alone every night, and I openly welcomed the times when Tyrone was by my side so I didn't have to.

The mere thought of Tyrone's name caused a smile to form across my face. He truly was heaven sent in my eyes, and there was no wrong that he could do. It had been a long time since I had trusted a man as much as I trusted Tyrone. When he said he was out, I didn't ask him with whom or where he was going. I took his word. I had finally allowed myself to once again believe in the laws of love. Even when he was dating the girl he told me about, it was me that he called to check up on, asked to come over and spend time with, and ultimately wanted to be with; although I'm sure he probably did the same for her. The important thing is she was out of the picture, and I didn't have to worry about sharing him anymore.

As my musings of Tyrone faded, I quickly finished dressing so that I could head to the studio to meet with Uniyah. Today would be the first time that we'd work with one another since her last performance. I was really excited to see what she was bringing to the table and even more excited to reveal to her what I'd been working on. Plus, I had a surprise for her.

In my recordings, I had begun to incorporate more live instruments and strayed away from the synthesized and digital instrumentations that accompanied my keyboard. With our break, I had nothing but time. I even started taking some vocal lessons to strengthen my voice, which Tyrone told me were already pretty darn good.

I headed out the door, destined for the nearest train station. After climbing aboard the train, I turned on my iPod and hummed along to the tracks that I had recently produced. I began writing the lyrics as they spontaneously came to my mind. It was funny how my prior work reflected how much I was longing to be in love. Now all of my lyrics were about *being* in love. I switched to some of the tracks that Uniyah and I had previously recorded earlier in the year. As I listened to each of them, I made mental notes of areas that needed to be re-recorded.

I loved Uniyah's voice and the sultry, yet soulful, way it brought my songs to life. To add some diversity to the tracks, I had contributed to singing the background vocals along with Janelle from time to time. As I listened to my voice, which blended nicely with each track, I noticed how insecure and timid I sounded. Hopefully, my new inner peace and added confidence would now show through in my vocals.

As the train came to my stop in the West End, I quickly

jumped off and headed to the studio, anxious to get to work. I couldn't wait to update her on the changes I'd gone through and about Tyrone falling in love with me and me with him. I was anxious for her to tell me all about the guy she was currently involved with as well. Over the past couple of months, outside of the studio, Uniyah and I had become more phone buddies than anything else. But even in our brief conversations, I could truly hear the happiness in her voice. I prayed that she had finally found that special someone she could now call her own.

As I stood in front of the studio, I couldn't help but wonder if things between Uniyah and I would ever go back to the way they originally were. As the old cliché goes, "only time would tell." I opened the door and headed toward the studio but stopped when I heard the sound of female voices laughing. I cracked the studio door and saw Uniyah and Janelle acting crazy as usual. I didn't realize how much I truly missed hanging around them until that very moment.

"Hey, no clownin' around in here," I joked, startling them both.

"Hey, Brandon!" they replied in unison before the round of hugs we gave each other.

"Y'all ready to get to work?"

"I'm always ready," Uniyah stated.

"Just say the word," Janelle countered.

As we sat scattered around the studio, we listened

intently to the track that I had been working so arduously on. I usually criticized my own work, but as I listened to the track I was happy there was nothing I wanted to change, which was a first. I watched both Uniyah's and Janelle's faces as they listened as well, but both were expressionless. They didn't make a sound or even tap a foot. I felt myself growing nervous and insecure at the thought that I was the only one feeling my creation. Then Uniyah turned to me with watery eyes.

"Brandon, that joint is on point! I haven't heard something that intense in years. And more importantly, it's radio friendly."

"I agree, Brandon, this song is hot," Janelle added. "I think you got a hit with this one."

I could do nothing to sustain the joy I was feeling in my heart. I had prayed that morning on what avenue to pursue and had decided that I'd begin shopping the song to some of the local recording labels in hopes of acquiring a writing deal. I just needed to hear an approval, and I'd gotten two with Uniyah and Janelle.

"I am so glad y'all like the track. I just hope one of the record companies like it too but, in the meantime, we still need to get down to business!"

No sooner after I made that statement, there was a knock on the door. Heading to open it, the rap group Real Deal entered. I had taken the initiative to reach out to their manager so that we could put together the collaboration that they wanted. As the group entered, we gave one another some dap and we all familiarized ourselves with one another.

I ushered both Uniyah and Janelle into the recording booth and handed them lyrics to the song. The two of them would be laying down the background vocals, with Uniyah taking the female lead. I got them warmed up and when their harmonizing was in sync, I started playing the track.

I could feel things slowly growing back to normal. I had two of my closest friends back in my life and, most importantly, I had a man that loved me for me. I couldn't imagine how things could get any better.

Forty Three
MARKUS

I struggled to see through the sleet as I made my way to Uniyah's place to pick her up. I'm a Florida boy and didn't quite know how to drive in this type of weather. I was trying my best to focus on the road and not on what I was about to say to her, which would certainly break her heart. I had thought long and hard about my decision and, in the end, I had to admit I was truly in love with Brandon. He was in my thoughts and prayers all the time.

I turned up the volume of the radio in an attempt to drown out my screaming conscience, which was trying to convince me that things would be easier if I just stayed with her instead. I could go on to obtain the wife, house, two kids, and dog that society told folks they *should* desire. But no one knew my desires better than me, and I had to follow them, as hard as that was going to be. Besides, even if I went ahead with a life with Uniyah, I would eventually break her heart, chasing after what I really wanted instead of what everyone else told me I should want. Even with that reasoning, my soul was telling me that, in the end, my picturesque fantasy would only end in heartache and pain and I didn't want to cause Uniyah any unnecessary pain.

I jerked the wheel to the left in a vain attempt to get control of my ride as I slid on a patch of black ice. I thought of pulling over to the side of the interstate to wait out the storm so I'd have better visibility, but fearing being even later to Uniyah's, I chose to press on. Relaxing and trying to clear my thoughts so that I could give my full attention to the road, I leaned back in my seat. Then I heard a loud bang. My car jerked to the right, to the left, and then began spinning out of control. The last thing I remembered was being yanked forward and my head hitting the dashboard before I blacked out. When I awoke—fading in and out of consciousness—I could hear the sound of a siren in the distance and someone talking over me, but I couldn't make out the words they were saying. Someone was shining a light into my left eye, and I heard myself telling them to stop it but apparently they weren't listening because they repeated the same action in my right eye. I tried to move my arms but I couldn't, so I tried telling the voice in the distance to hand me my cell phone so that I could call Uniyah, but the voice was ignoring me again. As the light moved away from my eyes, I lost consciousness again.

❖❖❖

Fully awake, I was slightly frightened since I didn't recognize any of my surroundings. I took a deep breath and tried to calm myself down as I looked around, ignoring the sharp pain in my head and neck. The beeping machines, pale green curtains, and metal furniture left no doubt that I was in the hospital. I tried to remember why I was there, and my mind began racing a mile a minute reliving the accident all too vividly in my head.

Although I didn't remember all of the details, I remembered that I was driving to pick up Uniyah to take her to dinner, but I never made it. I didn't know how much time had passed, but I had to get to a phone to call her and let her know I was okay—or so I hoped.

I forced myself to sit up and braced the side of the bed as the pain in my head bounced from left to right. I couldn't believe that standing up could be so excruciating. As I tried to make my way toward the door, my body collapsed to the floor and the IV that was in my arm came out. Just as my knees hit the floor, Uniyah walked through the door with a cup of some hot liquid, most likely tea. Seeing me on the floor, she instinctively dropped the cup and rushed to my side to assist me back into the bed. Once I was situated, she raced out of the room to get a nurse to re-insert the IV and to wipe up the blood that was currently seeping through a bandaged wound.

I was quite taken aback as she returned with a male nurse who, even through the pounding in my skull, I noticed was quite attractive. I had to catch myself from staring too long as to not bring any suspicion to Uniyah, but that was hard as the male nurse wiped away the blood from my torso—close to my groin—and re-inserted the IV in my arm. The entire time he cleaned me up, I noticed he was diligently trying to make eye contact with me. He was trying to see if I played on his "side of the field" or not. After he was finished, I whispered a barely audible "thank you," and he exited the room, leaving Uniyah and me alone.

I glanced at her and saw the look of concern plastered all over her face. Even with her appearance a little haggard, she still looked beautiful. There was no possible way that I would be able to break her heart. She was too precious. I tried to break the silence, but she placed a finger on my lips to quiet me.

"Don't try and talk, baby. Just relax," she stated.

I did as she instructed and soon drifted off into a deep sleep.

The next time I awoke, I thought I was dreaming as Brandon was sitting across from me staring into my eyes. I blinked hard so I could focus, and my eyes had not deceived me: it was Brandon in the flesh. The pace of my breathing increased and I felt small beads of sweat form on my brow as he approached.

"Brandon, what are you doing here? Where's—" I stammered.

"Uniyah went home to freshen up," he interrupted me, obviously knowing what I was going to ask. "You've been asleep for a whole day, and she asked me to come and sit with you while she ran home. Imagine my surprise when I came into the room and realized that her Markus was my Tyrone."

"B, let me explain."

"My name is Brandon!" he corrected me. "This shit is fucked up, Tyrone. Oh, uh, excuse me, *Markus*. I told you that Uniyah was a close friend and that we worked together. Did you honestly think that you could date both of us without us eventually finding out?"

"B, I mean Brandon, I didn't realize that you two knew one another until recently," I lied, struggling to sit up in bed, my head still pounding. "In the beginning, you never mentioned Uniyah by name and when she talked about you, I didn't think that she was talking about *you*. It wasn't until the night of her performance when I saw the two of you hugging that I came to the conclusion that you two knew one another."

"And knowing this, you still continued to deceive the both of us and even had the audacity to tell me that you were in love with me? By the way, let me thank you for the fucked-up birthday gift!"

"Wait, I didn't know who or what I wanted until you basically forced me to decide, and I knew that evening that I was definitely into you more than I had ever been into anyone else. Brandon, when I told you that I was— and still am—in love with you, it wasn't a lie. It's the truth," I confessed.

I watched as a tear formed in his eye and slid down his

312 Timothy Michael Carson

face. The one thing that I told myself that I would never do, I had done. I had hurt Brandon and possibly wrecked a wonderful friendship. My actions were selfish, but I truly didn't know how to stop all of the lying after finding out the truth. But I probably needed Brandon more than he needed me.

He wiped the tear from his face just as Uniyah made her entrance into the room.

"Hey, Brandon, thanks for staying here with Markus while I went home to shower and change clothes."

"No problem, Uniyah. Look, I'd better be heading home. I got a paper due for school."

"Wait, Brandon, let me formally introduce the two of you, now that Markus is awake."

"That's not necessary, Uniyah. We've already talked, and I must really get going."

"Well, all right. Are you okay, Brandon?" Uniyah questioned as she leaned in to give him a good-bye hug.

"Yeah, my contacts are just bothering me. That's all," he lied, trying to explain away his red, swollen eyes.

As I watched Brandon try his best to act nonchalant, I wondered why he didn't blow my cover to Uniyah. Although I didn't want to see her hurt, I was almost relieved when I thought that the truth would be out on the table. I could then confess my love to Brandon, and Uniyah would know that, although what she and I shared was indeed special, it would have to come to an abrupt end. But Brandon's silence forced me to have to explain the situation to Uniyah myself. I was going to have to do my own dirty work, and it served me right.

I watched as Brandon embraced Uniyah and walked out of the room—and possibly my life forever. As he left, Uniyah stepped to my bedside and leaned down to kiss my forehead. Her presence didn't rejuvenate me as much as Brandon's had. He had warmed my body and now a sudden chill had run up my spine.

"Good news, baby. The doctor is going to release you today, and you know I'll be right there to nurse you back to health," she informed me.

I forced a smile on my face as she embraced me. Once I had fully recovered, the first thing I'd have to concentrate on was getting Brandon back.

Words couldn't even express the way I was feeling. Never in my wildest dreams did I think that the man I was falling in love with, my best friend was falling in love with as well. I thought I would faint when Uniyah opened the door at the hospital and I walked toward the bed where Markus—who I only knew as Tyrone—lay before me unconscious. I never imagined that I would feel so betrayed or feel the pain that came from a broken heart again. Tyrone—Markus—was supposed to be "the one."

He was supposed to be the one that ended my heartaches and lonely nights. He was supposed to be the one I could build a future with. Even though I never truly believed that was possible, he had given me reason to hope. I couldn't believe that I could be so gullible. I wondered at times what I'd done in my past to deserve this continuous karma of heartache. All of my previous relationships had ended due to infidelity, deceit, or both, and it made me wonder if the problem somehow lay in me and not them.

I crawled into a corner of my bedroom, with my knees pulled tight against my chest. I sat in the darkness as Mary J. serenaded me with her soulful voice. If anyone could relate to what it was that I was going through, it was definitely her. Tears ran from my eyes again and my heart was hurting so bad it was almost unbearable.

Part of me wanted to drown my sorrow with a bottle of liquor while another wanted to end all of my pain with a bottle of pills. I was full of hatred and, yet, still possessed love for Markus. I was always the one to tell people, "You just don't fall out of love overnight. Falling in love with someone is a process and when things end abruptly, the feelings unfortunately don't end as quickly. A person has to go through the process of falling out of love with a person, too." While deep in thought, I fell asleep, only to be awakened hours later by a cold chill. I stumbled through the apartment as darkness surrounded me. I made my way into the bathroom, flipped on the light switch, and squinted as I stood before the mirror, forcing myself to look in it. I looked horrible. My eyes were swollen and puffy, dried tear stains streaked my face, and my nose was red and clogged. I turned on the water in the tub, as the first step to washing away the pain I was feeling—or at least the evidence of it.

As the tub filled, I stepped away, lit some candles, and then placed them strategically throughout the bathroom and apartment, hoping the aromatherapy from the scented candles would relieve some of the tension that was building up inside of me. I wanted a glass of wine so bad, but

I didn't want to make any decisions inebriated. Things between Markus and I weren't completely over, and I still had some thinking to do.

As the scent of French vanilla filled the bathroom, I turned off the tub's water and hastily began stripping away my clothing. I didn't take any time out to admire my physique or to see if all my hours at the gym were paying off. I just wanted to feel the slight burn of the hot water on my skin, relaxing my muscles and easing the building pressure growing within.

I slowly lowered my body into the water, allowing it to adjust to the temperature. Once partially emerged, I laid my head back against the wall with a washcloth folded gently across my eyes. I sat in silence as the steam pacified and temporarily relieved me of my stress. If I could, I would've stayed in this state permanently.

Thinking back over things, everything made sense. Things like Markus refusing to come to the studio, regardless of how many times I asked; or the many excuses he made when I tried to get him to meet Uniyah; and why he made such a big deal when I wanted to chill at his place. I couldn't fathom how in the hell he could date the both of us and not feel guilty.

He met Uniyah at a straight club but met me over the Internet. Atlanta was full of single attractive women, but it was also full of single black men who preferred the company of other single black men. Still, how could I fall for someone that my own girl was dating?

I quickly lathered up, rinsed the sudsy foam from my

body, exited the bathtub, dried myself, and then headed back into my bedroom to lie across my bed. I had to come to terms and grasp reality. Things between Markus and I needed to be resolved and, unfortunately, before I could make a sound and solid decision, we had to meet and talk things through.

I had questions that I needed answers to and, if nothing more, I needed closure. Markus had said he cared for me and that he would never do anything to hurt me. But if that was the truth, I was definitely experiencing the pain of "when the truth lies."

I could lie across the bed all night, coming up with question after question and wracking my brain for answers, or I could get the answers that I desperately needed. If I were to have peace of any kind, I was going to have to contact Markus to get some resolution. I was going to reach out to him the same way we reached out to each other in the beginning: by email.

I powered up my laptop, quickly opened my Internet browser, and logged into my AOL account. I clicked "Compose" on my email window and began to type a message to Tyrone.

To: Tyrone
From: Brandon
Subject: Meet me!
We need to talk. Meet me at the gym Wednesday evening at 5 pm.

I fought with myself as to whether or not to type more

than the one-line message, but the things I had to say to him, I needed to say in person. There would be no more hiding behind text or instant messages, or emails. I needed to look him in the eyes; to know what we shared was real.

Forty Five
UNIYAH

I was ecstatic when the doctor finally relented to my request and allowed Markus to be released into my care earlier than intended. I thought the opportunity would give us more time to bond. With him working late at the office, trying to impress the senior partners, and my spending time in studio sessions, dance class, and voice training, it was amazing that we had the little time we did to spend with one another. That's why two days after Markus' release from the doctor's care, I was surprised when he insisted on spending the rest of his time recuperating on his own.

He hit me with the classic "I need some space" line. It was a phrase no girl in love ever wanted to hear; especially days after you'd given up the goods. I was floored—more like pissed—when he uttered those words to me, and felt like someone had ripped out my heart.

I truly felt all alone and had no one to counsel me or give me advice. For some odd reason, Brandon wasn't answering his phone or returning any of my phone calls. Janelle was overwhelmed with work and when she wasn't working, she was busy trying to find her own Mr. Right.

It had been three days, six hours, and twenty-three minutes since Markus had delivered that devastating news to me. I hadn't left my apartment since and had canceled every studio session, dance rehearsal, and voice lesson for the remainder of the week. I had to figure out what the hell "I need some space" meant. Was I not supposed to call him anymore and basically wait by the phone for him to call instead? Was I not supposed to try and reach out to him to let him know that I deeply cared for him and missed him being in my life? Basically, what in the hell did "I need some space" *mean*? I remembered Brandon telling me that he went through something similar with a past lover, and, in the end, they broke up.

I was beginning to realize that it was simply a cop-out; a way for a guy to say he wasn't feeling the relationship anymore. Basically, he was letting me down easy. After he uttered that statement, he hadn't called, emailed, even sent me a damn text message, as impersonal as that was. Everyone warned me to not fall so deep, so fast but, like a fool, I had done exactly that. Now here I was— hair unkempt, funky from not bathing, and my face stained with tears. I had all of the classic symptoms of a broken heart.

I dragged myself out of bed and managed to shower. If Markus wanted to call it quits, then he was going to have to do so face-to-face with me. This bullshit about him needing space wasn't going to fly. I needed him to look me in my eyes and tell me why he was doing this to us.

After bathing, I quickly dried and tied a headwrap around my hair. I was in no mood to be cute. I wanted answers and I wanted them now. I quickly grabbed a pair of sweatpants, a T-shirt, and some sneakers, and made my way to Markus' place.

I weaved in and out of the evening traffic, hurriedly making my way across town. I was breaking every traffic law that the state of Georgia had in place but, at the moment, I didn't give a damn. I was a bitch on a warpath. I cut off other cars, pushed the gas when the light was yellow, and only yielded at stop signs.

I made a forty-minute trip in almost twenty minutes. I impatiently waited for a resident to pull up to the security gates and tailgated them into the condominium. I didn't want to give him any chance to deny me access to the answers or the questions that I had. I didn't want him to have any time to come up with any lies or excuses to pacify me. I merely wanted the truth; regardless of how much it hurt. He owed me that much.

As I pulled to his high-rise, I noticed that his rental car wasn't parked in his designated parking space so I patiently backed into an empty space hidden by the shade of a tree and waited. I had the radio on and was paying no attention to the topic that the disc jockeys were discussing. It was hot and the humidity was causing me to perspire, so I rolled down my windows and patiently waited for Markus to arrive.

I waited until the sun went down and the sky was illuminated by a full moon. Yet, there was no sign of Markus. The tears once again began to flow from my eyes as reality set in that there was possibly someone else in the picture. I remembered the night prior to his accident; he'd told me there was something he needed to discuss with me. Then, days later, he needs space and here I was sitting in the dark at two a.m. with no sign of him returning.

Surely, he wasn't at the office at this time of night. Slowly things were beginning to come together in my mind. All the late nights at the office; all the nights he couldn't come over until the wee hours of the morning; acting shady the times he did come. Not to mention all the times that I'd call his cell phone and he wouldn't answer, only to explain he was spending the evening at home; although there'd be no answer there either.

I'd make up excuses or simply overlook things because I was so in love and chose to believe the bullshit he was feeding me instead. I figured our entire relationship was nothing more than a game. All the times he told me that he cared for me, were probably his way of breaking down my defenses so I'd have sex with him.

After all, it had been nearly six months, and I still hadn't met the infamous "Jay" that he spent so much time with playing basketball and going to the clubs with.

I'd suggested several nights where we all could hang out and have drinks, but there was always some reason why "Jay" couldn't make it. Now I wondered if this "Jay" was really a she.

I had been sitting in the car for over five hours, and I was tired. I pulled out my cell phone and dialed Markus' number. I wanted to know where he was. After the fifth ring, he finally answered.

"Hello?" he answered in a sleep-laden voice.

"It's Uniyah. I realize that it's late, but I wanted to know if I could come over so that we could talk about us."

"I don't think that's a good idea. I had a late night at the office, and I have an early start in the morning. Can I call you tomorrow? We can get together for lunch or something and talk."

"I'll call you," I said flatly as I slammed my phone on the dashboard. A single tear ran down my cheek as I turned the key in the ignition. I had been sitting outside of his condo and watching it like a hawk. He had not come in or gone out. He had just lied to me. I had to face the hard facts: things were apparently over between the two of us.

Forty Six
MARKUS

I tried my best to wait as patiently as I could for Brandon outside of the gym, which was both odd and funny. I'd never been one to chase after anyone, and yet here I was chasing after Brandon. I'd realized that there was hope for us, after I received his email while I recuperated at Uniyah's place.

I had no idea what I was going to say to make him stay with me, or how I could convince him to give me another chance. I had to do and say whatever it took for us to be together. Somehow, I had fallen in love with him and couldn't imagine my life without him in it.

I glanced at my watch and noticed that it was ten minutes after our agreed upon time. It wasn't like Brandon to be late. I began to get nervous, thinking that maybe he had changed his mind about us meeting to talk. Then I saw him exiting the gym, looking just as breathtaking as he had when I first set eyes on him.

Something about him made my heart race, my tongue thicken, and my body perspire. He was everything that I had dreamed about, except in my dreams I always thought it would be a woman that would make me feel this way.

I exited my rental car and tried my best to look as casual as possible. I watched Brandon search the lot for me and when our eyes met, I froze. My legs wouldn't move. I felt like I was standing in drying cement. I watched as he made his way to me without an ounce of emotion on his face, and I couldn't help but wonder if he still shared the same feelings for me that I shared for him.

"Let's go for a ride. I'm driving," he instructed. Since he said it more as a directive than an offer, I followed his lead without question.

I handed him the keys and struggled to the passenger side of the car. I still hadn't fully recovered from my car accident, which left me pretty banged up. As we drove away from the gym and got onto the interstate, he didn't utter a word. I didn't try to spark any conversation either. This was his meeting, and I was letting him call the shots. He reached down and turned on the radio and, ironically, Babyface's old jam, "Never Keeping Secrets," was on. Brandon reached down and turned up the volume. I assumed it was his way of sending me a message. I stared out the window and listened to the lyrics of the song.

I wasn't sure where we were headed. I debated on inquiring just to hear him speak, but decided that silence was best. I began to think that maybe he was driving me to Uniyah's place, or to his place, where Uniyah would be. I didn't want a confrontation, and I began to panic.

"Uh, B, I mean, Brandon, where are we going?"

My question was followed by silence and, when I was about to ask the question again, he simply stated we were going to his place so that we could talk.

"Is Uniyah going to be there?" I nervously stammered.

"Would you like her to be?"

"Brandon, stop playing games. Why can't we talk now about what's on your mind or about where *we* stand?"

"Where *we* stand, huh? I don't know where *we* stand and that's why *we* need to talk. As for Uniyah, I didn't tell her that I was meeting you today. Honestly, I don't quite know what to tell her, in regard to you, or in regard to us."

For the remainder of the ride, I sat in silence. It was obvious that Brandon was still harboring some ill feelings. Not once did he glance in my direction or acknowledge my presence until we got to his spot and he handed me the car keys before exiting the car and heading to his apartment door. I was reluctant about going inside, as I was still expecting an ambush from him and Uniyah. But my uneasiness was laid to rest after I walked into his apartment and saw we were all alone.

I closed the door behind me and made my way over to his sofa to take a seat across from him. I was so nervous, yet energized, as I sat a few feet away from him. I was astounded at how being in the same room with him made me feel good.

"Why didn't you tell me?"

"That I was dating someone else?" I questioned.

"No, I knew that. Why didn't you tell me that it was Uniyah that you were dating?"

"Honestly, I was being somewhat selfish. I enjoy the vibe I get when I'm with Uniyah, but with you, the feelings are so much more intense. I can't stand to be away from you or to not hear from you. As things progressed, I was certain that I'd lose both of you, and I couldn't fathom the idea of you not being in my life. When we met, I never imagined that things would progress to the level that they have. I had never been with a guy before and never thought it was possible to actually fall in love with one."

"You keep telling me that you love me, but how do you expect for me to believe you when everything that our relationship was built on was a façade? I didn't even know your real name."

"Everything between us wasn't a lie. Tyrone was real. He was and is a part of who I am. I can't force you to believe that what we shared, and that I hope we still share, is real. Me being here should show you that it was more than just sex or about being a player. If that were the case, I would've charged you and Uniyah to the 'game' and moved on. But, B, I'm here. I'm fighting for a chance for there to *be* an us."

"What am I supposed to tell Uniyah? How could I be with you and keep her as a friend?"

"B, honestly, I don't know. That's why I didn't want to tell you when I first found out. I'm certain of one thing; I'm not allowing you to get away from me. You're everything that I ever wanted in a lover, and in a friend. I'm scared as hell because I don't know how to proceed."

"I can't throw away the friendship that I have with Uniyah. She's like a sister to me," Brandon argued.

"Then I'll be honest with Uniyah and tell her the truth. I'll tell her that you didn't know I was dating her."

"And what if she gives me an ultimatum and tells me that it's either you or her? How could I choose?"

Brandon's questions were ones that I had asked myself time and time again. I knew that if I told Uniyah about my life as Tyrone, she'd want nothing to do with me. I also figured that she'd want Brandon to do the same. They would both have to make their own decisions and, unfortunately, I didn't have a say in the matter. My worst fear was about to come true. I was going to lose both of them and, more importantly, Brandon.

We went back and forth with the what-ifs. None of my ideas seemed plausible where everyone came out unscathed. The evening sun had already set, and we sat in silence while the moonlight lit the room.

"What are you thinking about?" Brandon asked, breaking my train of thought.

I took a moment to evaluate how I truly felt before answering. "I'm scared, B. I'm scared of losing you and maybe destroying a friendship that you and Uniyah share.

I'm scared that I've hurt Uniyah and can't go back and change the way things are going down."

Brandon stood up and extended his hand to me. "Let's sleep on it. We can't make a decision that's going to affect more than you and me within a few hours."

I took Brandon's hand and allowed him to lead me into his bedroom, where we undressed, and then snuggled up next to each other in bed. I don't know how long I stared at him as he slept before I drifted off as well. I couldn't get over how good it felt to be with him again. And with that, I realized what I had to do.

waited patiently for Markus to arrive at our designated meeting place. I had ignored all of his attempts
to contact me the last two days because I didn't want
to face the inevitable. I needed some "me time" to recu-
perate and to pull myself together first. Finally, after
building up enough courage and strength to address him,
I returned his calls and agreed to meet him for lunch at
Applebee's by Perimeter Mall.

I had arrived thirty minutes early and decided to nurse
a green apple martini while I waited. I wasn't much of a
drinker aside from an occasional drink when I needed to
unwind but, over the last few days, the liquor had helped
to numb the pain. The only drawback was the hangovers.

Waiting patiently and trying not to think of what was
about to go down, I pulled out my cell phone and checked
my voicemail. There were several messages from Brandon,
stating that he urgently needed to speak with me. I
wasn't in any mood to counsel anyone on the laws of
love. I wasn't so sure that I knew them myself. I had
another message from Janelle, asking me to return her

call. She was worried about me. The last thing that I needed was for her to be giving me her "hate men" speech, and talk about how they are all nothing more than dogs.

I checked the time on my phone display, before placing it face down on the table. Like a hawk, I watched the traffic outside the window. I wanted to know exactly when Markus arrived. With every passing minute, my fury grew. I'd finally relented and had given myself to him physically, breaking my vow of celibacy, only to be informally dumped. I felt used and deceived; especially after learning that, days after his request for space, he had already replaced me.

I couldn't wait for him to arrive as the rage within me reached its zenith. I jumped when I felt a light touch on my shoulder. Somehow Markus had slithered into the restaurant without me seeing him and had caught me totally off guard. I gripped my drink with both hands to stop myself from slapping that damn smirk from off of his face. How dare he show up and smile in my face when I've been sleepless for days! How dare he smile at me when my heart was in shambles! I wanted him to hurt just as much as I was hurting, and I was determined that he would.

"Hey, how are you, Uniyah?" he casually asked as he slid into the booth across from me.

How am I? Could he not tell from the bags under my eyes and the redness that surrounded them?

Before I could answer the question, the waitress interrupted us and asked Markus if he wanted anything to drink. He ordered a glass of water with lemon, and I asked for another martini. I was grateful for the interruption; it gave me time to better collect my thoughts. I didn't want Markus to know that he had gotten the best of me. I wanted this meeting to go as casually as possible.

"I'm doing as good as could be expected," I answered after the waitress walked away.

"I'm sorry to have brought any unneeded stress into your life; especially at this crucial time. I know how earnestly you've been auditioning for record labels and sending out copies of your demo trying to get signed."

"So, if you understand all the pressure that I'm under, then why hurt me like this?"

He looked deeply into my eyes before answering. I had to look away before I allowed a tear to slip from one of mine. "Never let them see you cry" was my motto, but I was on the brink of a mental and emotional breakdown. Besides having Markus pull this stunt, I had been turned down by numerous record execs, saying that they already had a complete roster of female artists. Most of the letters I was receiving were more interested in the producer and songwriter—which happened to be Brandon.

I was at an all-time low, feeling as dejected as humanly possible. The one person that I thought would never bring me any drama or stress happened to be Markus and, instead, he was the one tearing my heart in two.

"Let's not talk about my musical aspirations. Let's focus on why we're here; to discuss the state of our relationship. Out of the blue, you told me that you 'needed some space.' This was merely weeks after the 'whirlwind' weekend you created for me, making love to me for the first time *and* telling me that you loved me. Then two days after I waited on you hand and foot as you recovered from your accident, you suddenly have an epiphany that I no longer make you happy?"

"Uniyah, that's not exactly the case," he rudely interjected.

"No, let me finish," I demanded. The liquor was finally kicking in, and I hadn't even started on the second glass that the waitress had placed on the table.

"How dare you tell me that I'm misstating the facts? Two nights ago, I sat outside of your apartment until the wee hours of the morning. When I finally realized that you weren't coming home, I called you. I'm sure you remember that phone call," I added cockily with a chuckle.

I felt like I was speaking for all the women that had been through a similar situation or had to deal with bullshit excuses from the men who claimed they loved them. I didn't know about them, but I was definitely tired of the lying, the disappointment, and the heartache. I just wanted some relief. Feeling bold and courageous I pressed on.

"Do you remember what you told me in that conversation?" I asked, knowing fully well that he did. "You told me and I quote, 'I had a late night at the office, and I have an early start in the morning. Can I call you tomorrow? We can get together for lunch or something and talk.'"

I paused so my statement could sink in. I wanted him to truly feel where I was coming from. From the look on his face, I could see that he was starting to, but it still wasn't enough. A little pain wasn't satisfying; I wanted him to feel a *lot* of pain.

"At first, your statement hurt me and then it angered the hell out of me. I couldn't understand how you could lie so easily to me as if it was second nature. As if our whole relationship was built on a lie. I will admit one thing though: your lie brought about some much needed clarification. It made me think of all the late nights at the office, all the excuses why you couldn't come to the studio; it made me think of all the bullshit you'd fed me."

"Uniyah, please lower your voice," he said. "You're correct. I did lie to you, but please believe one thing if you don't believe anything else. When I stated that I cared for you, I wasn't lying. I was telling the truth. Recently, I came to realize that you are more of a dear and close friend. I wasn't sure how to tell you and, when I had finally built up enough courage to do so, it happened to be the night of the accident and I didn't get an opportunity."

I couldn't believe what he had said. It had totally taken

me by surprise and, before I could stop myself, I had flung the remainder of my martini into his face. With my free hand, I slapped him. Stunned by my own actions, I stumbled from the booth and furiously made my way out of the restaurant, trying to hold back the tears that were waiting to burst from my eyes. They did as soon as I exited the restaurant and made it to my car. Now it was me who needed "some space" and there was no time like the present to get away and get it.

Forty Eight
BRANDON

I scurried around my apartment, trying to clean up the cluttered mess. The last few days had been hectic as hell, with all of the drama with Markus. I was totally confused as to how we should proceed. I hate to admit it, but I was strongly considering risking my friendship with Uniyah to explore where my relationship with Markus would lead. It wasn't like I'd be doing anything different than what Uniyah had done the night she last performed. She had put her own interests before our friendship and didn't consider the repercussions.

Maybe I was wrong for feeling like that, but it didn't seem fair that I should have to choose between the two of them. I wondered if she would continue to be with Markus when she found out that he was bisexual. That was unforgivable for most women, but there were still many that thought their pussy had the power to change a man's sexuality. But I'd discovered, once folks turned down that road for whatever reason, including curiosity, there wasn't any turning back.

I glanced down at my watch and quickened my pace

in cleaning. I threw clothes in the closet without hanging them and quickly tossed the comforter on my bed, leaving more lumps and bumps in it than I should have. Markus was to arrive within minutes and I was a little nervous. I wasn't sure where we would go or where the future would lead us, but I was curious to find out. I wanted my chance at love and I wanted my friendship with Uniyah to continue. I just didn't know if both were possible. I heard a car pull up, and I took a deep breath. I waited for Markus to knock on my front door, but waited a few seconds before answering when he did. I didn't want to seem overly anxious.

I looked around my place and was satisfied with the mood I'd set. The lights were low, and the sounds of Kenny G's "Besame Mucho" from his album *Rhythm & Romance* played softly in the background. Markus knocked a second time, and I finally opened the door. When we saw each other, we instantly embraced and shared a passionate kiss, as if we hadn't seen each other in years. The chemistry between us was thick and he looked astonishingly handsome, despite the worried look he wore. Something was definitely on his mind.

Before I could tell Markus to come inside, my cell phone began to ring. I motioned for him to have a seat and walked over to check the caller ID. It was Uniyah finally returning my calls. Deciding to call her back later, I turned it off and placed the phone on the charger located in my bedroom, and then turned my attention back to Markus.

"Something's wrong," I stated as I took a seat next to him.

He grabbed my bare foot and began to massage it. "I tried to tell Uniyah earlier this afternoon about us, and it didn't go too well."

"What do you mean, it didn't go too well? What happened?"

"Well…," he began before my house phone started ringing.

I sighed and signaled for Markus to hold on, and then headed into my office to find my cordless phone so I could turn the ringer off. I didn't want to be disturbed by anyone, even if it was a life or death matter. I quickly headed back to the living room and took my original place beside Markus.

As he continued to massage my foot, he began to tell me how things had unfolded. Uniyah could be very emotional, but I was surprised to hear she had behaved in such a way. Then again, after her admission about what she had done to Keno, nothing should have surprised me. He also told me how she had admitted to staking out his apartment the last night he'd stayed over at my place. I remembered his cell phone ringing that night, but was too sleepy to remember what he muttered into the phone. But I was happy that I didn't. Had I known it was Uniyah that had called, I would have felt even more horrible.

"Well, what were you going to tell her in regard to us?" I asked, almost not wanting to know his answer.

He paused and stopped rubbing the balls of my feet. "I was going to tell her that I had deceived the both of you and how I was truly sorry for doing that. I was going to tell her that although I cared for her deeply, I didn't care for her in the same manner that I cared for you. I was going to ask her to allow you and me to continue being together without holding ill feelings toward either of us—especially toward you. I wanted her forgiveness, her understanding, and, in some way, her approval."

I looked at him disapprovingly. That was a lot to ask of someone who believed that they were the love of your life, and the skepticism must have shown on my face.

"I know, B. I know. I thought that there was some way for things between all of us to be normal. It would take her some time but, in the end, I thought that she'd at least want you—if nobody else—to be happy. I've been reading too many E. Lynn Harris books."

"Markus, I don't—," I began but was interrupted by a knock at the door. I stared at Markus and he stared back at me. I wasn't expecting anyone and had no idea who could be stopping by out of the blue. I slowly rose to my feet and headed to open the door. When I looked through the peephole and saw who it was, a knot formed in the pit of my stomach and my skin grew cold.

Forty Nine
UNIYAH

I raced through the streets of Atlanta trying to get home. The tears continued to fall from my eyes as Markus' words played over and over again in my head. He was supposed to be my savior from heartache and pain. Instead, he had been the one to bring me both. I had never had anyone pursue me as hard and as long as he did, only to be discarded like used garbage once he got what he wanted. I felt like I had been robbed of all of my dignity.

At that moment, life seemed so unfair. *Love* seemed so unfair. I didn't know who to turn to, so I lay in bed, staring at the ceiling while the tears fell continuously. I sobbed as the memories that Markus and I shared played over and over again in my head until I fell asleep.

When I awoke, the sun had set and I felt so alone. I dragged myself into the kitchen and fixed myself a drink. This time my choice was cranberry juice and vodka. I went back into my bedroom and threw the framed picture of Markus and me to the floor. I wanted no memories of him. His haunting smile lingered in my head and depressed me even more.

I grabbed my phone and dialed Brandon. I needed to hear his voice to keep me sane and calm. I needed for him to tell me that things would work out and that I was overreacting. The phone rang and rang, but there was no answer. I paced around the apartment, feeling restless. I began to throw all of the things Markus had bought me during our courtship into the trash—the cards, the flowers, and the stuffed animals. I didn't want any reminders of him. But through all of my hate, I still wanted him to call and say that he had made a mistake; I wanted him to call and say that he indeed loved me like I loved him.

I tried to calm myself down but as the liquor began to control my senses, I became more upset. I needed to get him out of my thoughts. I picked up the phone and dialed Brandon's cell phone number. After a couple of rings, it went to voicemail. I then tried his home phone and it too went to voicemail. Dialing his cell phone again and without it even ringing, my call was sent directly to voicemail.

"Aww, hell nah!" I shouted as I dropped my phone to the floor. Whenever Brandon had needed me, I was there for him. And now that I needed him, he was un-available *and* avoiding my phone calls? "You ungrateful sonofabitch!" I screamed.

I ran into my closet and threw on the first thing I found, which happened to be some old jeans and a T-shirt. Unconcerned with my appearance, I grabbed my car keys and headed out the door. He was going to be there for me, whether he liked it or not. Before I started the car, I tried calling Brandon again on his home phone before I went over to his place to give him an earful. As I expected, it rang and rang. "Damn you, Brandon," I shouted as I put the car in reverse and backed out of my parking space.

As angry as I was at him, I prayed he would be home when I got to his place. I felt like being around somebody who truly loved me would make me feel better. He was the only man that had never hurt me or deceived me.

As I made my way down the freeway, I heard thunder in the sky clap and could smell the rain that was on its way. I hated this damn unpredictable Atlanta weather. One day it was warm, the next it was cold, then the sun was shining, and before you knew it, there was a treacherous thunderstorm in the middle of fall. As soon as I pulled into Brandon's complex, it began to pour. The rain pelted down from the sky, pounding on the top of my car and windshield. I circled around to the other side of Brandon's building and found an open parking spot.

As I ran through the rain toward Brandon's apartment, something caught my eye and I stopped in my tracks. It looked like Markus' rental car was parked outside of the building. I walked around the car and confirmed my suspicion after I saw the rental sticker on the back. Did Markus know someone that lived in the same complex as Brandon? The irony perplexed me. I began to wonder if they were friends, and if Brandon knew something about Markus' "other relationship."

I thought back to how quickly Brandon had exited the hospital room that day when I got back. Was he helping to cover Markus' tracks? Had Markus threatened him to keep quiet? The thoughts continued to run through my head as I made my way to Brandon's front door.

I knocked and waited for an answer. Just as I began to fumble in my purse for the spare key he had given me, Brandon opened the door. I stopped in my tracks after I pushed past him and saw Markus sitting on his couch. My breathing became rapid. It felt like my heart was going to burst out of my chest as I felt myself growing dizzy. Trying to find my balance, everything suddenly went black as I collapsed to the floor.

Fifty
MARKUS

This can't be happening, I thought to myself as I rushed to Brandon's side to help lift Uniyah from the floor. I never thought that it would be me who'd be at the root of all of this drama. While Brandon fanned her with a magazine he'd grabbed off his end table, he instructed me to go into the kitchen to get a glass of water and a damp towel.

I did as he requested, handed both to him, and took a step back. I didn't know what to do, and I needed to get my thoughts together. I wish she had allowed me to tell her about Brandon and me at the restaurant so we could have avoided what was happening at this very moment. Uniyah moaned as she began to gain consciousness. I inched further into the corner, out of her sight. At that point, I wished that I were invisible.

"Uniyah, are you all right?" Brandon asked with deep concern. You could see the worry etched all over his face.

"Br-Bra-Brandon," Uniyah stuttered. "What happened? Help me up. What's going on?"

"Shh, it's okay," Brandon coaxed, pulling a pillow from his couch and resting her head on it.

I felt scared *and* guilty as I stood there helpless, watching. I had caused all of this madness, and I wanted to be there beside Brandon, comforting her. I still had deep feelings for her; even though I was in love with Brandon. What she and I had shared was real; it simply wasn't right.

"What's wrong, Uniyah? Why are you crying?" Brandon asked as he saw tears well in her eyes.

"It's over. I didn't even see it coming. There's someone else in the picture. I found out the other night, and he confirmed it this afternoon," she rambled.

"Slow down, Niyah. You're rambling. What's over and what didn't you see coming?"

"Markus and I are over. He told me that he didn't care for me as a man loves a woman but more like someone cares for a friend. It broke my heart to hear him say that. Then when I came over here, I thought I saw his car parked outside and I swore when I came in, he was sitting right there," she said, pointing to where I had been previously seated. "God, my mind must be playing tricks on me." She sighed before resting her hand on her forehead.

"You weren't imagining it, Uniyah. I'm here," I said, coming out of the corner that I was standing in. I wanted this to be over, for once and for all. I was tired of being a coward. I didn't know what the outcome was going to be, but I wanted to know my destiny before the night was over. I wanted to know whether or not I was going to be in Brandon's life, or if I was moving on without him.

As Uniyah made eye contact with me, she pushed Brandon away and struggled to stand up. "What the fuck is going on? Are you telling me that you two know each other?" she asked, glaring back and forth between Brandon and me.

"Niyah, maybe you should have a seat so I can explain things."

"No, you stay the fuck away from me. Brandon, you too! I trusted you. I loved you like a brother and you betrayed me? You knew how much I loved Markus. You were friends with him this entire time and knew about all his head games?"

"Uniyah, wait!" I yelled. "He didn't know."

"Know what? That you were cheating on me with some other trick?" Uniyah shouted.

Brandon remained silent as tears began to flow from his eyes, and I realized that I had to come clean with the truth. From Uniyah's words, I realized she still hadn't figured out the other person *was* Brandon. I felt myself begin to perspire as I prepared to drop a bombshell on her worse than she could have ever imagined. I didn't want to, but I had to.

"Uniyah, it's not what you think. I lied to the both of you. Please listen and let me explain. It isn't Brandon's fault. It's all mine."

Uniyah's eyes bore into me, and I could truly feel her hate and disgust.

"Uniyah, I met you and I thought you were my ideal woman. I told my mother about how perfect you were and how good you made me feel. I thought you were the cure to my nightmares, my drinking, my insecurities."

"What nightmares? What are you talking about?"

"Uniyah, please!" I shouted and paused to catch my breath. I was scared to continue but I had to get everything out while I still had the courage. I needed to hear myself admit out loud what I had done and what I had become. "Uniyah, I'm bisexual."

Uniyah shook her head in disbelief, but I continued before she could interrupt.

"I met Brandon online, not long before I met you, and I connected with him in a way that I never had with anyone else. I had never felt the way I did toward anyone and, especially, not any man. But I couldn't deny the attraction. I was drawn to him and being around him felt natural. But he never knew me as Markus. I told him my name was Tyrone: my middle name.

"I never revealed to him that it was you I was dating, just as I never revealed to you that I was dating him as well. The more time I spent with the both of you, I slowly began to realize that you two were acquainted. I didn't even know to what extent until the night of your performance, when I saw you two hugging. I didn't know what to do. I had deep feelings for you and I had deep feelings for him, and I didn't know which of you I wanted more at the time. I didn't know how to tell you both the truth without getting hurt. I was selfish in only thinking about how I would fare in the situation, so I continued to date both of you. But I had to accept that Brandon had my heart."

Uniyah sobbed uncontrollably as she inched back toward the front door. I walked over to comfort her, but she screamed for me to stay away.

"Look, Uniyah, I was being a man when we made love. I told myself that if we did that, then you would stop the attraction that I had for Brandon; that you would make me fall for you and want no one *but* you. But after we were done, I realized that I still wanted Brandon."

"Uniyah, I didn't know until after the accident," Brandon interjected.

"Why didn't you tell me then? We aren't supposed to keep secrets from one another, especially something like this!" she screamed between sobs.

"I don't know, Uniyah. I was initially shocked when I first walked into the hospital room and saw that *your* Markus was *my* Tyrone. I was overwhelmed as to how we could have fallen in love with the same man without either of us knowing. I went into seclusion, trying to sort things out and trying to figure out how to proceed. Even now, I don't know what to do. I love him just as much as you do. I want him in my life just as much as you want him in yours, but I know that this isn't possible at all. I can't happily be in love with him and have a nourishing friendship with you at the same time," Brandon explained.

"Did you sleep with him?" Uniyah demanded to know,

looking back and forth at both of us, but the question was directed at me.

"Uniyah, we have been intimate," I admitted.

"I didn't ask if you two had been intimate. I asked if you two had fucked," she crassly stated.

In unison, we both nodded our heads to answer her question.

Uniyah looked at me and then at Brandon. "How could you let him do this to me? You think you're the only one he's slept with? He could've infected the both of us with all kinds of STDs! Brandon, how could you let him do this to me? To us?" she asked rhetorically before turning and storming out of the door into the pouring rain.

But before either of us could answer, she was gone.

L ying alone in my bed, I couldn't stop thinking about my life and its current state. Everything seemed to be surreal. There wasn't a single night that went by that didn't find me thinking about what I had done to Uniyah or the destruction that I caused to her friendship with Brandon. The two of them had a bond unlike no other, and I had selfishly taken that away.

The worst of it all was that I had become another down low brother that infatuated society. Isn't it ironic? I had destroyed two lives and all I could think about was being another stereotype. I had tried unrelentingly to reach out to Uniyah, but it was as if she had cut all forms of communication with the world. When I attempted to call her numbers, the prerecorded messages informed me that the numbers were no longer in service. When I tried to write her letters, they all came back stamped "return to sender." I never met her parents or family members so I couldn't ask them to let her know that I was trying to reach her. It was probably for the best; I didn't need to bring her any more undesired stress.

I had run into her friend, Janelle, one evening at the club. When she saw me heading her way, she made a beeline toward the door. It was no secret about what had gone down. I'm sure that she held ill feelings toward me as well. Her friends were at odds, and I was the sole reason for this.

My relationship with Brandon turned tumultuous after Uniyah found out about the two of us. For four months we tried to make it work, but things would never be the same. The smile I fell in love with had disappeared, and the brightness in his eyes had vanished. It was like he was someone else. He spent a great deal of time in the studio writing and producing, and when he wasn't there, he was moping around. I had done everything in my power to bring him out of his funk, but no matter what I conjured, nothing seemed to work. Deep down I knew what the problem was. He was missing Uniyah.

I know that he blamed me for their demise. Part of me wanted to inform him that he had a choice. When he saw me lying in that hospital bed, he could've walked away then. But seriously, what good would throwing stones do? We argued nonstop, and this was something out of character for the both of us. Before things went downhill, the two of us only had minor disagreements that we were capable of working out. Regardless of how hard I tried, our relationship came to an unfortunate end. I don't know why I had convinced myself that he and I truly had a chance. Uniyah was a great part of his life and, regardless of how much he loved me, there was nothing I could do to replace the bond the two of them once shared.

Turning over in my bed, I glanced at my digital clock. The bright red numbers informed me that it was only 10:23 in the evening. Although the nightmares hadn't returned, my nights were still filled with tossing and turning. I wasn't at peace and wouldn't be until I made things right between Brandon and Uniyah. Hopefully, the sleeping pill I had taken two hours prior would begin kicking in.

Just when I dozed off, the piercing ring of my house phone brought me out of my sleep. Groggily, I glanced at the clock. It was 11:15 p.m. Who in the hell was calling me at this time of night on a weekday?

"Hello," I bellowed into the receiver.

"Now, I know I raised you better than that. Why are you yelling into the phone like that?" the soft angelic voice of my mother questioned.

"I'm sorry, Ma. I haven't been sleeping well, and I took a pill to help me get a few hours of rest."

"Baby, what's wrong? Is something on your mind? When you were younger, you'd have trouble sleeping if something was weighing on your heart."

If only she knew what that was. I desperately wanted to share with her what I had been going through and the damage I'd caused, but I didn't quite know how to tell her. "It's just a big project I'm working on at work.

Once it's over, I'm sure everything will go back to normal," I fabricated. This was an act that I was becoming a master of.

"Don't stress yourself too much."

"I won't, Ma."

"I'm not going to keep you much longer. I wanted to let you know that your brother won't be able to come with me next month. He couldn't get the leave from his job, but guess who's going to drive up with me?"

"I don't know. Who?" I asked, trying to conceal my lack of interest. I wanted to pull the covers back over my head and fall into a deep stupor.

"Your cousin, Miller, is going to accompany me. I hope you don't mind. This will give the two of you an opportunity to get reacquainted, just like when you two were younger. He's been asking about you a lot and says that there's something that he needs to get off his chest."

Suddenly, I became nauseous and started feeling clammy. I couldn't believe that the past that I had been trying so arduously to suppress was resurfacing once again. What was it that Miller had to get off of his chest?

"Ma, how about I splurge on a first-class ticket and fly you up here so you don't have to endure the drive?"

"I don't mind the ride. Why? Is something wrong with Miller taking your brother's place?"

"No, I think this pill is kicking in. I better go before I fall asleep over the phone."

"Hold on. Why is it that every time I mention your

cousin, you get standoffish and have to abruptly get off?"

"Look, there's a lot you don't know and a lot you don't need to know."

"Markus, what is it? What aren't you telling me?"

"Ma, I have to go."

I hurriedly hung up the phone. I ran into the bathroom to run some cold water over my face. As I was returning back to my bedroom, my phone began to ring again. When it ceased, my cell phone started ringing. I could hear my mother's ring tone. I hit the IGNORE button.

I couldn't believe that my past was coming back to haunt me and the biggest thing that I'd kept a secret from my mother was about to come to light. I needed to protect her from the truth at all costs. I had to find a way to eradicate my cousin from our lives, for once and for all.

BRANDON

Words couldn't describe the pain and turmoil that I was feeling. Out of all the shit I've done in my life, nothing compared to what I had done to Uniyah. My actions were so out of character, and no matter how upset I was, no one deserved the pain that I had subjected her to.

Day after day, I had tried to formulate an adequate

apology that would get me back into her graces. But the truth be told, there was nothing that I could say or do that would allow her to trust me again. Although we both had been victims of Markus Tyrone's deception, when all the facts came to light, I had chosen him over her.

Deep down I recognized that this was selfish, but I wanted to be in love so bad. I remembered how happy she had been whenever she spoke about him and the positive things he had done for her emotionally. I hoped that if I continued dating him, I'd experience those same feelings.

Sadly, my past love life hadn't been filled with good memories and, selfishly, I had only thought about my own happiness. In doing so, I had alienated my friendship with Uniyah and lost someone that was as close as a sister. I would communicate with Janelle often, but out of respect to Uniyah, we didn't discuss her. I could understand Janelle's logic. I had lost the right to know about Niyah's life and whereabouts when I decided to pursue my brief relationship with Markus Tyrone.

Brief was definitely an understatement. Whenever I looked him in the eyes, I couldn't stop myself from wondering if he felt any remorse for the pain that he had caused, or if he ever felt guilty for all the lies that he had told to capture my affection. I didn't know what to really believe when it came to him. Our entire relationship had been built on lies and there was nothing that we could do to change that. The man that I had fallen in love with was not the man that I lay next to at night.

Whenever I was in his company, I felt like a complete stranger. Looking in the mirror, I didn't recognize the man staring back at me. I had lost myself, lost my values, and lost the sense of friendship, all in a vain attempt to find love.

I closed my eyes as I felt the plane stabilize in the turbulent wind. With my earphones on my ears, I let my iPod play a mix of recordings that Uniyah and I had worked on throughout our studio sessions. I would be lying if I said that hearing her voice didn't make my eyes mist.

Without Uniyah in my life, I tried to engross myself in my studies by taking online classes to finish my degree. I spent whatever free time I could in the studio. I'd do anything to not be in the company of Markus Tyrone. I came to realize that there was no better way to get out my frustrations than to put it on paper. Most of what I wrote had a very melancholy feeling.

Over the last few months, I had become a weak and pathetic lovesick individual. There was no doubt that I needed to find out who I was, as a person and as a man. I have begun to learn how to truly love myself so that I can allow another to love me as well. I used to think my happiness could be equated with being in a relationship. Like many romantics, I failed to realize that you can't rely on someone else to make you happy. Happiness must

360 Timothy Michael Carson

come from within and that individual you bring into your life should only enhance your sense of happiness.

Allowing another the power to make you happy, as I had done with Markus Tyrone, only gives that individual the power to strip away that happiness. In the end, that individual will successfully move on to another and you'll be stuck listening to Mary J. and Keyshia Cole singing about their woes. There comes a time when an individual has to take the lead and take charge of their own life and state of happiness. For me, that time was now!

Without any notice, I had packed my apartment up. What I couldn't fit into my suitcases, I had placed in storage to get at a later time. I changed my cell phone number and closed down my email accounts. The only people that could reach me would be those that I held dear in my heart. At this time those individuals were only family and Janelle.

I needed to break away from Atlanta. The time I had spent there had brought me more heartache and pain than it had good times. Looking back now, I've come to see the time was a complete loss. When I took in the inventory of what I had acquired, it only amounted to having one friend, a shitload of heartache, no degree, and no record or publishing deal. I'd never be able to regain my lost time, but I could stop wasting it. I needed to remove myself from Atlanta in order to grow as an individual, a writer, and as a musician. I had to turn my fear of growth into a motivation for growth.

During my escape from Atlanta, I'd do my best to find a way to reach out to Uniyah and to let her know that I was sorry for the way things went down and, more importantly, ask her to forgive me for being such a disloyal friend. It would be an arduous process, getting her to forgive me, and even more strenuous trying to get her to forget my dishonesty so that we could try and salvage our friendship.

For Markus Tyrone's sake, he better hope that the distance between Uniyah and me will trigger a much-needed change in both of us. No matter how much I tried to let things between him and me go, I was still infuriated with him. He'd never once apologized for the way things had gone down, or even tried to show any type of empathy for my loss of a great friend. Deep down, I knew that he was only out for himself. He didn't care who he hurt, and he didn't care who he trampled on as long as he got what satisfied him.

If my friendship with Uniyah couldn't be saved, then I'd personally ensure that Markus Tyrone Greene suffered in the same manner as I had!

UNIYAH

I left my sound check and headed to my downtown Atlanta hotel to relax before tonight's performance. This was the first time in six months since I had been back to Atlanta. Stepping foot back in the city wasn't the easiest thing to do, but I'd learned that in order to be successful, I had to rise above all the drama. Walking around with a broken heart and not knowing who to trust was very vexing and emotionally fatiguing.

I never thought I'd have to endure the things that I'd been forced to. Losing my best friend, and someone that I thought was the love of my life, at the same time, was an almost unbearable task to bear. Even to this day, I questioned the Man above on why I was forced to experience such things.

Words couldn't express the way I felt about Markus. In my wildest dreams, I'd never imagined that I'd be a victim of a "down low" brother. It was one of those things I thought could happen to everyone but myself. Now I recognized that I was as vulnerable as anyone. I had tried to get back into the dating scene but the pain of the betrayal was too deep to shake, and I needed more time to heal. Fortunately, I used that time and energy to give my best to my music and was happy to be reaping the benefits of my labor.

I loved Brandon, but immediately after things had come to light, I hated him. I hated him for his betrayal and disloyalty. I had been in his corner on numerous accounts when he'd suffered heartbreak after heartbreak. I'd nurtured him and counseled him so he could get back out and love again.

Looking back now, I can see that my hate for Brandon

was also tinged with jealousy. I was jealous that Markus had chosen him over me. Although I have no problems with those who have alternative lifestyles, I do believe that the natural order of things is for man and woman to unite. So I was at a complete loss as to how Markus could choose to be with a man over a woman.

Brandon was a great person, and prior to Markus, he was the quintessence of what a true friend was said to be. I didn't fault him for falling in love. I faulted him for allowing his desire to be in love to come between our friendship. From what Janelle tells me, it ultimately wasn't worth it. His relationship only lasted a few months. I'm not sure what was going through his mind, or why he thought the relationship would work. It was built on nothing but lies.

Easing into the back of the record company's complimentary limousine, I buried myself into the luxurious leather seat. The afternoon sun was beaming, and I could tell it was going to be a beautiful day. I had about six hours before I had to be back at the Fabulous Fox Theatre to do my forty-five-minute opening set. Although I hated the smallness of the venue, it was only a matter of time before I was headlining my own tours. Plus, opening up for soul singer Eric Benét definitely wasn't a bad thing.

My opening set would set the groundwork for the release of my debut album, *When the Truth Lies*. My current single, "Why Me," was in heavy rotation, and the follow-up single would ensure that I'd cross over into popular music and state my claim as a force to be reckoned with in the music industry.

Staring out of the tinted window, I couldn't help but to reminisce about the events of the last year. I had done a lot of things that I wasn't necessarily proud of. I convinced myself that I did these things to advance my singing career and love life. Many would probably think that I deserved what happened to me. Let's be honest, I wasn't an angel. I had almost torn a family apart when I became involved with David, I had traded oral sex for a chance to win a singing competition, I'd stabbed Brandon in the back, and I had gone to great extremes to reap revenge on Keno and his deceptive ways. With all this being said, no one deserved to be subjected to the type of pain and hurt that Markus had inflicted upon me. But who the hell was I to try and control karma?

But when all was said and done, I realized that through life's ups and downs, the good times and the bad, loves lost and loves gained, that even if the "truths" of others were a lie, the only truths that really mattered were the ones we told ourselves. And my truth was that through it all, I had made it.

It was quite unfortunate that as I rose to success, Markus Tyrone Greene would soon be revealed to all for everything that he is—a liar, a cheat, and an under-cover down low brother!

ABOUT THE AUTHOR

Timothy Michael Carson is a Florida native and the author of *When the Truth Lies* and *Love's Damage*.

He has his undergraduate degree in journalism, with a public relations concentration, and a minor in English from Georgia State University.

Timothy is a poet, freelance journalist, and the founder of Ready2Speak Books. He is presently working on his third novel, *After the Smoke Clears*. Visit the author on Facebook.

WHAT'S NEXT?

Many said it was unheard of
A majority thought it unobtainable
But with a dream and a vision I take grasp
Forging forward in my quest for success
Failure never was, nor is, an option
Most thought it nothing more than a fantasy
But it is with faith in a higher being
That I'm able to turn my dream into reality
With flying colors, I pass life's test
The battles leave me fatigued
But to defeat, not once do I ever think to acquiesce
With determination, I strive to be the best
Taking a step forward in front of the rest
When it's all over
I can't help but ask myself,
"What's next?"

—Timothy Michael Carson

A WORD FROM THE AUTHOR

Writing for me has always been a passion. It's the one thing in this world that I can see myself doing for free. For me, writing allows a sense of freedom and uncensored expression. Emotions that I don't know how to verbalize always seem to be expressed through my writing.

In the process of writing this story, I've had the privilege of encountering many young and aspiring writers of all genres. Many of them were afraid to put their stories out for the world to read, and a few simply were afraid of rejection. For each writer that has asked about my journey and what might be in store for them, I simply will say, "Be prepared."

The publishing process is a long and arduous road that you must not be afraid to travel along. You will encounter a few bumps along the way and you may not. No matter what you encounter don't give up.

To everyone who has picked up *When the Truth Lies*, I thank you and ask that you never give up on your dreams or allow anyone to stifle your voice. Many told me I'd never write a book. Many told me that I'd never be published. Fortunately my destiny is not determined by them, it's determined by a higher being. This is the case for *everyone* trying to live out a passion.

Always remain true to yourself and always believe in yourself.

Sincerely,

Timothy Michael Carson

Next month, don't miss these exciting new love stories only from
Avon Books

In My Wildest Fantasies by Julianne MacLean

An Avon Romantic Treasure

Rebecca Newland is desperate to escape a loveless engagement. Devon Sinclair is his family's only hope for averting crisis, but a forced marriage can't be the answer. When Devon rescues Rebecca on a stormy evening, their happiness may depend on their ability to save each other.

Not the Marrying Kind by Hailey North

An Avon Contemporary Romance

Harriet Smith and Jake Porter went to their graduation dance together, but Harriet was devastated to find out Jake had only asked her on a dare. Sixteen years later, Jake's back in town. Harriet thought all she wanted was to make him pay, but happily ever after may be the sweetest revenge of all.

Blackthorne's Bride by Shana Galen

An Avon Romance

When a drunken priest marries the wrong couple, Lady Madeleine's escape from her money-hungry suitors is hardly a consolation. Her new husband, the Marquess of Blackthorne, is fleeing an infuriated duke. But will the struggle to save their marriage, as well as their lives, prove to be too much?

Taken by the Night by Kathryn Smith

An Avon Romance

Six hundred years have taught Saint one thing—it is better to stay away from humans, and save himself the pain of loss. Ivy is no stranger to vampires or the passions of men, but Saint is the first to tempt her. As they search for a killer and fight to protect those they care about, Ivy and Saint will risk everything for a chance at a love that will last forever.

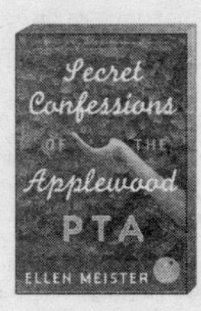